CASH
RULES

CASH RULES

THOMAS LONG

URBAN BOOKS
www.urbanbooks.net

Urban Books
10 Brennan Place
Deer Park, NY 11729

ISBN-13: 978-1-60162-015-6
ISBN-10: 1-60162-015-2

First Mass Market Printing: August 2007
Printed in the United States of America

10   9   8   7   6   5   4   3   2   1

1

Takeisha (T-Love)

It was the summer of 1999. Baltimore City was blazing hot and the humidity was thick in the air. It was nothing for a playa to walk down the street and see a pack of young dime pieces out on any corner, posted up and wearing the shortest of shorts and mini-skirts. The less we wore the better. Nothing was left to a man's imagination because us sistahs had all of our natural fineness out on full display. Thick hips, thin waists, phat asses, and firm round breasts were everywhere. The summer was like a fashion competition between us ladies to see which one of us could out-dress the other in the most revealing gear. I, Takeisha Jenkins, was one of many females caught up in this craze.

I had just turned 18 years old and graduated from Western High School. I wasn't a straight-A student, but my grades were good enough to get me a full academic scholarship to go to Howard University in the fall. I planned to major in business management. It had been my dream since I was a little kid to one day run my own business. I wanted to start my own record label and build an entertainment conglomerate that would become as large as Russell Simmons and his Def Jam Records empire.

My two best friends, Latrell and Danita, and I had been hanging tight since the third grade. We all grew up in the same neighborhood in East Baltimore and did virtually everything together. We partied hard together, ran the streets together, and got into all kinds of trouble together. We were inseparable. If one of us got caught doing something, then all of us took the charge together. If any chick dared to step to one of us with some BS, then she had better be prepared to take a major beat-down from the whole crew. We all planned to attend Howard University together.

Not to be bragging or anything, but I knew I had it going on. I stood about 5' 4" tall and weighed a solid 140 pounds. I had a thick set of thighs like Big Lez, the girl who used to dance in Mary J. Blige's earlier videos. My ass was firm, but it had a little jiggle to it when I walked. Guys just loved that shit. Their eyes damn near popped out of their heads trying to get a peep of my ass when I walked by. My breasts stood upright like two missiles preparing for take off. I had thick eyelashes and a set of pretty brown eyes that made many men wanna spoil me to death once they took one glance into them. My pecan complexion meshed well with my light brown hair that came down to my shoulders. To top it all off, my cute dimples gave me an innocent look that was hard for any young balla to resist.

Latrell was almost the same complexion as me and had a similar build. In fact, the physical resemblance between the two of us was so evident, we could easily pass for sisters. However, our personalities were drastically different.

I always got the best grades in school, and was usually the ringleader in any of our escapades. I had a laid back, smooth type of personality that usually got me whatever I wanted. Latrell, on the other hand, was the loud, around-the-way-girl type of chick who loved to make dramatic scenes. She cursed like a sailor, smoked blunts like a dude, but was still fine enough to be considered a dime piece.

Danita was a beautiful, chocolate-coated honey with an even skin tone that gave off a radiant glow. She brought to mind images of Naomi Campbell in her heyday. With her slender build, she didn't attract the kinda attention that Latrell and I did, but she could still hold her own. Her greatest strengths were her bright smile and innocent, shy personality. She was more of a follower and usually went along with us in whatever we were doing just to fit in.

When one of us was weak in a certain area, another member of our crew would pick up the slack. I guess you could say our different personalities complemented each other and made our friendship that much stronger.

The main thing that we had in common was our love for rap music and the hip-hop culture. For as long as we could remember, our love affair with hip-hop existed, and it had no intentions of dying out anytime soon. We argued back and forth all the time about who was the best rapper and the sexiest among the top male MCs. I was a die-hard Tupac fan. Latrell loved The Notorious B.I.G. Danita thought that Jay-Z was the greatest rapper that ever came into the game. There was a never-ending debate between us about who was the best, and it still goes on until this day.

When we were around 15 years old, we polished up our lyrical skills and decided to try our hand at the rap game. We formed a group called the KS Crew. The "KS" stood for "Killin' 'em Softly." We played off of our good looks, and rugged hood style. Even though we were fine enough to be runway models, we spit lyrics that were like fire. I became T-Love, Latrell became Luscious, and Danita was known as D-Boogie. We had built a reputation around Baltimore City in many rap battle ciphers for having the illest lyrics. We easily took out most of the best male competition. The only one that held his own in a battle with the KS Crew was a dude from West Baltimore by the name of Scar.

Scar was older than us by six years. This brother was fine in every sense of the word. He had the whole package—good looks, height, and muscles all over his sexy physique. He got into working out regularly from being locked up so many times in his life. He had thick, wavy hair and a piercing set of eyes that could look right into your soul. His distinctive Indian hue came from his maternal grandmother, who was half Cherokee Indian. His entire upper torso was an art show, showing off his multiple tattoos.

His government name was Nathan Jones, and he definitely had what it took to make it in the music business. He used the stage name Scar because he felt that once he beat you in a rap battle, you would be scarred for life. His lyrical skills on the mic were unquestionable. He could hold his own with any rapper, on any street corner, or even one that was on BET.

Unlike many rap artists who rapped about living the thug life, Scar was really living it raw and uncut. He was married to the streets, and even if he got a major record deal, he never planned to cut his ties to the hood or the game. He was addicted to the money like a crackhead hooked on that glass dick. The fact that he practiced what he preached only made his credibility as a gangster rapper that much more authentic and would increase his popularity.

It was in 1997 when we first met Scar. We were all at the Paradox nightclub to participate in a freestyle battle. The winner of the contest would be awarded $1000 cash and ten hours of free studio time. We were on the mic doing our thing as usual, destroying anybody that dared to touch the mic before us or after us. When it was Scar's turn to rhyme, he stole the show. For the first time, the KS Crew was upstaged and he took home the first prize.

Even though he beat us in the battle, we also gained his respect. He particularly took a liking to me, even though I was only 16 years old. We began messing around not too long after that night, and became a couple. We clicked instantly. He took the group under his wing as his protégés.

Scar and his manager, Ace, signed the KS Crew to a management agreement. According to the terms of our contract, they had two years to get us into the studio to record a demo CD and shop it to record labels for a deal. In exchange, they would get twenty percent of our earnings as a group. If they didn't get us a deal before the contract expired, then we were free to go elsewhere and try to get a deal on our own.

In the time that we had worked with Scar, he taught us a lot about the music business. He helped us develop our identity as a group. He showed us how to improve our stage performance and how to write songs that appealed to a particular audience. We spent a gang of hours in the studio working on different tracks before we came up with the tightest three songs to use in our demo package. We signed our deal with them in 1997, and the past two years had been a lot of hard work and struggle for us that was about to pay off.

Scar had several major record companies looking to sign him to a recording contract. Ace had gotten him a gig to open up at the Baltimore Arena for DMX and the Ruff Ryders crew. To share the bill with a crew of their stature was major. DMX was the hottest MC in the game, and Ruff Ryders Records was the label that had the biggest buzz on the East Coast. DMX had just dropped two number one albums in the same year. No artist had ever done that before.

It was an honor for Scar to share the same bill with them. He had to represent for B'more to let niggas know that it's cats in this city that got real lyrical skills. It was put up or shut up time. If Scar got a deal after this show, then we were next in line to get put on. All we had to do was sit back and wait for the chips to fall into place.

On the day of the show, me and my girls were at

my house getting dressed for what we hoped would be the biggest night of our lives. We were all trying on outfit after outfit, trying to find the right ensemble to wear. We had to be dipped from head to toe. Earlier in the day, we all went to the hair salon to get our heads done. Next, we got fresh manicures and pedicures, all paid for by Scar. He treated me and my girls like queens, and we loved every bit of the attention.

"Girl, your man sure knows how to treat a girl like a lady. I bet the dick is the bomb too, ain't it?" Latrell asked.

This wasn't the first time that she asked me some shit like that. I knew she had a thing for Scar since we first started working with him. In fact, she was pissed at first when he chose to get with me instead of her. However, she knew how I got down, and to cross me over a nigga would've been foolish on her part. We were too close to let some dick come between us, but, every now and then she let some slick shit come outta her mouth about getting with Scar, and I quickly checked her ass.

"Ho, you'll never know. That dick belongs to me," I said in return. I laughed out loud as I gave Danita a high five.

"Nah, for real though, yo, I can't believe that Scar is gonna let us get on stage with him at the show tonight. This is like a dream come true. This was supposed to be his chance to shine. He be looking out for us for real! " Latrell said.

"Yeah, my man handles his business. He wanna let us do our thing and get some exposure by piggy-backing off of him. Plus, you know he's trying to get on my good side after I caught him cheating with that stripper bitch," I replied.

About two months ago, I was at the movies with Scar when his cell phone kept ringing, but he wouldn't answer it. I didn't say anything about it to him, but I noticed from the red light blinking on his phone that the caller had left a voice mail message. I had managed to get Scar's password to his voice mail system without his knowledge. When I checked his messages later, I found out that the message was from a girl named Poochie. In the message, she went on and on, talking about how much fun she had sucking and fucking him the night before after she gave him a lap dance at the Cathouse Gentleman's Lounge. When I confronted Scar about it, he denied it at first, but then had to 'fess up when I wouldn't let it go.

This wasn't the first time that I caught him cheating, and it sure wouldn't be the last. He always bought me expensive gifts to make up for his mistakes and I gladly accepted them. The only thing that I loved more than Scar was his money. I was a real material girl at heart. Besides, with his help, the KS Crew was going straight to the top and about to be paid in full. I would have to put up with his cheating ways for now. I could dump his no-good ass at a later date.

We had finished getting dressed and were ready to leave for the show, looking fine as ever in our skin-tight jeans and matching fitted shirts. When the limo driver started blowing his horn outside, we made a mad dash for the front door.

The limo was laid out—bottles of champagne on ice, food trays neatly prepared for us to snack on. The stereo system was blasting a copy of our demo to get us pumped up for the show. This would be a night the KS Crew would never forget.

When we arrived at the Arena, we were escorted backstage by security. Along the way, we were awestruck to be in the presence of so many celebrities. The entire Ruff Ryders camp was there, including the LOX, Eve, and Drag-On. Busta Rhymes was there. Redman and Method Man were also in the house. Faith Evans and Carl Thomas breezed through. It was a star-studded affair, and the KS Crew was right in the middle of it all, loving every minute of it.

When we made it to Scar's dressing room, he was rehearsing his routine with his DJ, Killa. His face lit up when he saw me walk into the room.

"Whaddup, wifey? I see y'all made it on time. That's what I'm talking about. Black women where they supposed to be when they supposed to be," Scar said. He took me into his arms and kissed me.

"Hey, sweetie. You know I was gonna be here on time for you. Just know you still in the dog house," I reminded him as I whispered in his ear. He shot me a sly smile to acknowledge the fact that he was at my mercy for right now.

"You know we couldn't miss you blessing the mic tonight, Big Daddy. You know we're ready to get on stage and do our thing," Latrell said.

You know I'ma tear the house down. I hope y'all got ya act together. I'm opening the show. They say that I got twenty minutes to do my thing. I'ma let y'all shine after I do three joints," Scar said. He was a man of his word.

Our faces lit up like Christmas trees. Scar told us what songs we were supposed to perform, and we began rehearsing our lines. Someone knocked on the door to let Scar know that it was time for him to hit the stage.

"Baltimore City, are y'all ready to have a good time tonight?" the MC asked the crowd. They responded with loud cheers to show their excitement.

"Well, we got something special for you tonight. Before we bring out the Ruff Ryders crew to do their thing, wc got some local talent for y'all. This cat that I'm about to bring out has had y'all bouncin' to his new single, "Thug Passion", for the last two months. You hear it on the radio every day, all day and now you get a chance to hear him do his thing live. Put your motherfuckin' hands in the air for my main man, Scar."

"Thug niggas ride while these bitch niggas cry. If you feelin' what I'm saying, then put your pistols to the sky. You gotta feel my thug passion."

Scar sang the hook for "Thug Passion" a cappella while he was still behind the curtain. The beat dropped, and everybody shook their asses to the groove. Scar stepped onto the stage from behind the curtain and the crowd went crazy. He ripped off his wife beater and threw it out into the crowd. The bitch that caught it almost fainted. Girls were throwing their panties on the stage. Dudes were going bananas, shouting out what hood they came from. As he was singing his verses, the crowd began to sing along. After he finished "Thug Passion", he went into his next two songs and got a similar response.

After he finished his set, it was our turn to rock the mic.

"Baltimore, I appreciate all the love y'all been

showing me. Because of y'all, I done sold 5,000 copies of "Thug Passion" outta my trunk on the streets in two months. Now, that's love right there. Right now, I wanna bring out my female thugs to bless you for a minute. They've been making a little noise around town in a lotta local talent shows and MC battles. Some of you might have heard of them. Let me hear you make some noise out there and show some love for the KS Crew!" Scar screamed at the top of his lungs.

We seized our moment in the spotlight. All of that nervous energy went right out the window when we hit the stage. We were born to perform.

Scar had given us seven minutes to do our thing, and we made the most of it. We performed "Gangstress" and "A Thug's Lady" for the crowd. When the fellas saw how fine we were, they sang the chorus right along with the females in the crowd. History was being made that night. After the set was done, the hometown crowd gave the KS Crew a standing ovation for about a minute. The Ruff Ryders came on after us and ripped the show as expected.

Backstage after the show, everybody showed us all love. Several record executives handed out their business cards to Ace. They were interested in not only signing Scar to a record deal, but also the KS Crew. If any of these CEOs that were at the show talked the right talk and showed us the money, I was ready to sign on the dotted line.

After we left the arena, we all headed over to Syndee De Marr's restaurant for the after-party. It was a spot on Baltimore Street that catered to an eccentric crowd. It was black-owned and they specialized in New Orleans style Cajun dishes. Scar had rented out the entire restaurant to celebrate. Only a few of his select associates were invited. Big things were about to happen for Scar and the KS Crew. The door to success seemed to be right in front of us. All we had to do was turn the knob and walk right in.

You could say that it was written in my genes that I would have a future in the entertainment business. My mother and father were members of a band called The Backsliders back in the early 1980s. My mother, Rosa, sang lead vocals, while my father, Harvey, played the drums. The group had a couple of hot singles that made it onto the Billboard charts before they broke up. I had fond memories, as a little child, of being on the road with my parents when they were out on tour. Unfortunately, as the band members went their separate ways after their record sales dropped, this also marked a drastic change in the Jenkins household.

After the band broke up, my mother received several offers to record a solo album. She was a stunningly beautiful woman with an insatiable craving for the spotlight. Unable to find work as a musician in any band, my father wanted to settle down with my mother and devote his time to raising me. They had made a sizable amount of money while performing; enough to live comfortably for a good while. However, after my mother went against my dad's wishes and signed a contract with a record company out in LA, this created turmoil in my young life. My parents' relationship was never the same. They wound up getting a divorce when I was 9 years old.

The divorce was a bitter situation that scarred my relationship with my mother. When my mother chose her career over her family, I was confused and felt betrayed. Her living all the way out in California didn't help the situation either. She agreed to give my father full custody of me because she felt as though he could give me a more stable home life while she pursued her career. I would rarely see her in the coming years. She would call and say that she was gonna send me a plane ticket to come to LA to visit, but never did. Over time, I totally blocked my mother outta my life and refused to even accept her phone calls.

Rosa's music career flopped as quickly as it had started. She only recorded one hit record as a solo artist. Her record sales were poor, and the record company dropped her after only one album. For the next few years, she found herself trying to recapture the spotlight, but with little success. She began singing in lounges and sleazy bars.

Feeling depressed and unable to accept reality, she began delving into cocaine and heroin to escape her misery. She became involved in numerous dead-end relationships with up and coming musicians and producers who promised to jumpstart her career. For her troubles, all Rosa wound up getting was a roll in the hay and an expensive drug habit. They would ply her with drugs in exchange for sexual favors.

My father told me all of these details about her life even though I didn't want to hear it. I guess he hoped that I would change the way I felt about my mother. However, that wasn't gonna happen.

When I was 14 years old, my father dropped a

bombshell on me. I had just come home from school and was in my room doing my homework when my father said that he had to tell me something important. My mother had died of a drug overdose in a Hollywood motel. At first I felt sad, and cried alone in my room over the course of a few days. I wished she had been more of a mother to me instead of putting her career before her family. That was selfish of her. I needed her to be here for me, but she never was. Over time, my tears of pain turned into resentment. I vowed that I would never be like my mother.

My father and I had become extremely close over the years. We were like best friends. My dad took the money he made from his performing days to buy a modest house in East Baltimore on Biddle Street. He also opened up a record store in Security Square Mall. After his divorce, he had became a member of the Nation of Islam and changed his name to Rashid Salaam. I think that his religious conversion was his way of getting in touch with his African roots. He never forced his newfound religious beliefs upon me, but allowed me the freedom to choose my own spiritual path. He did an admirable job as a father, raising me the best that he could. He never remarried because my future was his only priority in life. I always hoped that some woman would come along and make my dad happy, like he used to be before my mom left.

Rashid didn't approve of my dating Scar for two reasons. First of all, Scar was six years older than me. He wanted me to date someone closer to my age. In addition to that, a drug dealer was not the type of young man that he wanted me to be involved with because of his dangerous lifestyle. Despite his reservations about our relationship, he stated his views adamantly to me and stepped back to allow me to make my own mistakes in life as a part of the growing up process.

Rashid knew that I smoked weed and drank liquor when I went out and partied with my girls. It worried him some because he didn't want me to wind up like my mother. He told me he hoped that I would outgrow my attraction to thugs and the street life. He prayed that I would find a respectable young man to settle down with and have kids in the future. In spite of what he considered to be my bad choices in men, he knew he couldn't be too mad with me since I hadn't gotten pregnant and I graduated from high school. With the high rate of teenage pregnancy in Baltimore City, that alone was a blessing.

My dad also knew that whether he wanted to admit it or not, I had not only inherited my mother's good looks, but also her stubborn ways. He knew that to challenge me too much, or to give me an ultimatum, would only push me away. He didn't want to make the same mistake that he thought he did with my mother, making her choose between her family and her career. He partially blamed himself all of these years for my mother's demise. I knew that it wasn't his fault, and that she was the one who made the foolish choices in her life that led her to an early grave.

One particular day, I was in my room going over my verses for the songs that we planned to record in the studio later that night. Over the last month or so, Scar had us in the studio every day, trying to lay the right tracks behind our vocals. The two songs we performed at the show had caught the attention of several record executives who were there. They, however, felt that the music behind our lyrics was a little wack. Consequently, Scar and Ace brought in a production team from New York, named the Smith Brothers, to lace us with some hot beats.

Smith Brothers Entertainment was comprised of three brothers: Charles, Joe, and Elliott. Charles and Joe were identical twins, while Elliott was their older sibling. They were industry veterans who had worked with the likes of A+, Chico Debarge and the legendary Raekwon, from the Wu Tang Clan. Charles and Joe went to Morgan State University with Ace, and they always swore that they would one day work together.

As I rehearsed my lines in the mirror, I noticed Rashid standing in the doorway. He watched me rehearse with a look of pride on his face that only a father could have. I felt a little awkward and embarrassed that I got caught singing into my hairbrush.

"Daddy, you scared the life outta me. The way you be sneaking up on me, I'ma start thinking that you the police," I said. I walked toward him and planted a big kiss on his cheek. My daddy was my hero, and would always be the first man in my life.

"You better be glad that I'm not the police because I would lock your behind up, right along with that criminal boyfriend of yours," he joked. I poked my lips out to let him know that I didn't think he was funny.

"Daddy, don't start," I said.

"I'm just teasing you, baby girl. Let me hear what you were just working on. Let me see if you got skills or not," he said. Even though he was in his mid-40s, Rashid was hip for his age. He loved rap music. He saw it as a positive vehicle for disadvantaged ghetto children to make it outta the hood.

I turned up the radio and flipped to the track I wanted to rhyme to, then I ran down my verses for him to hear me represent. As I went on, I could tell that he was impressed with my passion for music and my flow. He started bopping his head to the beat. When I was finished performing for my harshest critic, I turned the music off and flopped onto my bed, awaiting his opinion.

"So, what you think?" I asked.

"That was hot, baby girl. I loved it. You just need to go get me some soap so I can wash out that trash mouth of yours," he said.

"Daddy!" I whined. I grabbed a pillow off my bed and started another one of our pillow fights. Rashid managed to wrestle the pillow away from me, and tickled me into submission.

"I give, Daddy. I give!" I yelled. We both laughed hysterically.

"No, for real, I liked the song, Keisha. I just wish that you would write about more positive things. All you youngstas talk about is how many blunts you smoke, how many bodies you caught, and how you gonna kick somebody's ass. You're way too pretty a girl for that."

"But Daddy, look at where we live at. All that's around us is drugs and crime. I'm just writing about what I see around me," I reasoned. That was no lie because up the street and around the corner from where we lived had become an open-air drug market.

"I understand that part of what you're saying. I just wanna hear you use your music to talk about making a difference in the community, that's all," Rashid said.

"I will. One day, I will. When I get to be big and famous, then I can talk about all that stuff. For right now, gangsta rap sells. It's what's hot."

"I hear you, baby girl. I hear you. Good luck on your studio session. I have to run to the mosque and take care of some business. I'll see you later," he said. We embraced and said "I love you."

Rashid made his way out the front door. I picked up the phone and called Latrell and Danita on a three-way call.

"What y'all hookers doing? Are you getting ready?" I asked.

"I'm dressed, T. I'm just waiting on you," Danita said.

"Well, I just got up. I was out with Tank last night. I ain't get in until four this morning. Partyin' and bullshit. You know how that goes. Besides, you know that Scar is gonna be late anyway," Latrell said.

"Yeah, that's true. His ass is always late, but y'all still just be ready around four o'clock. I'm trying to finish up these tracks so that Ace can submit the new demo to these record companies," I responded.

"I'm feelin' that, no doubt," Danita said.

"Me too. Then we can start getting some paper," Latrell chimed in.

"Exactly," we all said at the same time. We were in the rap game for the money. That was without question.

About 30 minutes after I got off the phone with them, Scar pulled up outside of my house in his brand new Yukon Denali. He took his last toke off of a nicely rolled blunt as he rang my doorbell. I came to the door in an oversized T-shirt with no panties on.

"Damn, baby. Is it like that?" Scar asked as he eyed my phat ass when I turned around and lifted up my T-shirt. He grabbed me into his arms and cupped my bare ass with both hands, one on each cheek. Whether he was a dog or not, he was my little puppy, and he put his dick game down with authority.

"Always for you, Daddy."

We barely made it into my room before we made the house hotter than an Arizona desert. Scar stuck his tongue so deep down my throat that it was a wonder I didn't choke. I pulled off his Sean John sweatshirt and revealed his muscular chest as I ripped off his wife beater T-shirt. He pulled my shirt over my head to expose my C-cup breasts, then took my bulging nipples into his mouth one at a time. I moaned in sheer ecstasy when he bit them with subtle force. My whole body shivered when he turned me around and spanked me on my pear-shaped ass. I liked it rough, rugged, and raw, and that was just how Scar gave it to me every time.

Scar pushed me onto the bed face first and positioned me with my ass up in the air. He loosened his belt and let his pants drop down to his ankles as he entered me from behind. I started biting on the sheets to muffle my screams, and grabbed onto the headboard to keep my balance.

Scar looked at himself in the mirror, admiring his performance. He was 10 inches deep into the pussy. He had my young pussy sprung, and he could do whatever he wanted with it.

"Bitch, you like the way that feels, don't you?"

"Yes, Scar, you long-dick motherfucker. Oooh, you just don't know what the fuck you do to me."

"You a dirty whore, ain't you? Say you a dirty whore! Say it, slut!" He spanked my ass until it started to turn red.

"Ooooh, I'm a dirty whore. I'll be whatever you want me to be. Just don't stop giving me that dick!"

"Damn, my legs is gettin' tired as shit," Scar said.

Fucking me doggy style had his ass drained. He pulled himself from in between my legs and backed away from me. I laid out flat on the bed as he kicked his boots off and got totally naked. He instructed me to come back to the edge of the bed and to lay with my head hanging upside down. He got up on the bed and put my legs high up in the air as he reinserted his pulsating penis into my tight pussy, standing over top of me. I used my hands to balance my head on the floor as he began to fuck me with a vengeance.

We went at it for another 15 minutes before Scar released his cum all over my face. He flopped down on the bed out of exhaustion. I rolled all the way onto the floor and curled up like a baby. If my daddy only knew how freaky his little angel was, he would be in shock.

"Damn, nigga, you beat this pussy up. What time

is it?' I asked. Scar looked at his Presidential Rolex watch and told me it was 3:30.

"Come on, baby. Let's take a shower real quick. You know we gotta get to the studio," Scar said.

I got up off the floor and grabbed him by the hand, leading him into the bathroom. We showered, got dressed, and were off to pick up the rest of the crew for our studio session.

2

Latrell (Luscious)

Takeisha and I had been through a lot over the years, ever since we became friends in the third grade. It still made us laugh to think about how we met. We got into a fight over a boy that we both liked, Travis Martin. He was a cute, medium-complexioned boy with curly hair and fat cheeks that all the little girls loved to squeeze. All of the girls in our class had a crush on him. He would constantly be bombarded with notes from them, asking for him to be their boyfriend.

Having been raised in a household with two older brothers, I was a tomboy growing up. Even though I was a pretty little girl, I was as mean as could be. I would bully the other girls, and some of the boys, outta their lunch money. The fact that I was a little bigger than most of the kids in my class and I had two older brothers that everybody was afraid of worked in my favor. One day in class, I took it upon myself to tell Travis that he was gonna be my boyfriend. He had no choice but to accept my invitation or else face getting his ass kicked by a female.

What I didn't know was that Travis had developed a crush on another little girl in our class. He had taken a liking to Takeisha since the first day of school. She always wore her hair in the cutest little ponytails and her clothes were always neat. Even though she was only 8 years old, she seemed to have a lot of mature, feminine qualities about her. I couldn't stand her little prissy behind.

I began to notice that Travis was paying a little bit too much attention to Takeisha and became jealous. He would do little things like pull her chair out for her to sit down or share his snacks with her. Sometimes he even helped her with her classwork.

One day, when I noticed that Travis was staring at Takeisha a bit too long in class, I decided that I had enough. It was time for me to whip Takeisha's dainty little ass. I approached her after class and told her that I wanted to fight her after school let out. Little did I know that Takeisha was hardly afraid of me and was waiting for the invitation to fight. We were about the same size, so there would be no excuse for whoever lost. Everybody in the class heard about the fight and eagerly waited for the school day to end.

When the final bell sounded, everybody rushed out the front door into the playground area. They wanted to get the best view of the main event between us. When we made it out to the playground, the crowd got exactly what they were waiting for. I made the first move, hitting Takeisha flush in the mouth with a sharp right hand. Her lip was busted and blood began to spill as she fell to the ground.

When I tried to jump on top of her, I was met by a swift kick to the chest and I fell backwards to the ground. Takeisha quickly got to her feet and pounced on me, kicking me anywhere her feet would land. I curled up in the fetal position to try to block the kicks. I caught Takeisha's foot after several kicks had successfully landed, and tripped her to the ground. From that point, we were both on the ground, and took turns getting the upper hand on each other.

The fight was an even match until Ms. Hawthorne, a teacher at the school, broke it up and took both of us to the principal's office. My reign as a bully was over and Takeisha had gained my respect. We both were suspended for a week from school and felt pretty stupid about the whole fight afterwards. Neither one of us won the heart of Travis. That belonged to his mother, who vowed that none of the fast little girls in his class would corrupt her baby boy.

Soon after we became friends, we took shy, skinny little Danita under our wing. She had moved into the neighborhood with her mother from North Carolina in the middle of the school year. Her parents had just divorced, and her mother came up North for a fresh start. A little country girl, she appeared to be lost in Baltimore because it was much faster-paced than Tarboro, North Carolina.

When she first started school, the other kids used to tease her because of her dark skin and her mismatched clothes. However, when Takeisha and I took a liking to the new girl and befriended her, all of the teasing ceased instantly. If she was a friend of ours, then everybody knew that to mess with her would mean that they would have to deal with the two best fighters in the class. Over time, we made Danita a little tougher and taught her how to stand up for herself.

At first, we felt sorry for her being that she had no friends at all, but after we kicked it with her for a minute, we saw that Danita was good peoples. We used to go over her crib after school and her moms used to feed us all that good down south food like chicken, macaroni and cheese and collard greens.

I lived two doors down from Danita with my mother and two brothers. My father, Slick Willie Collins, was incarcerated for life on a murder charge. He used to run numbers and pimp women in the Seventies and early Eighties. He got into a dispute with another pimp from the West Side over one of his women and wound up shooting the man six times. I was six years old when that happened. I would visit my father in jail about four times a year, but I was raised by my single mother.

My mother, Latoya, was his bottom bitch. She was a fine redbone chick with hazel eyes and hair down to her shoulders. Her ass and thighs were her best assets, and she used them both to her advantage.

Virtually from the cradle, Latoya taught me and my two brothers, Derrick and Willie, Jr., how to survive out in the streets. She never worked a regular job, but survived off of welfare, boosting designer clothes, or finding some horny old man and beating him outta his social security or retirement check. One could say that I got my conniving ways honestly. My mother taught me everything I knew about using what was between my legs to get what I wanted. She gave me game that most of these hoes out here wished they had got from their mothers so that they would be able to know how to deal with these lame-ass niggas out here. Make no mistake about it, Latrell Collins was one bitch that was out to get hers at any cost, and it didn't matter who got in my way. The only people that I wouldn't cross were my mother and my girls.

My brothers were in and outta jail most of their lives on various drug charges. They were doomed to the inescapable fate of so many young black men caught up in the cycle of the thug life. I ain't gonna front because I was just as bad. I wasn't above breaking the law to get that cheese. On occasion, I would run up North for some of my hustlin' niggas to pick up a coupla bricks of that white shit if they paid me right. However, I knew I couldn't rely on gettin' fast money from the drug game forever. I knew if you fucked around long enough that eventually the boys in blue would come around to lock ya ass up. Jail wasn't a place that I was ever trying to call home. I just hoped that this rap shit kicked off so that I could get outta the hood.

It was around 3:45, and I had grown tired of waiting on Takeisha and Scar. I sat on my front step and smoked a blunt before I decided to knock on Danita's door. She lived with her mother and her stepfather. Her mother, Donna, was a nurse and worked long hours on the job. Being from the South, she was deeply religious and tried to impose her beliefs on Danita, but after living in Baltimore a few years, Danita began to learn the ways of the streets and rebelled against her mother's strict rules. Her mother would never put her out, but would constantly pray that God would deliver her daughter from the evil spirits of the world.

The two main evil spirits that she believed corrupted her daughter were me and Takeisha because we had her involved with what she called "that evil rap music" and the lifestyle of partying and gettin' high. Danita wasn't as wild as we were, but she had her moments.

I knocked hard three times on Danita's door. Her mother answered with major attitude.

"Lord, child. Why you beating on my door like some foolish heathen? Danita, one of your hoodlum friends is here to see you."

"How are you doing, Mrs. Robinson? I'm sorry, I didn't mean to disturb you," I said. Mrs. Robinson was cool even though she nagged a lot.

"Come on in, child. Pull your pants up, walking around looking like one of them crazy little boys. I know you been out there smoking them funny cigarettes. I can smell it all over you. Don't let me find out you got my little girl doing that, too. Neither one of y'all is too grown to be put over my knee. Go on in the back. She's in her room listening to that demon music."

I pulled up my pants and tried to straighten my clothes a bit. As crazy as I was, I would never disrespect my elders.

I made my way through the house to Danita's room. I spoke to Mr. Robinson, who was in the living room watching TV. When I got to Danita's room, she was sitting on the bed with a pen and pad in her hand. She was writing some new rhymes. The radio was blasting Jay-Z's first CD, *Reasonable Doubt*, which was a hood classic.

"What's up, girl?" I said to Danita.

"Nothing much. Just waiting on y'all so that we can go do our thing in the studio," she responded.

"Let me see what you working on." I checked out the lyrics Danita was writing on the pad. "Oh, that sounds kinda tight. I ain't think you had it in you. I thought that your moms had you in here writing some gospel rap and shit."

"I see you got jokes today. Real funny. But you know I'll rip you in a battle any day," Danita said. No doubt about it, I might have had more hood in me, but I was no match for Danita's flow.

"Yeah, yeah, choir girl. We'll see when we get to the studio. What's up with you and Larry?" I asked. Larry was Danita's boyfriend.

"Same ole, same ole. Nothing new," she responded.

Danita and Larry had been dating for the last two years of high school. Larry was what you would call a good guy. He ain't run the streets or break the law. He worked for his father in his auto shop and planned to take it over one day. She didn't see him much because of his work hours.

Danita wasn't the type of girl, like me or Takeisha, to date several men at the same time because they had money. She believed in true love and planned to one day get married to her Prince Charming. Fuck that love shit. I'll take a nigga with money that's down to kick that shit out any day.

"You need to cut that zero and get with a balla like me and Takeisha," I said.

"I'll pass on that. Y'all got too much drama for me. That just ain't my style."

As we were talking, we heard a loud horn blowing outside. It was Scar and Takeisha, 30 minutes late. We gathered our stuff together and headed toward the front door. When we got outside, we jumped into Scar's truck and rolled down the windows. The leather seats and fully equipped interior were straight luxury.

Scar sparked up a blunt and everybody took turns hitting it. The hydro was on point. Tupac's "Picture Me Rollin' " was playing in the background as we rode to the studio. Everybody was higher than a motherfucker. Smokin' 'n ridin' was all that our young lives were about.

3

Scar

"Hey, yo, turn my mic up a little bit so that I can hear myself in the headphones," I said to Keon, the studio engineer. He adjusted the volume on the microphone until I was comfortable with how I sounded when I was rehearsing my vocals.

I had taken some of my money from hustlin' and built a state of the art recording studio in Northwest Baltimore, off of Rogers Avenue. I called it Bulletproof Production Studio and it was located inside of a row house that I had purchased dirt cheap. I figured that since I had the money, it was senseless for me to pay someone else to rent studio time when I could have my own spot. That way, I wouldn't have to be pressed for time when I wanted to lay down a track.

I used several local producers to lay down tracks for me. In exchange, they would get some free studio time to do their own thing. I spent about $50,000 to make sure that the studio had the top musical equipment on the market. Names such as Roland, Akia, Alesis, and Korg were listed on the various drum machines, keyboards, sequencers, and digital recording devices in the studio.

The beat came on in the headphones and I started to do my thing.

They call me Scar, nigga,
I cut you fools like a switch blade.
Understand it, let it be known,
I'm in this game to get paid.

The feds wanna knock me,
'cause my name be ringing on the block.
The Tech-9 a do'em fine,
if they wanna get shot.

Pistols poppin' off,
these niggas is soft in this game.
A straight gangsta like Pacino,
when I'm bringing the pain.

Catchin' bodies like Gotti,
but I'm a fiend for that weed smoke.
Check my resumé in them streets,
you see I ain't no motherfucking joke.

That was the first section of a new track I was working on called "Straight Gangsta". It was the last cut I wanted to add to my demo CD.

Everybody felt the verse I just laid down as they bobbed their heads to the track. Weed smoke was mad thick in the air and everybody was catching a contact. I had my top lieutenants, Spanky, Trevor, and Chucky, as well as the KS Crew up in the place. I wanted my protégés to do a feature on the song. The KS Crew couldn't wait for their chance to hold the mic down and shine.

T-Love went first with her rhyme and brought just as much heat as I did. Next, it was Luscious's turn to spit. She laid down a sexy, gangsta verse that was hot enough to put Lil' Kim and Foxy Brown on notice. D-Boogie closed out the track with lyrics so fierce that everybody was shocked they came from Danita and her cream puff self.

After everybody finished their verses and the hook was laid down, high-fives were passed around the room as the track played in the mega speakers positioned all around the studio. This track would definitely be a hit in the near future.

"Scar, that joint is off da chains. Don't none of these cats out here want it wit' you on the mic!" Latrell said. I knew my shit was straight butta, and she just cosigned what I felt.

"Yeah, I know I taught him well," Takeisha said. I grabbed her around the waist and lifted her onto my shoulders.

"Put me down, fool. You crazy as shit," she said. Her kicking and screaming made me drop her down onto the couch.

"Yeah, but you can't get enough of my crazy ass, girl," I shot back. I plopped down and began to tickle her. She laughed uncontrollably until tears began to fall down her cheeks. All of T-Love's friends knew that if you wanted her to give up a secret or to make her do something, then all you had to do was tickle her nonstop, on her sides, until she couldn't take it anymore.

"A'ight, y'all lovebirds, save that for the hotel. We need to be focused on business here," Trevor said.

Trevor was my ace boon coon. We had been hustling together since forever. The whole front of his mouth was laced with platinum like Baby from the Cash Money Millionaires. He loved to floss for the bitches, and that's why you would never find him out in public wearing less than fifty grand in jewels on his small, compact frame.

We had been through all kinds of drama together out in the streets, and Trevor loved catching bodies. He got his violent streak from watching his moms get her ass beat by her many boyfriends when he was growing up. Whenever I needed to bring somebody a move on the physical tip, he was eager to do the job. He was like a pit bull because when he locked in on your ass, it was all over for you.

"Word, man. I'm trying to get my flow on. Y'all holding me up," D-Boogie said. Everybody stopped what they were doing and turned to face her. We were shocked at how bold Danita was becoming. She was finally coming outta her shell.

"Yeah, let's get back to making these hits. I wanna send the demos out by the end of next week. We gotta make sure they tight," Ace said.

That was all the motivation the girls needed to be on point. We had a lot riding on their demo and our expectations were high. Without hesitation, they made their way into the vocal booth and began to lay down their verses one by one.

First Latrell laid down her verse.

Flame thrower, tittie shower,
the body's banging from head to toe.
A paper chasing honey from the hood,
I'm taking all these niggas' dough.
You wanna play, you gotta pay,
ain't a damn thing free over here.
Jealous bitches, they wanna see me,
this heart don't pump no fear.
But, ho, I will take ya man,
when I let 'im hit it from the back.
He'll leave you standing on the sideline,
while I'm countin' them stacks.

All three joined together for the chorus.

A gangsta bitch, when I switch,
my fine ass is making niggas fiend.
I like the diamond rings and things,
Strawberries and whipped cream.

A .22 inside my garter belt,
and I ain't scared to squeeze.
The KS Crew, motherfucker,
bringin' all these rap bitches to they knees.

Next, T-Love took her turn at the music.

I told y'all before,
that this mami like it raw.
I like my niggas in wife beaters,
hardcore, saying fuck the law.

A sophisticated lady,
but I'm shady as hell.
Street credentials is essential,
that's why our records sell.

Blowing up in every hood,
it's all good when we come through.
To all my niggas serving hand to hand,
I'm sending this one to you.

Ain't nothing else to say,
except cut that seven-figure check.
Give it to you how you want it, daddy,
Juicy got you crazy, all nice and wet.

After another chorus, D-Boogie let it flow.

Next up on the mic,
I be the one, D-Boogie, the assassin.
Pushing all the hottest whips,
dressing in the latest fashion.
The quietest one in the bunch,
but don't be fooled by the pretty smile,
'cause I be Killin' em Softly
with my rugged-ass style.
Relentless pursuit of that cheddar,
it keeps me out on the grind.
Slim and petite figure,
you wish your girl was this fine.
Dark chocolate skin tone,
it's smoother than butter.
A ladylike diva,
but you know I keep it gutter.

Me and my boys vibed to the track as the girls finished up their verses for "Gangstress." I felt proud watching my shorty do her thing. The beat was hot and the lyrics matched perfectly. The new track that the Smith Brothers laid down was much better than the original one I got from some local cats. I paid the Smith Brothers ten grand in cash, plus future royalties for all the songs that they produced.

As they were walking outta the vocal booth, my cell phone started to vibrate on my hip. I answered the phone and it was Rock, one of my workers. He called to tell me that he was low on product. I walked outta the room to get some privacy. I let Rock know that I would get at him in the morning to replenish his supply. That nigga was on some foul shit, but I would deal with him when I saw him.

When I returned to the main recording room, Takeisha stood near the door with her arms folded and her lips twisted.

"What you looking at me all wild-eyed for, girl?" I asked.

"Let me speak to you for a second, in private," she responded. We walked out into the front area of the studio to be alone.

"So, what's up?" I asked her.

"Who the fuck was that on the phone? Was it one of your bitches?" she asked.

I knew Takeisha loved me, but she was growing tired of my cheating ways. However, she wasn't no angel herself. A few months ago, she had a little thing going with this cat named Ringo, another young hustla in the game who was making some chips. He knew that Takeisha was my girl, but he didn't care.

She met him at the club, Choices, one night when she was mad after catching me cheating once again. Ringo was one of them Christopher Williams typa brothers with his light skin and grey eyes. She thought that I would never find out about her and Ringo fucking around, but that was a joke. Guys talk just as much as females and her rendezvous, as well as others that she had in the past, got back to me. However, I said nothing to her.

I really didn't care because her messing around on the side made me feel less guilty when she caught me out there. Nonetheless, I still played the role like a playa was supposed to do.

"That wasn't no female. That was my man, Rock. You wanna see the number? You can call it yourself. You're starting to be real paranoid. Stop buggin' out on a nigga," I responded.

"Fuck you, Scar. You can't tell the truth if it would save your sorry-ass life," Takeisha said.

I extended my arm out to give her my cell phone so that she could make the call. At first she pushed my hand away, but then she snatched the phone outta my hand. She dialed the last incoming number on my phone. She just knew that she had caught me slippin' again, but when Rock answered the phone, Takeisha felt stupid. She reached out to hug me, but I pushed her hands away.

"I'm sorry, baby. You the one that got me all paranoid and shit. Don't be forgetting about that bitch, Poochie, and all the rest of them skanks."

"You talking about the past, T. I told you I ain't fucking with them other hoes no more. It's all about you. We about to get this money. Now, get your fine ass back in the studio so that we can finish this demo."

"Anything you say, baby," Takeisha replied.

I grabbed Takeisha around the waist and gave her a wet tongue kiss before we walked back into the studio. Everybody moved about in the studio and tried to act as though they were busy. In reality, they were all tuned in at the door, listening to the whole conversation between me and Takeisha.

"Y'all some phony motherfuckers. I know damn well y'all was listening at the door," I said.

They were all flat busted and said nothing. After a moment of silence, laughter filled the room.

After everybody had their fun, the KS Crew went back in the vocal booth to finish two more songs. About four hours later, all the songs for both demos were recorded. All that was left was for Keon to work his magic and mix the songs down to the final versions, then burn them on a CD. Once that was done, we would be one step closer to fulfilling our dreams.

It was 5:00 in the morning when we left the studio. I dropped the girls off at their cribs. Me and Trevor still had business to take care of before I went home to chill. We had to pay Rock's ass a visit.

When we pulled up at his crib, we planned to straight whip this nigga's ass. It was 6:00 in the morning when we broke into his house and woke him up outta his sleep. This nigga was straight violating and had to be dealt with. He was fucking with my money.

"Nigga, get your bitch ass up. Why the fuck is your count so motherfucking short?" I asked.

"Yo, chill, Scar. Hold up man. You know I would

never steal from you. How long we done known each other? Think about it, man. If the count is short, you might wanna look at your man, Trevor, here," Rock said.

For the past few months, when I sent Trevor to collect money from Rock, his count was always a little light. At first, it started out being $500 short, then $1,000, and now he was short by almost $2,000 on this last package.

When he saw that I wasn't buying his excuse that Trevor had stolen the money, Rock tried to blame it on the young boys that he had working for him. He tried to tell me that they weren't collecting the right amount of money when they were doing their hand to hand sales.

I wasn't feeling that excuse, either. I had been in the game long enough to know when a cat was starting to get a little greedy seeing all that cash pass through his hands. While it was true that I would clear at least 25 grand every week to keep for myself, I still wasn't having nobody stealing from me without facing ramifications and repercussions. I had to make an example outta Rock.

"Nigga, even if I believed that it was your li'l niggas that was fucking up the count, it's still your responsibility to handle that shit to make it right," I said.

I continued to tear up Rock's mid-section while Trevor held him up from falling to the ground. Blood started to run outta his mouth. His face was swelled up on both sides, like Martin Lawrence's face when he fought Tommy Hearns on *Martin*.

Little did Rock know that I had eyes on him all along. I paid Bunk, one of the young boys who worked for him, to spy on him. Bunk told me that

Rock was going around bragging about taking my money. He told me about all of the money that Rock flashed around them and spent on his girl, Rita. He would take her shopping almost every day. This nigga was out here trickin' with a bitch at my expense. It's a shame what some niggas gotta do to get some pussy, but I guess every nigga out here ain't built like me, able to get pussy on the strength of my game.

"Yo, this fool think we stupid. We need to take his ass over to the butcher shop and show 'im how we really get down," Trevor said. Hearing that, Rock almost shitted in his pants because he knew what that meant. His life would be over soon if he didn't do something quick.

The butcher shop was an abandoned house where Trevor and I would take niggas we caught stealing or who we thought were trying to take over our drug strip. We would work 'em over before killin' 'em. After we had finished torturing the poor soul, Trevor would chop him up into little pieces and throw the scattered body parts into the Chesapeake Bay. Trevor had a chainsaw that he loved to use on his victims. He got a thrill outta hacking up somebody's body parts and watching them squirm and bleed to death. He was into watching bloody horror movies all the time. He was my boy and all, but he had a sick sense of humor.

"Nah, man, please. Ain't no need for all that. I'll work for free for however long you want me to. I'll get you all your money back. I got like seven grand in my safe in the living room," Rock said as he begged for his life.

"Oh, you gonna get my motherfucking money back, nigga. That ain't even a question. You get a pass for right now. After you get my money, then I'll decide if I wanna let your punk ass keep breathing. As it stands now, you owe me thirty grand, and that's including the interest. Get up and open up the fuckin' safe and get me that money," I said.

Rock lifted his bruised body off the bed and hobbled toward the living room. When he finally reached the safe, he took out all of the money he had and gave it to me. In reality, even if Rock did get all of my money back, I was still gonna kill him, just on GP. I had a reputation to uphold, but I still wanted to get all of the money that I could from Rock before I killed him. My greed for money was stronger than my desire for revenge.

As we made our exit from Rock's house, my cell phone rang. It was Ace. I wondered why in the fuck was he calling me so early in the morning. He must have some good shit to tell me.

"Yo, what's up? Tell me what's good, man," I said. I put the key in the ignition of my truck and drove off.

"I got good news for you, bro. Things went better than I expected. I got a deal so sweet set up that I gotta tell you about this shit in person. They want you and the KS Crew. I'ma be back in town Friday to give you all the info. Keep your nose clean, man, because I got big plans for you, Scar."

"Nah, me and trouble don't get along. I'm just an innocent little church mouse. I ain't trying to hurt nobody out in these streets," I replied. I was rubbing my sore knuckles from the beating I just put on Rock.

"I hear you. I'll get at you when I get back in town."

"Peace," I said and hung up the phone. I dropped Trevor off at his crib and made my way back to my condo out in Woodlawn. Since Takeisha would be out with her girls later on, I planned to hook up with one of my other tender young dime pieces to have a little fun of my own.

4

Takeisha (T-Love)

The KS Crew always looked fly when we went out. I had on a lime green short set that showed off my phat ass, thighs and shapely breasts. Latrell wore some skin-tight rhinestone-covered jeans with a baby tee that had the word "Luscious" written in glitter across her chest. She had the outfit specially designed by her girl Tiffany, who had her own boutique called Exclusively 4 U, in downtown Baltimore. Danita wore a mini-skirt that came down to the upper part of her thighs and a strapless top that showcased her soft, even-toned shoulders and back. She had a pair of legs that any model would kill for.

We were on our way to Choices to get our groove on. Latrell had borrowed Tank's Lexus GS 300 for us to front in tonight. Even though we were all under the age of 21, it didn't matter. As sexy as we looked, none of the bouncers dared to ask for ID. Their eyes were too busy watching our shapely figures and pretty faces as we walked by them.

We made our way to the bar to order our drinks. I ordered an Amaretto Sour with a twist of pineapple. Latrell ordered a Mai Tai, mixed heavy with rum. Danita had a Strawberry Daiquiri. She only drank when we went to the club because she had a bad episode a few years ago when she drank too much hard liquor. Since then, she made sure that she watched how much liquor she drank when she went out.

One night when we were at a house party, this dude named Pick talked Danita into drinking Tequila shots with him. Latrell and I were nowhere to be found as we were in the party having fun on our own. Danita had a thing for Pick and thought that he was cool, so she went along with him. After she had about four Tequila shots, Danita was silly drunk and basically open for anything. Seeing that she was not in her right mind, Pick took advantage of the situation. He coerced her into following him into one of the empty bedrooms in the house. After they were there for about ten minutes, he had managed to talk her into getting outta her clothes. She was drunk, he was looking sexy to her, so she was all too with it. Needless to say, they wound up getting their freak on. After they were done and Danita was half-conscious on the bed, Pick had some slick shit up his sleeve.

Pick had planned to run a train on Danita with two of his other boys. While the lights were out, he slipped outta the room and left the door open for one of his boys, Tony, to slide in and get a piece of

Danita's fine ass. Danita was too drunk to know what was going on. Tony had succeeded in getting his clothes off and was about to mount Danita when he was startled by a hard knock at the door.

It was me and Latrell to the rescue. We had felt that something was up because we hadn't seen Danita for a while in the party. Christie, another girl from around the way told us that she overheard Pick and his boys talking about running a train on Danita. When we found out where she was and what Pick had planned for her, we had to go and save our girl.

Luckily, we made it to the bedroom where she was in time to save her from gaining the label of neighborhood skank. We quickly grabbed her highly intoxicated behind outta the bed and got her dressed, then took her back to my house to sleep off her stupor. The next morning, when she found out what she almost did, Danita swore to never drink that much again.

"Let's see what kinda fine niggas is up in here tonight. I'm trying to dig in somebody's pockets deep," Latrell said as she made her way to the dance floor. Danita and I grabbed our drinks and followed behind her.

We were dancing up a storm as the DJ played a mixture of hip-hop and R&B. Several guys had approached us throughout the night, offering to buy us drinks. Of course, Latrell and I gladly accepted most of them and sent those same guys on their way afterwards. We had damn near sweated out our fresh hairdos, but we didn't care. We were out to have a good time, and that was exactly what we did.

It was about 3:00 in the morning when we

started to get tired. We were ready to leave. Latrell had met her quota, getting phone numbers from six different dudes that had balla potential. She planned to call each one of them to see which one was down to spend his money on her. I wasn't too far behind her in the number department, getting four of my own. I hadn't planned to use any of them right now, but I would hold onto them for an emergency situation. The next time Scar and I were on the outs, I would give one of them a call to take me out or to buy me an outfit to make me feel special. Several guys approached Danita, but she didn't give her number out or take any. Her heart belonged to Larry.

"Yo, tonight was off the hook. I had mad fun up in there," I said as we headed home.

"Me too, girl. Niggas was sweating us all night. I definitely got my mack on, and I know you did. Miss Tight Drawers back there was being all anti and shit. She all in *looove* and whatnot," Latrell said, referring to Danita.

"Don't hate on me, hooker, 'cause I don't fuck with every nigga that got a Benz that's tryin' to holla. By the time you wanna settle down, your shit gonna be worn out," Danita shot back. Latrell shot her a mean stare. After a few seconds, we all had to laugh. No matter what, even though we had our differences, we were the best of friends.

"Leave my girl alone. If she wanna be in love, let her. She ain't like your cold-hearted ass," I said. I always took up for Danita when Latrell teased about her goodie-two-shoes ways.

"D, you know I'm just fuckin' with you. You know you my girl," Latrell said. We shared a group hug. This was definitely a Kodak moment to be treasured.

"I just thought about it. I ain't going home. You can drop me off at Scar's house. He said that he was gonna be home all night watching the baseball games. I'm trying to get my swerve on. It's been about three days since he hit me off," I said.

"A'ight, that ain't even a problem," Latrell replied.

Latrell made her way onto North Avenue to get to I-83. Danita had fallen asleep in the back seat by the time we pulled up outside the front gate of Scar's apartment complex. I entered Scar's private code and the gate swung open. Within no time, we were outside his building. I gave Latrell a hug and jumped outta the car.

Scar had given me the key to his condo after the last time I caught him cheating. It was his way of trying to regain my trust. As far as I could see, he had been faithful since the incident with the girl, Poochie. I usually called before I came over, but tonight I chose not to. I was drunk and felt extra horny. I planned to put this pussy on him like he never had it before.

5

Scar and Takeisha (T-Love)

Scar was knocking the lining outta Fredericka's hot, young cunt. With every thrust of his member, her screams of passion got louder. Her pussy was wetter than a waterfall after he ate her out for about a good hour, non-stop. She returned the favor and gave him some head that was outta this world. They did it in every imaginable position. Even though she was only 17 years old, Fredericka handled herself between the sheets like a wily pro. The fact that she took two tabs of Ecstasy before they got started only increased her level of arousal.

"Damn, Scar, I love that shit! Bang this pussy out, baby. Oooh yeah, just like that!" Fredricka yelled. Scar gave her just what she wanted as he continued to beat that young pussy up.

About three weeks before they finally decided to hook up and do the damn thing, Scar met Fredericka in Owings Mills Mall. He saw her walking by herself and figured that she was a prime candidate to be his next victim. She was wearing a pair of booty-huggin' Daisy Dukes with a midriff shirt that showed off her flat, Janet Jackson like abs. Her nipples were showing through her shirt and made him grow hornier by the minute as he watched her walk. She had a reddish-brown complexion and an hour-glass figure. He noticed her freshly pedicured feet through her open-toed sandals. She wore her hair in micro braids that came down to the middle of her back. After admiring her fineness for a while, he proceeded toward her to put his mack down.

"Hey, what's going on, shorty? Can I holla at you for a second?" Scar asked.

"It depends on what you got to say. My time is precious, so make it quick," Fredericka said. Her feisty attitude made Scar want her more.

"I feel you, ma. I ain't trying to hold you up or nothing. My name is Scar, and all I need is ya name and ya number and we can continue this conversation at another time when you're not so busy."

He could tell that she was a sack chaser. Scar peeped her checking out all the ice he had on and knew she was down to hook up. She was the kinda girl that liked to be on the arm of a balla, and Scar was that nigga. He put the bait out there and waited for her to nibble on it.

"Well, my name is Fredericka, Mr. Scar. Give me your cell phone, and I can program my number in there so I can be sure that you don't lose it," she said.

Since the day they met, they had spent countless hours on the phone. The conversations usually got hot and set the stage for them to finally hook up and have some booty-spankin', headboard-bangin' sex.

"Damn, shorty, this pussy is what's up. You ain't lie when you said this shit was like the Atlantic Ocean. This pussy is wetter than a motherfucker," Scar said.

They were going at it like two dogs in heat when the door swung open behind them. They couldn't hear a thing because the music was so loud. Takeisha stood in the door, with her eyes wide open, watching Scar fuck another woman with her legs pointed toward the sky. She thought about all of the times that he had her in the same position. She knew that he had cheated on her, but to actually see it for herself, it hurt her deeply.

She slowly walked away from the bedroom door. The moans and groans from Scar and Fredericka's fuckfest echoed in the background. It made her stomach turn. She was crushed. Her heart was broken. In spite of all the drama he put her through, she really loved Scar.

When Takeisha reached the kitchen, she looked underneath the sink to retrieve a big steel pot. She filled it to the rim with water and placed it on the stove to heat up. Tears were running down her cheeks and she cursed Scar out in every foul way imaginable under her breath. She wanted this motherfucker to die for playing her out like that.

Why the fuck would he give me a key to his house and have some other bitch up in here? she thought as she waited for the water to boil.

After it came to a boil, she turned off the gas burner and removed it from the stove with the potholder. She slowly began walking back toward the bedroom, becoming more enraged to hear that they were still going at it like animals. When she reached the bedroom door, she gingerly walked into the room to see Scar's backside facing her, fucking Fredericka missionary style. Without thinking, she hurled the pot of boiling hot water toward the bed. The heat from the hot water burned up against Scar's back. Fredericka's exposed legs were also treated to a warm surprise. They both yelled out in agony.

"Aahh shit! What the fuck? Who the fuck is that?" Scar screamed as he turned around to face the person who had just poured the blazing hot water on him. When he saw who it was, he instinctively reacted and slapped the living shit outta Takeisha. She flew backwards from the impact of the blow and landed up against the wall.

"I'm glad that shit burned your lying, cheating ass, motherfucker. Fuck you and your bitch," Takeisha yelled.

Enraged, Scar ran toward her and hit her with full force, anywhere and everywhere that his blows would connect. Takeisha tried to cover up as best she could. She got in a few solid blows of her own, but they had no effect on him. He had never hit her before, and she had never seen this side to him.

"Bitch, who the fuck told you to come over here without calling? You wanted to catch a nigga cheating, well, you got exactly what you was looking for," Scar said.

"Why the fuck do I need to call if I'm supposed to be your girl?" Takeisha said.

He didn't bother to respond to her question. He continued to pound on her like he was fighting another dude. Her face was swollen and bloody. His back was raw from the hot water, but his pain was blocked out by his rage.

Even though he was dead wrong, he still had to save face. She came to his house uninvited, which was a major violation in his world. He gave her the key to his house because she was his main girl, but he still figured she would never come over without calling first because she had never done that before.

Fredericka attempted to get off the bed and make it toward the bathroom with her clothes when he motioned for her not to leave.

"Nah, shorty, you ain't going nowhere. This bitch right here is about to leave. You was invited, she wasn't," he said.

He grabbed Takeisha by her hair and dragged her ruggedly toward the front door. He pushed her out into the hallway.

"Now get the fuck outta here, with ya sneaky ass. Don't think that I ain't know about your ass fuckin' with that nigga Ringo and them other cats," he yelled at her.

Takeisha couldn't really say shit because she too was cold busted. She sat on the ground with a blank look on her face. She wondered how he found out about her messing around. There was nothing else to say. The way things looked now, they were through.

"You limp-dick bastard. Fuck you and your two-dollar ho. Don't call my fucking house no more begging me to take your tired ass back," Takeisha screamed at him from the other side of the door.

"There ain't a chance of that happening now, ho. Oh yeah, as of right now, the KS Crew is through. Your contract with me and Ace is cancelled," Scar said.

"You can't do that, nigga. We got a signed contract!" Takeisha yelled.

"Well, I can show you better than I can tell you. Y'all careers are over as far as I'm concerned," Scar replied.

Feeling dejected, Takeisha walked away from Scar's door. Not only had he slammed the door in her face, but he also slammed the door on her opportunity to get a record deal. She wondered how she could explain this to her girls. Her world was turned upside down over this one incident.

What the fuck am I gonna do? she wondered as she walked down the stairs and outta the building.

6

Takeisha (T-Love)

Still pissed off after I made my way outta his building, I ran my house key along the side of his truck, leaving him with an unpleasant reminder of me. Every woman knew that if you wanted get back at a man for hurting you, you destroyed his most prized possessions—usually his car or his home. Why men continually left their most valuable possessions in harm's way, within reach of a scorned woman was a mystery that would remain until the end of time. That wasn't all I had cooked up for him, though. There would be more drama to come. His ass wasn't gonna get off that easy.

I walked toward the front gate and outta the condo complex in a shambles. I managed to call my father at home to come and pick me up. I waited for him at the Royal Farms store up the street from Scar's apartment complex. When Rashid saw my face, the man that I saw before me wasn't the calm father that I was used to seeing. I got into his car and he just went off. I had never seen him this angry before.

"That nigga hit my baby girl? He did this to your face? Is he still in that fucking house? Where the fuck does he live?" Rashid asked in a fit of rage. He was ready to get some of his Muslim brothers together and pay Scar's ass a late-night visit.

"Calm down, Daddy. I don't want you to do nothing stupid. I'm a big girl. I know how to handle this situation. Trust me, he won't get away with this. When I'm done with him, he's gonna wish that he never messed around on me."

"That ignorant ass nigga don't know whose daughter he done put his hands on. It's niggas like him that make all of us black men look bad. He had another woman in his house, is that what y'all were fighting about?" he asked. I nodded my head to answer his question.

"I hope you learn a lesson from this situation here. You need to leave them no-good, hoodrat, drug-dealing destroyers of our people alone. They don't have no respect for themselves, to sell poison to their own people. Why would you think that a man like him would treat you with any respect? I know I done raised you better than that. After tonight, I better not see that nigga anywhere near you or his ass is mine." Rashid yelled.

"You're right, Daddy. I know you're right. I'm done with him," I said. I leaned up against his shoulder and began to cry. He turned his car off and wrapped his arm around me.

"It's all right, baby girl. I'm sorry for yelling at you. I only want the best for you. It's time for you to start making better choices in men. That fool is on the fast track to a deadend road, and would only take you right along with him. The only place selling drugs will get you is either death or the penitentiary. I'll be damned if I let some no-good, lacking-knowledge-of-self snake like him take my baby girl down with him. I would give my own life before I let that happen."

"Daddy, I love you. I swear I wish you knew how much I really do love you. You make me feel so special," I said. I raised up off of his chest and wiped away my tears with my left hand. My father just smiled and turned the key in his ignition to start the car.

Before we went home, we stopped at IHOP to get something to eat. We talked for a while about me going to college in the fall. He told me about how things were going at the store. After we finished eating, we headed home. I was eager to get into my bed and sleep the day away. My mind and body were tired. My face was sore, and I knew I would have bruises on it from that motherfucker hitting on me like I was a goddamn man.

I put some ice on my eye, which was bloodshot red and swollen. I lay across my bed to get some rest, wishing that our fight was just a bad dream, but knowing that it wasn't. I thought about some of the good things I liked about Scar as well as the bad. My mind was twisted up right now. Part of me hated him, and the other part loved him. I had to decide which side of me I would listen to.

After I tossed and turned for a while, I drifted off to sleep. Not until the next day did it really sink in that my fight with Scar had possibly cost us the chance of a lifetime. Since I had been dating him, he was the guiding force behind the KS Crew's career. His money and industry connections were our ticket to the big time. I had no idea what we were gonna do now. Going to college in the fall was looking more and more like a realistic option at this point.

I had to figure out a way to break the news to my girls. I knew that they would be pissed off and disappointed.

7

Latrell (Luscious)

My mind drifted off elsewhere as I lay in the bed with Tank. I stopped by his crib when I dropped T and Danita off after we left the club.

I had been messing with Tank for the last year, off and on. He never sexually satisfied me, in any way. I only dealt with him because he liked to spend money on me. I often joked with my girls about Tank having a two-inch dick. When he was inside of me, I barely felt his puny dick and had to fake orgasms all the time just to get the sex over with.

Tank was a midlevel hustler with a nice, small drug operation in South Baltimore. He had a crew of about ten dudes that worked for him. He used to be a star basketball player at the legendary Dunbar High School until he blew his knee out in the middle of his senior year. Before that, more than a hundred schools were looking to recruit him to play ball for their program. Some said that he was the best point guard to come outta Baltimore since Skip Wise.

With his basketball dreams shattered, Tank turned to doing what he knew would make him a lotta money—selling crack. Like Biggie Smalls said, "Either you're slingin' rock or you got a wicked jump shot." That saying was true for him and most of the other dudes that I knew from around the way.

On several occasions, Tank had me pick up and transport drugs from New York City, by way of Amtrak train or the Greyhound bus. I wasn't no scared bitch. Fear never lived in my heart. My mother raised me to be that way. When it came to gettin' money, I was down to do whatever. If it was money to be made, then I was down to get mine. In my world, love didn't have a place. Like the Wu Tang Clan said, cash clearly ruled everything around me.

"So, what's up, Latrell? Did I beat that coochie up last night or what?" Tank leaned over and asked me. He ran his hands across my firm backside.

"You know you did, baby. You had me cummin' all night, even in my sleep." I rolled over and licked on his chest in a teasing fashion. I laughed inside as I gassed up his ego. If there was one thing I got from my mother, it was her ability to run game on a man.

"Oh, shit. That feels good. You better stop before you get my man all hard again. I gotta go take care of some business in a few," Tank said.

"Can I get some money to go shopping? I wanna go buy something sexy to wear for you. I know you wanna make me happy, don't you?" I asked in my most sexy voice.

"Damn, girl. You must think I'm a walking ATM machine and shit. Here your ass go. Take this and buy something that you know is gonna turn me on when I see you in it." He gave me twenty crisp hundred-dollar bills outta the wad of money sitting on top of his dresser. Getting his money was just too easy.

"You got that, sugar dick. Anything for you," I replied.

As I watched Tank get dressed, my cell phone rang. It was Takeisha and Danita on the other end. I noticed that Takeisha was crying as she tried to speak.

"What's up, homies? Damn, T, why you crying and shit? You and Scar had another one of y'all arguments last night?" I asked in a joking manner.

By Takeisha's response, I could tell that this was no laughing matter. She ran down everything that went on at Scar's house the night before.

"Damn, that's fucked up. You shouldn't have went over without calling, though. You know how niggas are. They ain't shit. He ain't even worth you crying over. Man, suck that shit up and move on," I said.

I hope she is done with him. Now I can get a chance to fuck his ass.

"Latrell, whose side are you on? Our homegirl needs our support right now. If he gave her a key and was doing the right thing, she shouldn't have to call before she came over," Danita interjected.

"I'm just keeping it real. When you go to somebody's house without calling first, you liable to see anything when you get there. Besides, it ain't like

T wasn't getting her some dick on the side. She wasn't no Miss Perfect like your ass," I said.

"Fuck you, Latrell. Who the fuck are you to judge me? I called you for support, not to get no fucking lecture. If I would have known that this was how you was gonna carry it, I wouldn't have called you. I'm fucked up right now," Takeisha said. Her voice sounded muffled as she tried to talk and fight back her tears at the same time.

"Girl, stop playing. You know we all family. It's KS Crew for life. I'm over at Tank's house. I'ma have him drop me off at your house. I'll be there in like a half-hour. We can talk more then. Is that cool?" I asked. In the back of my mind, I wondered if this little incident would fuck up my chance to get a record deal.

"I'll see you when you get here," Takeisha replied.

When I saw her later, I couldn't believe that Scar beat my girl up like that. I felt bad for her. No woman deserved to get hit by a man. If that was me, I woulda killed his ass. I felt kinda guilty for all of the times I wanted to get with his ass. I knew that T felt fucked up inside. I knew just the right thing to take that nigga off her mind.

"Yo, y'all wanna go shopping or what?" I asked.

"We ain't got no money, girl," T said.

"I didn't ask if y'all had any money. I got this. You dealin' with a boss bitch over here," I said. I pulled out the knot of money I just got from Tank and showed it to them.

"Girl, you is off da chains. You broke that nigga Tank off for some change I see. If you treating, then I'm trying to go shopping with you. Let's get the hell outta here," T said.

We walked up the block to get a cab and went to

the mall to take Takeisha's mind off her troubles. Looking fly in a new outfit just had that impact on any woman who had a flair for the finer things in life. A lot of niggas would say that I was heartless, and they would be right, but when it came to my girls, I had a soft spot. They were the only ones I fucked with like that.

8

Ace

I sat in the bar area of Mackenzie's Restaurant waiting for Scar to arrive. It was now 2 p.m. and Scar was an hour late for our appointment. I was growing tired of him missing appointments with me when we had business to discuss. I figured that Scar was probably out late the night before drinking and smoking trees with his boys or holding court at the Cathouse with a group of strippers. His lifestyle was gonna eventually become a problem for both of us.

I saw Scar as a raw talent with unlimited potential for a long career in the entertainment industry. He had the rugged good looks that would go over well on the movie screen. He had the street credibility to back his hardcore rhymes. A lot of Hollywood producers looked for rappers who had actually lived the life to play roles in urban gangster movies. They didn't need a lot of training because all they did was reenact on screen the realities they lived out in the streets. Many had tried, but no one had stepped up to fill Tupac's shoes. Once I secured him a record deal, I planned to start shopping Scar around to any young up and coming movie director willing to give him a role.

I was on my second Hennessy and Coke when I saw Scar stroll in the front door with Trevor and Chucky following closely behind him. My face got tight as I wondered why the hell Scar had to bring his riff raff homeboys with him everywhere he went. They had no motivation to do anything positive in life. The hood and the street life was all they knew and the only reality they wanted. With all the money they made out in the streets selling drugs, none of them had ever traveled out of the country to see the world or owned any valuable long-term assets. It's one thing to have lived the thug life and to talk about it on records, but to still be involved in that lifestyle when you have a legitimate means to make as much, if not more money was foolish. I just hoped that my many lectures to Scar would pay off and make him change his circle of friends. If not, a stiff prison sentence was all that awaited him in the long run. Either way, I planned to ride my cash cow until the wheels fell off.

"Well, it's about time, man. You're only *one hour* late for our appointment," I said sarcastically.

"My bad, dog. I had to go to the hospital last night. I just got out this morning," he said. Scar sat down slowly on the bar stool, in obvious pain.

"What the hell happened to you? Oh Lord, do I really wanna know?" I asked.

"Nah, it ain't what you think. This wasn't no street shit. That bitch Takeisha caught me fucking last night and threw a pot of hot water on my ass," Scar said.

He went on to explain what exactly went down. Trevor sat to the side and just couldn't stop laughing his ass off. I tried not to laugh, but I gave Scar a look that said *I told you she was gonna get you one day for playing with her heart.*

He said his back was still in pain from the burns caused by the hot water that Takeisha had thrown on him. He had bandages on to cover his burns until they healed.

He and Fredericka were both treated at Sinai Memorial Hospital. Her burns were less severe than his were. She got away with a few minor burns on her legs that would heal in a couple of days.

"Well, I'm glad you're all right. Now, let's get down to business. I got you a sweet deal set up with Marquee Records. They wanna give you a record deal with a $750,000 cash advance up front. They wanna guarantee to release your first two albums and have an option on the next five. Plus, they wanna sign the KS Crew to a deal, too, with a $250,000 advance. Now, you know you gotta go fix this little situation with ya girl, right? You might have to kiss a little ass, man," I said.

"Fuck that. That bitch burnt me. I'm glad I whipped her fucking ass. I ain't tryin' to see her crazy ass again. Fuck the money they offering for them. Just do the damn deal for my shit," Scar responded.

I wasn't hearing that, because Scar was fucking with the twenty percent manager's fee I would get if the KS Crew signed the record contract. I had to do something to change his mind. Dealing with these ignorant-ass street niggas was a headache sometimes. They tend to let their machismo stand in the way of sound business decisions.

"Think about the money, man. A hustla like yourself ain't gonna let all this loot get by without gettin' ya cut, are you playa? Not only that, you better hope that she don't call the police and try to get you locked up," I said.

"You heard what the fuck I said! Do the deal for me. Fuck them bitches. I made them hoes and they ain't shit without me. They all gonna suffer for that bitch's mistake. We can find another group of rap bitches to take their place. T can fuck around and call the police if she wants to. She's gonna come up missing. You might come up missing too if you keep pressing this issue," Scar said.

He gave me a cold-hearted stare to let me know that this issue was no longer open for debate. Trevor wrapped his hand around the pistol tucked in his dip to further solidify the message. I liked money, but I loved my life. I knew Scar could end my existence at the drop of a dime if he wanted to, so I took heed to his warning. The KS Crew was a dead issue at this point. I turned my focus back to my top money client.

"A'ight, boss. If that's what you want, then so be it. Let's eat. Excuse me waitress, bring us a bottle of your best champagne, please," I said.

The waitress returned with the champagne and we all shared a toast. About thirty minutes later, our food came out and we ate like hogs while I broke down the specifics of the record deal that was being offered. Scar liked what he heard, and was glad to finally get a chance to show that he was as good as any MC out in the field already. I just hoped his ass could stay out of trouble long enough for us to cash in on this chance to be in the limelight.

9

Takeisha (T-Love)

About a month had passed since my big fallout with Scar. I hadn't heard from him, and I made no effort to call him either. My mind was telling me to forget about him. He was a no-good, cheating dog that I should be glad to have outta my life. However, my heart was missing him like crazy. He was my first love. While it was true that we both messed around on each other, we still shared an inexplicable special bond that couldn't be erased by all the drama that went on between us.

Despite all of his faults, he treated me royally. He spared no expense to make me happy. To a girl who thrived off of being spoiled, that meant more than almost anything in the world.

I had cried myself to sleep many nights since our dreadful confrontation. I tried to put up a front to my girls that I was getting over Scar by dating other guys, but my heart told another story.

Rashid happened to walk by my bedroom and saw me stretched out across my bed, staring into space as though I had lost my best friend.

"What's up, baby girl? You got time for your old man today?" he said.

"Hey, Daddy. I always got time for you. You're the one man I know will never disappoint me," I responded.

"You better never forget it. I'll always be here for you, no matter what. I know you're not still thinking about that sorry bastard. You need to be glad that he's outta your life," he said.

"I know, Daddy. It's just hard. You were young and in love once. It's just hard letting go when you care about someone. You haven't let go of Mommy all of these years," I responded. As soon as those words left my mouth, I wished I could take them back, even though it was something I had felt inside for a long time. It kinda slipped out. I obviously struck a nerve, because Rashid's facial expression changed drastically.

"Point taken, sweetheart. It has been hard for me to get over your mother. However, that's a different situation. We shared a life together for a long time. More importantly, our love for one another produced a beautiful gift. That gift was you. Scar is just one of many men you will come across in your life. You're still young and got a lot of exploring to do. Don't get all caught up and let him make you into one of those psycho chicks," he said as he kissed me on my forehead. What he said was funny, and it was good advice from the heart.

"Daddy, you always know the right thing to say at the right time. You don't have to worry about me stalking him. Besides, as fine as I am, I got men lined up trying to get with this," I shot back.

"A'ight now, don't be too fast. I ain't ready to be no grandfather yet," he replied.

"I'm just joking, Daddy. But for real, what am I gonna do about my music now? Scar was handlin' everything for us. He owns the rights to the music that we did for him, and being that he ain't speaking to me, he probably won't give me our demo tape. What do we do now?" I asked.

"Never put all of your eggs in one basket. You should never have put all of your hope into him. If he doesn't wanna give you copies of the music that you did in his studio, you might have to chalk it up as a loss. Trust me, I've been through that scenario enough times back in the day. I wanted to tell you this, but I had to let you see it for yourself. If you're really serious about your music, then I can get you girls into the studio. I got an old partner of mine whose son happens to be a rap producer and has his own studio. I'll pay for everything. Business at the record store has been good to me. Consider it as an investment, but under one condition: you girls have to go to school. It's nothing wrong with following your dreams, but I want you all to have some education to fall back on," he said.

My face lit up. My father always came through for me. Why didn't I think to ask him for help from the jump? Oh well, it was too late to harp on what I didn't do. I had to take advantage of this chance he was about to give us.

"Daddy, you would really do that for me? I can't wait to tell Latrell and Danita. I just looove you so much," I said. I jumped off of the bed and gave him a big hug.

"Remember what I said. I wanna see some class schedules so that I know you girls are registered in school, now," he reminded me.

"That's a small thing, Daddy. We never intended not to go to school in the fall. I gotta get dressed so that we can go out and celebrate. Let me call the girls!" I said ecstatically.

Rashid made his way out of my room and I got on the phone to call my crew. I told them to be dressed in an hour and to come to my house because I had good news.

Like clockwork, Danita and Latrell arrived at my house in exactly an hour. They both spoke to Rashid and made their way to my room. The three of us gossiped for a few as we made sure that our outfits were in perfect order.

"A'ight, so what's the big secret, T? Are you and Scar getting back together?" Latrell asked sarcastically when we were seated at a table at The Cheesecake Factory.

"No, smart ass. My father has agreed to put up the money to get us into the studio so that we can record a new demo. He's gonna set everything up for us with an old friend of his," I replied.

"No shit! Are you serious?" Danita asked enthusiastically. I nodded my head to reaffirm what I had just said.

"That's some good shit right there. When do we get started?" Latrell asked.

"I'm not sure yet. He said that he would let me know by the end of the week," I replied.

"I got an idea. Let's see if we can get them cats, the Smith Brothers, to do some more tracks for us.

They were kinda cool. I was feeling their whole vibe. See if you can get their number from Scar."

I rolled my eyes at Latrell.

"Shit, I ain't say go fuck him or nothing. This is business, not personal. You know the drill, girl," Latrell suggested.

"Yeah, I feel you. I'll have to see about that," I responded. I wasn't even trying to go down that road.

"Or, if you can't get the info from him, I'm sure Ace will give it to you. They are friends of his," Danita chimed in.

"I said that I'll see about that. Damn. Let's talk about something else. I'm trying to have a good time," I said.

"Well then, you know we gotta celebrate tonight. My moms is gonna be gone for a few days doing her thing. I already got an ounce of weed at the crib. We can grab a bottle of Moet and get tore up tonight," Latrell suggested.

"Now that's proper! It's KS Crew for life!" we all said at the same time. The show was back on for us.

10

Takeisha (T-Love) and Scar

"**F**uck you, bitch. I ain't giving you nothing or doing shit for ya ass. You wanna be sneaking up on a nigga and playin' big girl games, then you get your own connections in this music business. I done destroyed all of the master copies of the music you recorded at my studio. I guess you could say that you're fucked, " Scar said to me.

I had called him to ask about getting a copy of our demo tape, or at least a hook-up with the Smith Brothers. It had been almost two months, and I figured enough time had passed since our fight. I thought maybe we could have a civil conversation about business, but now I saw that it was a bad idea. Scar acted like a total asshole. I would be damned if I let him carry me again and not say something in response. He must've forget that I could be a nasty motherfucker as well. Two could play that game.

"You're cheating on me and you got the nerve to carry me greasy like that? Fuck you, too, you sorry bastard. You destroyed all of our music? Well, the only person that you hurt was yaself, because that was ya studio time that was wasted, jackass. You're a silly, immature motherfucker. I thought that we could talk like adults, but I see that we one adult short on this phone," I said.

"Yeah, whatever. You played yourself, shorty. Just accept that shit. I wasn't the only one out here fucking around on the side. You and your li'l sneaky ass. It don't matter, 'cause all that's over with now. Time is money. You ain't making me no loot, so you wasting my goddamn time right now. I don't need ya ass because I got a deal now, bitch. Marquee Records signed me to a lovely deal. You're the one that gotta start from scratch," he replied, laughing at his own silly attempt at humor.

I didn't find a damn thing funny. His ass got a deal and we gotta start from scratch? Oh, this motherfucker had to feel my wrath. Just wait until I was finished with his ass.

"I'm glad you finally showed me what you think of me, Scar. Now I finally know what was really in your heart. You better watch ya motherfucking back, you faggot," I said as I angrily hung up the phone.

My heart was crushed that Scar would talk to me like that. Even though he knew about my indiscretions, he never confronted me about them before now. To me, that made me feel as though he really didn't care as much as he said he did. If he hadn't cheated on me, then I would have never done the same in return. The double standard that men have in relationships about being able to have their cake and eat it too was in full effect in this situation.

I had to face the reality that our relationship was over and it was time for me to move on with my life. He had to really hate me to try to destroy my music career. However, I would be damned if I let him stop me from achieving my dream. I picked up my phone and dialed Ace's number.

"Hey, Ace. This is Takeisha. What's going on?"

Through all of my ups and downs with Scar, Ace was always cool with me. We got along well. I liked his professional attitude and the way he handled his business. I wished we could get him to manage us, but I knew that was outta the question. Scar probably had his ass scared to come near us.

"What's up, shorty? How are you? I heard about your breakup with Scar. I'm sorry to hear about that," he said.

"It is what it is, Ace. The nigga got what he deserved. I know you can feel me on that. You ain't gotta say it because I know you work for him and all. You know him better than me," I responded.

I knew Ace had a hard job dealing with Scar and all of his drama out in the streets, from his being arrested to getting into shootouts with rival drug crews. Ace had to bail him outta situations more than enough times.

"Yeah, you know I was laughing my ass off inside when he told me about what you did with the boiling water. I told him that you was gonna get his ass one day," Ace said. He let out a loud chuckle. I had to look back and laugh my damn self.

"I just got off the phone with your bastard of a

client. He said he destroyed all of our material. He told me you got him a deal with Marquee Records. He couldn't wait to rub it in. I guess I should say congratulations to you, even though your client's an asshole," I said.

"Thanks, T. I shouldn't tell you this, but they wanted to sign y'all too. Scar vetoed the deal. You know how that goes. When a label wants an artist bad enough, they'll do whatever he wants to satisfy him. I'm sorry y'all had to get fucked in this situation. He pays me, so I gotta do what he says. Plus, I ain't having him and his psycho crew running up on me. Don't let it be known that I told you any of this info," Ace said.

I was even more pissed at Scar when Ace laid out the specifics of the deal that was offered for us. Just because our relationship was over, he let that shit stop not only us, but himself from making money?

He must be really feeling himself. He's gonna be feeling something else when I'm done with his ass.

"What's done is done. Ace, you know I ain't no snitch. What we talk about is between us. The KS Crew is some stand-up bitches. Besides, if they were willing to sign us, then I know that somebody else is gonna come along to pick us up. That's what I was calling to talk to you about. My pops is gonna work it out so that we can get into the studio to do a new demo. Do you think that you can hook me up with your boys, the Smith Brothers?" I asked him.

"Now that I can do. Hold for a sec while I find their number," Ace said. He looked through the phonebook on his cell phone and retrieved their number, rambling off the digits to me.

"Thanks, Ace. That was good looking out. I hope we can work together in the future. You're mad cool. I fuck with you like that," I said.

"You good peeps too, T. My boys are fair. They won't try to burn your pockets up. They thought that y'all were kinda hot and liked working with the group. Good luck with your project. If you need anything else, feel free to give me a holla," he replied.

"You got that," I responded.

"I'm out," he said.

As soon as I got off of the phone with Ace, I called the Smith Brothers. The phone rang several times and I got no answer. When the answering machine came on, I decided to leave them a message.

Yes, this is Takeisha Jenkins. Y'all did some tracks for my group, the KS Crew, recently. I hope you remember me. I got your number from Ace. Well, the reason that I'm calling you is because me and my girls are no longer working with Scar and Bulletproof Productions. We're doing our own thing. We were hoping that we could work with y'all again. I mean your tracks were hot. We have studio time set up and all. If you could give me a call at your earliest convenience, I would appreciate it. My number is 410-555-3234. I hope to hear from y'all soon. Be easy.

After I finished recording my message, I called my girls and gave them the 411. Latrell and Danita were just as excited as I was. Rashid had told me earlier in the day that he had arranged for us to lay down tracks at his friend's son's studio in Edmondson Village. He would only charge us $25 per hour for studio time. My father had agreed to give us $3,000 to pay for musical production for the demo. Now all we had to do was convince the Smith Brothers to work with us for that price and we were set. That was no problem. I could be extremely persuasive when I wanted to be.

11

Danita (D-Boogie)

I had been waiting almost two hours for Larry to arrive for our date. We were supposed to go to TGI Friday's to get something to eat and then go to the movies. I called his father's auto body shop and got no answer. He must have left work. His cell phone was turned off because when I tried to call him, it went straight to voicemail. There was also no answer at his house.

I was concerned because it was unlike him to be late and not at least call to tell me something. In fact, he was the one who got on me all the time because I took long to get ready whenever we went out. Larry was usually the reliable one.

Throughout all of the time we had been dating, I grew to feel a special bond with Larry that I'd never felt with another guy. He was different from most of the other guys that I had met. While all the other guys I came across were into hustling and the fast lifestyle, Larry spent most of his time with his father working on cars. He was a plain kinda man and not into wearing expensive clothing or a lot of jewelry.

Larry was kinda tall but on the thin side. I was tall enough to come to the middle of his chest. He had the smoothest sepia brown skin and thick eyebrows and wore his hair in a neatly combed Afro style that was tapered around the edges. His smile had a way of making me blush whenever he flashed his set of perfectly white teeth. He wasn't what you would call super fine, but he was fine enough for me. His personality made up for what he lacked in the looks department.

He was patient when it came to us being intimate. Most guys wanna try and hit on the first date, but not Larry. We didn't have sex until two months after we started to date. He said he wanted to wait until we got to know each other before we were intimate.

He was also charming and knew how to do little things to make me smile. For example, on my birthday last year, he took me to the zoo in Washington, DC to see the white tigers because I had told him how beautiful I thought they were. He would send me flowers for no special reason other than the fact that I was his girl. He just made me feel like I was a special part of his life. He surely was a special part of mine.

He never criticized me for hanging out with Takeisha and Latrell even though he knew they were gold diggers out to work any man who was available to get got. He just accepted me for who I was and how I acted around him. Even though he worked a lot, the time that we spent together was priceless, and something we both cherished. Larry was a perfect gentleman with me and always gave me the utmost respect. I never had to worry about him cheating on me with another girl like the guys that Latrell and Takeisha dated. Larry's heart belonged to me, and my heart belonged to him.

I drifted off down memory lane as I thought about when we first met and all the good times we had spent together. I thought about our first date when he took me out to the lake in Columbia and we just talked for hours about everything. I reminisced about the trip we took last summer to Kings Dominion and how much fun we had. I closed my eyes and thought about how he made my body feel when we made love. As I was going deeper into my trance, the phone rang and it startled me. I knew that it had to be Larry. Surely, he was calling to explain why he was running late.

"Hello."

"Hello, Danita. Is that you?" The caller sounded kinda rattled and uptight.

"Yeah, it's me. Who is this?" I asked.

"It's me, Sam," the caller responded. Sam was Larry's little brother.

"Sam, what's up? Where is Larry? He was supposed to be here hours ago," I said.

"D, I got bad news. Are you sitting down?" Sam asked.

"Yeah, I'm sitting down. What's wrong? Did something happen to Larry?" I could tell by the way Sam sounded that something wasn't right.

"D, Larry had an accident on his motorcycle. He was riding down Northern Parkway and got sideswiped by a eighteen wheeler. Larry's hurt real bad. He's in surgery right now. They don't think he's gonna make it," Sam said.

He went in further detail to tell me how it all happened. Larry's neck and spine were fractured in several places. He was bleeding profusely internally. Sam also told me about the female, who he didn't know, that was riding with Larry. She was killed on contact. I heard every word he said, but I was in a state of disbelief.

"Sam, you have got to be kiddin'. That ain't no shit to be playing about," I responded in a hostile tone.

"I wish I was, D. This is for real. My parents are there with him right now," he said.

"I'm on my way over there now. I'm coming to get you," I said.

Within thirty minutes, I pulled up at Larry's house to get Sam and we were on our way to the Shock Trauma Unit. While I was worrying if Larry was gonna make it, I also wondered who was female riding on the motorcycle with him. I would find out the answer to that question soon enough.

When we reached the hospital, I paid the cab driver and we made our way into the hospital. We took the elevator to the fourth floor, where I noticed Larry's parents walking down the hall toward us. Larry's mother was screaming hysterically and his father was trying to hold her up from falling to the ground. From his mother's reaction, I knew that Larry didn't make it. He died in surgery. My world was crushed, but this was only the beginning.

I later found out that the girl on the motorcycle with him was named Carla. Larry was seeing her on the side. They were leaving her house when the accident took place. This explained why he was late for our date.

I was completely baffled. Not only had I just lost my man, but I also found out that he was cheating on me with another bitch. I was totally messed up and didn't know what to think or do. When I told my mother what happened, she tried her best to comfort me.

"Baby, you're gonna be all right. I know this is gonna be hard for you. I know how much you cared about that boy. He was a nice young man, and it's shame he had to die so young. He's in a better place, though. I know you can't understand it right now, but God called him home. It was his time," she said. I wasn't in the mood to hear none of her religious BS right now. I didn't tell her the part of the story that involved Carla.

"Ma, I don't wanna hear that right now. I just wanna go to my room and be alone. I need some rest," I said.

The tears I cried had my eyes looking puffy, and I was an emotional wreck. I was unable to think clearly. After my mother said what she had to say for a few minutes, I went to my room, turned the lights out, closed the blinds, took off my clothes, and jumped in the bed. I just wanted to block the world out.

I must have slept through the night because when I awoke, it was morning. Takeisha and La-trell were in my room.

"Damn, girl. Are you all right?" T asked me.

"I guess so. I'm as good as can be expected. How did y'all get in here?" I asked.

"Your mother called us this morning and told us that Larry died. She figured that you might need us to help you get through this," she replied.

"Yeah, D, you know we couldn't leave you here to be alone in a time like this. Besides, even though I used to ride you about Larry all the time, he was a good dude. He wasn't like all the rest of these niggas out here," Latrell said.

"Thanks y'all. I knew my girls would have my back. However, that nigga wasn't the goody-two-shoes we all thought he was," I said.

"What you mean, D?" Latrell asked. I told them the whole story about Larry and Carla.

"That is so fucked up, D. When I thought that one of these niggas was about something good, he proved me wrong. That motherfucker deserved to die for playing you like that," Latrell said.

"How the hell you gonna say something that mean, Latrell? She don't need to hear that right now. Whether he was right or wrong, D loved him. She don't need to hear that negative shit from you," Takeisha said.

"Yeah, you right. My bad, D. I just hate to see you in pain like this," Latrell said. It was the best attempt at an apology that she was capable of making. I knew she meant well. She had my best interest at heart.

"It's all good. Part of me feels the same way, but I know it ain't right to wish death on nobody regardless of what they do to us. A broken heart can mend, but death is forever. I just need y'all to help me get through this," I said.

"Say no more. Whatever you need, you know we got you," T said.

We talked a little while longer. They lifted my

spirits a little bit, but I knew that only time could take my pain away.

Despite my anger over finding out that Larry was cheating on me with another girl, I still attended his funeral. Of course, my girls came along with me. I could still sense that deep down inside Latrell didn't wanna be there. I knew her too well. In Latrell's book, all men were dogs and good for only two things, either money or some dick. Her mother had instilled that mentality in her a long time ago. That was why she had never allowed herself to catch feelings for any guy she slept with. Latrell was forced to put her personal feelings aside after Takeisha reminded her that I needed their support as friends at this critical time in my life. I knew it was a battle for her to do that, but for her to come let me know how much love she had for me.

The weeks after the funeral were hard on me. I spent most of my time alone in my room in a gloomy state. I cried myself to sleep many nights. My mother suggested that I go to church with her to help me get through the healing process, but I refused.

I was beginning to feel as though Latrell was right, that no man was worthy of my love. If I could devote myself to Larry in all ways and he would still cheat on me, then any other guy would only do the same thing. What made me the most angry was the fact that he died before I even got a chance to confront him about what he did to me. It was as though our relationship was a chapter in my life that would never be closed. I began to build a wall around myself emotionally. I decided that I didn't need a man in my life at all. I would never allow another man to hurt me the way Larry did. I made up my mind to put my full energy into school and my music.

It was the end of August and school was about to begin. Takeisha's father had decided that since we had kept our end of the bargain and enrolled in classes at Howard University, we would need transportation to get back and forth to classes. He bought Takeisha a 1996 silver Honda Accord at an auction. He paid $7,000 cash for it. It had leather seats and was fully loaded with a 5-disc CD changer and power everything. His record store, Sounds Unlimited, had been doing well for the last few years, so he had the money to spend to make his daughter happy and help her along the road to doing something productive with her life. Takeisha had tried to talk him into buying her a used Lexus, but he wasn't hearing that. He knew how much attention that the car would draw from the police and the harassment we would endure. He chose to buy her the Accord because it was stylish and dependable. All in all, we were just happy to have a set of wheels to get around in.

Once the school year began, we made the daily commute from Baltimore to Washington, D.C. to attend our classes. Since this was our first year, we mostly took our prerequisite classes. Takeisha had already declared that she would major in business management. That would give her an opportunity to develop the right skills to run her own business one day.

I decided to study sociology. I was always the humanitarian of the bunch and into understanding what made people tick. I also planned to pursue a minor in English. That would help me improve my writing skills. I was an avid reader of poetry and novels. Some of my favorite poets included Nikki Giovanni and Jessica Care Moore. My bookshelf at home was filled with novels by Donald Goines and Iceberg Slim.

Latrell was the oddball of the group. She was undecided about what her major would be and had no plans to declare one anytime soon. She was more interested in hanging out with us and seeing what kinda parties were gonna be going on during the school year.

After classes were done, we would usually get together at Takeisha's house to write rhymes or rehearse our stage show. The weekend was when we would be in the studio laying down tracks. The Smith Brothers had agreed to produce three tracks for our demo CD for the agreed upon price of $3,000. They also said that if they were really feeling our demo, they would try to shop it themselves to some of their contacts in the music industry. Being industry veterans, they had a good relationship with at least one representative from every record label that signed rap artists.

They set a timetable to have a demo together by the end of the year. That gave them 90 days to work their magic with us to produce a bangin' demo. I hoped that they came through for us because after what I just went through, I could use some good news.

12

Latrell (Luscious)

It was around 8:00 in the morning on a Sunday when I woke up. I was tired from being in the studio late the night before. Normally, I wouldn't be up this early on a Sunday, but today I had business to handle.

Tank called me earlier in the week and asked me to make a run to New York to pick up a package for him. He came by my house Saturday night and dropped off the money for me to buy a kilo of cocaine. Tank trusted me enough with his money to know that I wouldn't steal from him. He was gonna pay me two grand to bring the coke back to B'more. When money called, I always came running.

I told Danita and Takeisha to go on and record without me that day because I had to take care of something for Tank. They knew I was up to no good. Takeisha warned me several times about transporting drugs for Tank, but I paid her no mind. She tried to reason with me that I was risking my freedom and the future of the KS Crew for my own selfish reasons. That argument went in one ear and out the other.

As I got up to get dressed, I heard a knock at my door. It was my mother. She must've heard me fumbling around in my room and got up to see what the hell was going on. She knew me well enough to know that I never got up that early without a good reason—and it was sure money. I figured that she wanted her cut of whatever I made because that was just her nature. We were two peas in a pod. If I were the mother and she were the daughter, I would probably do the same thing.

"Mm-hmmm. Where is your fast-ass going this early in the morning?" she asked as she stood in my doorway. Even though her hair was all over her head, my mother was still a fine-looking sistah.

"I gotta go make a run upstate for Tank. My bus leaves at ten. Why you up so early?" I asked.

"I couldn't sleep with all that racket you were making. I'm the one asking questions around here. You better be careful and watch your ass. You know if you get caught, that nigga is gonna act like he don't know you and leave your ass in jail. Why you ain't choose an easier hustle than that, girl? I thought I taught you better than that," she said.

"I do my thing and you do yours. You're good at what you do and I'm good at my game. I ain't got caught yet," I responded.

On the real tip, my mother knew I could handle my business out in them streets. She told me on numerous occasions that she was proud of me. She had trained me to be able to make my own money since I was ten years old, so I wouldn't be dependent on anybody else. She said she wanted her daughter to be a ride or die bitch who could always carry her own weight in this world. She taught me how to survive at all costs. I was a good student of all her lessons.

"I hear you, Miss Drug Lord. Just make sure you don't forget to pay the gatekeeper when you come back. I got some new clothes that you should be able fit," she said. She showed me a bag of clothes she got from her last caper at Macy's.

"Yeah, that's what I'm talking about, Ma. I can fit all these jeans right here," I said as I went through the bag of clothes. I found a couple of shirts in there to match.

My mother made her exit and went back into her room. I took a quick shower, threw on some clothes and made my way to the front door. I passed by my two lazy-ass brothers, who were knocked out on the living room floor, sleeping off their high from the night before.

I made my way to the corner and tried to hail down what we called a hack cab, when somebody from around the way used their own car to make a few extra dollars to take you wherever you had to go. The hack cabs charged a lot less than a cab company would. When I found a ride, I got him to take me downtown to the Greyhound station, and in a short while, I was on my way to New York City.

As I rode on the bus, I thought about my life

and the world around me. I wondered if there was a better world than the one we lived in. From my vantage point, it seemed as though everybody was on the take and out to get whatever they could from somebody else. There was no "real" anywhere to be found between anybody.

In the hood, I done seen homeboys kill each other over control of a drug strip. I'd seen fathers molest their own daughters. I'd seen cops plant drugs on niggas and beat niggas to death in the streets like they were animals. All I'd ever known all my life was drama, be it at home or in my hood. I guess that's why I was like "fuck it" now, and just out to get mine. This money that I was about to get was gonna buy me some fly-ass shit when I got back to B'more.

After I exited the bus in New York, I made my way through Port Authority to the trains. I was headed uptown to Harlem. When the train arrived at my destination, I exited the station and looked for the address Tank gave me. Once I found it, I made my way into the housing projects.

I entered the building and rode the piss-stained elevator, to the sixth floor. When I reached apartment 6B, I knocked on the door three times. A large Hispanic dude with jailhouse tattoos covering his bulging biceps answered the door with a loaded shotgun in his hand. When I told him who I was looking for and who sent me, I was allowed into the apartment.

The dealer I was to meet was named Miguel Salazar. He came out of the bedroom and greeted me with a warm handshake. Miguel was one of them pretty boy type of Latino cats with curly hair and striking facial features. He eyed me from head to toe, checking out my bangin' body. I could see he was impressed.

Miguel slowly counted the money in my knapsack to make sure the amount was correct. Once he verified it, he motioned to one of his workers to retrieve the cocaine from the back room. I put the cocaine into the knapsack that once contained the money and was on my way. The whole transaction was over in a matter of minutes. I made it back out of the building and headed toward the train station when a voice yelled out from behind me.

"Excuse me, Miss, we need to talk to you. Slow down for a second."

I turned around and saw two white males not too far behind me, dressed in jeans and white T-shirts with black nylon jackets. Right away, I knew they were narcotics detectives. Miguel and his drug operation had to be under heavy surveillance by the NYPD and the DEA.

My blood was pumping and my heart raced wildly. I loved the adrenaline rush as I tried to figure out how to ditch these fucking narcos.

I ran as fast I could and the cops gave chase. I knew I wouldn't make it to the train station, so I had to come up with another plan. As I ran, more cops joined in the chase. I made a quick dash toward 125th Street, onto the crowded sidewalks.

The cops now had their badges out in an attempt to make their way through the crowd of people. However, they were having a hard time. One of them got knocked over as he ran smack dead into a large brother that walked outta one of the stores on the block. All of the commotion that they caused had people moving frantically in every direction.

I took advantage of the madness that ensued. I moved faster than I ever had before in my life. My freedom was now on the line. I looked behind me and noticed the growing distance between me and the cops. They got caught up in the traffic on the streets.

When I reached 130th Street, I spotted a cab dropping off some passengers. I jumped in it as fast as I could.

"I need to get outta here as fast as possible. My husband is crazy. He's chasing me and wants to beat my ass. I'll pay you whatever you want to get me outta here," I said. I lied my ass off, but the fact that I was running and damn near outta breath when I got to the cab was enough to convince him.

"Don't worry, pretty lady. I'll take you wherever you wanna go. As long you pay me, I'll take good care of you," the cab driver said.

It was my luck that the traffic light was green. The cab driver put the pedal to the metal. When he saw me flash a coupla hundred dollar bills in the rearview mirror, he was satisfied that I would keep my end of the bargain. Them Arabs claim they don't speak good English any other time, but they know how to speak perfect English when money was involved.

He got me the fuck outta Harlem and I was relieved. Them narcos were left behind to figure out how the fuck I got away.

I would live to see another day of sunlight. Being a mule was starting to get a little more hectic.

I instructed the cab driver to take me to Grand Central Station. I planned to take the Amtrak train home to get back to Baltimore faster. A part of me got a thrill out of being chased by the police. It gave me a rush better than having sex. I was always told that my desire for excitement and danger would one day prove to be my downfall. That might be true, but it wasn't gonna happen today.

13

Scar

Life had been good since I signed my deal with Marquee Records. I was riding high on cloud nine. Nobody couldn't tell me that I wasn't the shit. The first rapper from Baltimore to get a record deal with a major label, I was treated like a Don everywhere I went.

Over the last few months, every club in the city wanted me to stop through and make a guest appearance. I did guest radio spots on 92Q and 95.5 to promote my album. *The Sun* newspaper and the *City Times* ran articles about my record deal. Brothers on every street corner, whether East Side or West Side, showed me love across the city. I had obtained a level of success that every thug nigga dreamed about reaching to leave the street life behind. Little did they know that I had no intentions of leaving the drug game behind. I planned to use my musical career as a smokescreen to make my drug money look legit.

Marquee Records laid out their plans as to how they were gonna promote my debut release. They planned to send me out on a twenty-major city tour that included radio interviews, guest appearances on a few music video shows, and signings at record stores like Sam Goody and Tower Records. They had already leaked the news to most of the hip hop magazines about my deal. I read in the new issue of *Source* gossip column that an unknown insider at the record label described me as the realest gangster rapper to come on the scene since the death of Tupac.

The executives at the company wanted me to give my input and be actively involved in the marketing campaign. Ace said they were so high on my potential to be a star that they were open to doing just about anything to make me happy. Very few new artists were given the opportunity to control their own debut project. I guess those rich white folks figured that as long as I could put up big sales figures, it was cool to let me be free to do my thing. I couldn't disappoint them. They believed in my talent, and just like I had all my life, I stepped up to the plate when my number was called.

With the recording budget that I was given to produce the album, I was able to utilize the services of some of the best producers in the rap industry. When I found out that the Smith Brothers were working with the KS Crew on their demo, I chose not to use any of the tracks I had bought from them. I wasn't gonna give them a chance to shine on my shit if they fucked with them bitches. Timbaland, Just Blaze, Dame Grease, and Swizz

Beats were just some of the major producers slated
to produce tracks on the album. I also planned to
have guest appearances on the album by Jadakiss,
Scarface, and another young up and coming rapper by the name of 50 Cent. I had a local producer,
named J Funk, and two local MCs, Basey and
Normskola, on the album to give the world a sam-
ple of the talent that Baltimore had outside of the
R&B group, Dru Hill. With all of the star power
and money that Marquee Records was putting behind this album, I couldn't lose.

I had been in the studio nonstop for the last six
weeks laying down tracks. Ace had worked it out in
my deal that all of the major recording would be
done at Bulletproof Studios. When the record
company gives an artist a recording budget, it has
to be used to pay for all the producers, musicians,
and studio time. What ever is left over is for the
artist to keep. With most of the recording being
done at my studio, I saved a lot of money on studio
time and this meant I could keep more money for
myself.

All of the final mixes and mastering of the songs
would be done at The Hit Factory in New York
City. I had eight songs completed and ready to be
mastered. I planned to record fifteen more tracks
and choose the best five out of the bunch. All in
all, the album would have thirteen tracks. The
name of the album was gonna be *Street Life All I
Know*. My theme was that coming from a broken
home and growing up in the streets, I only knew
one way to live, and that was the thug life. To me,
this wasn't a gimmick to sell records, but the reality of my life.

I had virtually been on my own since I was 13

years old. My mother died giving birth to me. My father, Nathan Sr., did his best to raise me, but his lifestyle wasn't much of a positive influence on me. My father was a straight hustla who was taught from birth to sell drugs. His father and my grandfather, Rudolph "Nicky" Jones, was an old school legend in Baltimore from the days of Little Melvin and Slim Butler. He ran one of the largest heroin rings in the city and taught his son the game from the time he was able to listen and comprehend his lessons. Nathan Sr., in turn, passed the game on to me.

My father was arrested in 1988 and sentenced to life in prison for racketeering and conspiracy to distribute heroin. He was serving his sentence in a federal prison in Colorado. Because of the distance, I never went to see him, but kept in touch with him through phone calls and letters.

I lived with my paternal grandmother, Lucille Jones, after my father's arrest. My grandmother was up in age and could do little to keep me outta trouble. A heavy-set woman, her diabetes and high blood pressure kept her bedridden most of the time. I always made sure that she was taken care of and got everything she needed.

An only child and out on my own, I took to the streets to survive. I got my gift with words from my mother, Roberta Wilson, who was a poet and activist in the Black Panther Party. The hard knock life that I came from gave me a wealth of stories to tell in my rhymes.

I was up in the studio with Keon giving a final listen to the finished tracks before I sent them off to be mastered. As we grooved to the tracks, my cell phone went off. It was Trevor calling, and he sounded amped up. I motioned for Keon to turn the music down for a second so that I could hear what Trevor was saying.

"Yo, a nigga is bugging right now. Five-O done ran up in all of our spots. They even hit our main stash house. We ain't got shit left now. PoPo done snatched up most of the crew. Niggas is down at Central Booking waiting to make bail. This shit is crazy, Scar!"

"How the fuck did this shit happen? Somebody gotta be tellin'! Calm the fuck down, T. Let me think for a second," I replied.

I was going up in my own head, trying to figure out who could've been running his mouth to the police. Somebody had to be talking, because for the police to come at us so strong, they had to have inside information. I knew that none of my top soldiers was snitching. All of a sudden, one name came to mind.

"Yo, where the fuck is Rock's ass at?" I asked.

Since I caught him stealing and was taxing every penny he made to get my money back, Rock was the only one outta my crew that had something to gain from the whole situation if he made a deal with the police.

"Come to think about it, when I went through there the other day, he said that he had to make a run to take care of something for his moms. He begged me to come back through tonight to pick up the loot. When I went back through the strip, his workers told me he had been gone all day," Trevor said.

That was all the convincing the two of us

needed to figure out who was responsible for the raids. We shoulda killed his ass when we had the chance.

"We gotta find that nigga, if he's still out on the streets. If Five-O got his ass, then you know that they coming for us next. I ain't sweating that shit, though. If they do come for me, my record company got lawyers to fight this shit. I got too much legit money for them to fuck with me," I said.

"Yeah, but what about my ass?" Trevor asked.

"You know I got you, nigga. Stop sweating so hard. Get your ass over here so we can put our heads together and figure this mess out."

I hung up the phone and motioned for Keon to turn the music back up. I sparked up a phat blunt and rocked my head to the mellow track blasting outta the speakers. I had to play it cool and smart because when I found Rock's ass, he was 187 with no questions asked. For ratting on me, that slimy motherfucker had to get got. I couldn't wait for Trevor to make it over to the studio so we could handle this situation.

14

Scar and Rachel

The next few days were kinda quiet for Scar. He had seen the story on the news about the drug raids. However, there was no mention of his name or Trevor's. There was still no word on Rock's whereabouts. Trevor was laying low at his girl's house until this situation cooled down. Scar had arranged for his top workers to be bailed out. His young, hand-to-hand cats would have to eat their charges. That was just a part of the game. Besides, he knew that them young, starving cats saw doing a bit as a way to earn them some stripes and respect out in the streets.

The upstairs area in Scar's studio was a decked-out two-bedroom apartment. It was his own little haven when he was too tired to go home after a long studio session. The living room area was laid out with a butter-soft leather sofa and love seat and a 55-inch big screen TV. His bedroom, where he did most of his entertaining with his female company, was a playa's dream palace. He had a king-sized bed equipped with silk sheets and a Gucci comforter. An artist painted the wall facing the bed with a full-sized portrait of Scar performing shirtless in front of a crowd, his platinum, diamond-encrusted Bulletproof medallion hanging from his neck. There were mirrors on the ceiling and the headboard. He had a mini-bar positioned next to the bed, fully stocked with Hennessy, Tanqueray, Belvedere and a host of drink mixers. This room was his private domain, and no one dared to disrespect his throne.

He had just woken up after an all-night romp with Rachel, one of his new concubines. She was a 20-year-old wanna-be model he met one day while he was on Greenmount Avenue kickin' it with some of his boys. Rachel was a true ghetto diamond, thick in the waist and pretty in the face. Calling her a dime piece wouldn't do her enough justice. On a scale of one to ten, she was a fifteen. The only problem was that she had the intelligence of a mannequin.

As fine as Rachel was, Scar didn't care if she could add two plus two together. As long as she was down to spread them sexy-ass thighs of hers, then he was down to tell her whatever her dumb ass wanted to hear. He promised that he would make her a star in one of his music videos. He told her that her modeling career would jump off once everybody saw her in one of his videos. She fell right into his trap and believed the pipe dream he sold her. He had no plans to make her a star. He just wanted to get his freak on with this fine, young, tender thing.

It was 10 o'clock in the morning and he was in the living room watching Scarface, his all-time favorite movie, on DVD. Rachel was in the kitchen, butt-naked, cooking him some breakfast. He liked to watch her parade her plump ass around the house in her birthday suit. His dick was fully swollen when she came into the living room to bring him a glass of orange juice and tell him that breakfast was ready. He pulled her down onto the couch for a quickie before they ate.

"Damn, Scar. You act like you ain't get enough of this good pussy last night. Let me find out I got you sprung on the squirrel tongue," Rachel said. She knew that he loved to eat her out like she was an all-night buffet.

"Yeah, you got me open a li'l bit. It's me and you, baby, straight to the top. Now, climb that big ass over here onto this love muscle that I got sitting here waiting for you," he replied.

Rachel got on top of him and rode him like his dick was the last one left on the Earth. Needless to say, they forgot all about eating breakfast.

"Ooooh, Scar. I can feel your dick all the way up in my stomach. I just wanna cum all over that big monsta, nigga," Rachel said. She screamed in sheer ecstasy and felt pleasure like never before. It was as though the gates of heaven had just opened up to her.

"Make that pussy cum for me, bitch. I wanna see that shit running down my leg," he yelled as he smacked Rachel on her phat ass. Minutes later, he came inside of her and she did the same. He lay across the couch, breathing heavily.

Rachel got up and went into the bedroom. Little did Scar know that he was being set up in a major way. While she was in the bedroom, Rachel ripped her underwear and tore the T-shirt she was wearing the night before. She wrinkled up her jeans to make it look as though it was done in a struggle. She messed up her hair and thought about something sad from her past to make herself cry. She punched herself in the eye and scratched her arms. She planned to make it appear as though Scar had raped her. The rough sex they had last night and earlier that morning would help her case.

The night before, Scar left her alone in the studio while he went upstairs to take a business call. Rachel took advantage of the opportunity to do what she was paid to do. She planted a kilo of cocaine, packing vials, and banded money she had hidden in her large overnight bag. Everything was planted behind the recording console in a box containing wires and cords for the recording equipment.

Her job was complete. A drug charge and a rape charge together would spell sure disaster for Scar. After she was sure that she had her story together, Rachel dialed 911 on the phone in the bedroom and told her story to the operator.

"Yes, this is 911. How may we help you?" the operator asked.

"Yes, operator, please help! I've just been raped! I don't wanna talk too loud because he's in the other room. This nigga is crazy! You've gotta help me!" Rachel said frantically in a low tone. Her nose was stopped up from her crying, making her voice sound more convincing.

"Calm down, Miss. You say that you've been raped? Did I hear you correctly?" the operator asked.

"Yes, his name is Nathan Jones. He's a rap superstar and a drug dealer. He goes by the name Scar. He also has a large quantity of drugs in the house. He had me tied up to the bedposts with two pillowcases. I managed to wiggle free. He doesn't know that I'm loose. Please send somebody to help me. The address is 4502 Grove Ave. I'm afraid that he's gonna kill me! Please help me!" Rachel said.

"I need you to be as calm as you can, Miss. Don't do anything foolish. Help is on the way," the operator said.

Rock had paid Rachel $5,000 to set up Scar, and she put on her best performance to accomplish the task. He and Takeisha had hooked up recently and came up with a brilliant idea to get revenge on their common enemy.

Rachel went to the same hair salon as Takeisha and they had become cool with each other over the years. Takeisha knew Rachel was the kinda girl that was down for settin' up a nigga to take a fall if the money was right.

It was no accident that she happened to be at the Inner Harbor the day she met Scar. Rachel had been following him around town and took advantage of the first opportunity to get his attention while he was alone. Takeisha knew the kinda females he liked and knew that once he saw Rachel dressed in a short mini-skirt with her titties popping outta her blouse, he wouldn't be able to resist pushing up on her.

Rock knew that Scar had two felony drug convictions and a third one would mean that he would serve an automatic 25 years to life, not even mentioning the time he would get for the rape charge. They had set his ass up lovely.

* * *

As he sat on the couch naked, Scar was startled by a loud thump at the front door. He had drifted off to sleep waiting for Rachel to come outta the bedroom. Scar threw on his robe and walked down the stairs to see who the hell was at his door. No one was scheduled for a studio session. None of his boys knew that he had stayed at the studio last night. He looked out the peephole of the door and was shocked to see several police cars in front of the studio, and several officers on the other side of the door.

"What the fuck!" Scar yelled.

When he opened the door, he was greeted by six of Baltimore's finest. His face was twisted up in disgust. He balled his fists up in anger.

"You better have a search warrant to be coming up in here like this. What the fuck do you want?" Scar asked.

Before he could think of anything else smart to say, the officers burst through the door and threw him to the ground. His face scraped up against the hardwood floor. Scar was in no position to fight back. The police outnumbered him six to one and they had him outgunned. His hands were handcuffed behind his back. If this were an average street fight with no guns involved, Scar would have given them a run for their money. However, it wasn't, so he was forced to submit to their will.

"Mr. Jones, we just received a call from a young lady stating that she was in the residence and had been sexually assaulted. She also said that you have a large quantity of drugs in the house," one of the officers, Detective Haines, said.

Detective Haines was a short, potbellied black

guy with a nasal voice. He breathed heavily as though he had asthma or smoked too many cigarettes. He obviously was the highest-ranking officer, as the others deferred to him.

"Rape? What the fuck I gotta rape somebody for? Me and my girl was up in here minding our own business. Drugs? I'ma rapper. I don't sell no drugs. You ain't gonna find shit here. Your fat-ass all outta breath from running up the steps. They need to train y'all asses better. Hey, Rachel, come down here, baby, and talk to these fools," Scar shouted.

Scar knew they were barking up the wrong tree because he never conducted illegal business outta his studio. After the cops raided all of his stash houses the week before, he hadn't bought any new product. He instructed Trevor to close up shop for a while until this whole situation blew over. There was no way he would come up dirty.

As for the rape charge, that was outta the question to him. All Rachel had to do was to come downstairs to verify his story. She didn't respond when he called her name, but he wasn't worried. He figured she must be in the bathroom or something. Feeling confident, Scar reclined back against the wall and cracked a smile.

"We'll see about that, big mouth. Rainey and Coates, you check the upstairs. Davenport and Lewis, you search the lower level. Rogers and Atkins, you check out this floor. I'll keep him on ice," Detective Haines said as he dispensed his orders to his troops.

"Do you know who the fuck I am? Do you know what my lawyers are gonna do to you when I finish suing the shit outta the Baltimore City Police Department?" Scar said, taunting Detective Haines.

"Quiet, asshole. We've been watching you for some time. I know exactly who you are. If you're clean, then you got nothing to worry about," Detective Haines said.

After about twenty minutes, Detectives Davenport and Lewis returned to the living room. The entire house was a mess. However, the detectives were smiling as though they had hit the lottery. In their eyes, they had done the next best thing. Davenport flashed the kilo of cocaine Rachel had planted. They also found the cash, rolled up in rubber bands, and the packing vials.

Scar was caught dead to right. He was fucked. Seeing what they had found, he jumped up to proclaim his innocence. It was too late because Rock and Takeisha's plan went down as expected. Scar's fate was sealed as far as they were concerned. Takeisha got her revenge and Rock had saved his life.

"Yo, that shit ain't mine! Y'all planted that in here. Why the hell would I be stupid enough to keep drugs in the house where I lay my head at? Get the fuck outta here with this crap!" Scar was yelling. Detective Haines began reading him his rights.

To add insult to injury, the other two detectives came down the steps with Rachel in tow, looking tore down and crying at the top of her lungs. When she saw Scar, she ran toward him and began hitting him with all of her might. The officers pulled her off of him and led her into the other room. She was cursing and calling him all kinds of crazy names like "rapist", "pervert", "asshole" and whatever other expletives she could come up with at the time. She did her best to appear to be traumatized.

"This bitch is crazy! I ain't fucking rape her. Somebody playing some sick games up in here, but I ain't the one," Scar said.

"Tell it to the judge, superstar. Tell it to the judge. You rap assholes are all the same," Detective Haines said.

Scar's mind was racing as he was led to the paddy wagon outside. He had to figure out how to get outta this mess. Once the press got a hold of this story, Scar knew his career was gonna be over.

When he got to the police station, he planned to use his phone call to reach Ace. He hoped Ace knew what to do to get him outta this jam. He would need all the help he could get. Spending the rest of his life behind bars wasn't what he had in mind, but who did? First, all of his drug spots got raided, and now he was arrested on some BS charges. Somebody was setting him up, but he had no idea who it was. He planned to find out.

15

Takeisha (T-Love)

"Thanks, girl. You really hooked a sistah up," I said to Linda.

Linda was my nail stylist. She worked at Chic Nails in Reisterstown Road Plaza. She was responsible for keeping the KS Crew's hands and feet looking invitingly sexy. I paid Linda $30, including a tip, for my manicure and pedicure and was on my way. As I walked toward the mall's main entrance, my cell phone rang.

"Hello. Who is this?"

"It's Derrick. Hey, beautiful. What's going on?"

"Nothing much. I just got finished getting my nails done. I'm on my way home to take a nap. I'm tired as can be." I was obviously trying to give him the cold shoulder, but he didn't get it.

"I can feel that. You truly are beautiful. After you finish getting your beauty rest, can we hook up later on tonight? I'm trying to be in the presence of your radiant smile once again. How come you never return my calls or messages?"

"I've been busy. My girls and I are supposed to go to the studio later on tonight. We gotta get this demo finished soon. I might have to catch up with you another time," I said. I wondered why he ain't take the hint that I didn't wanna be bothered. Damn, he was a bugaboo!

"All work and no play ain't good for the soul, ya know? Try to free up some time for me. I just wanna satisfy your every desire. Derrick is my name, and giving you pleasure is my aim."

Negro, please. Your corny ass can't handle all of this woman here! I thought.

"I'll see what I can do. Oh, hold up. I got another call coming in. Let me hit you back in a few."

I was relieved to get Derrick off the phone.

Derrick and his brothers owned a car customizing shop called Rims and Things, in Randallstown. I met him one day when I went there to get an alarm system installed in my car. From the time that I walked in the door, he was sweating me to no end.

He introduced himself and tried to play the balla roll, telling me he was a co-owner of the shop. Seeing through his weak game, I figured that he was an easy mark to use to get what I wanted. By the time I left the shop, I got him to not only put the alarm system in for free, but I got my windows tinted and a wood kit installed in my inside paneling. All I had to do was to go out with him and make it appear as though I was interested. That was an easy task for a woman of my caliber.

Derrick wasn't all that bad looking, but he just

wasn't my type. First of all, he was only 5' 6" tall and that was an instant turn-off. I liked my men tall, dark and sexy. Next, he was a square cat, into doing things like going to art shows and the opera. He was very bourgie and boring in my eyes. I loved a dude filled with thug passion that was rough around the edges. Derrick didn't appear to be the type of man I could rely on to defend my honor if I needed him to. Finally, he had an annoying habit I picked up on instantly. When he picked me up for our date, I couldn't help but laugh at his driving skills.

Derrick drove with two hands on the steering wheel, never changed lanes, stopped at every stop sign, and did the speed limit. He was a straight geek. His wack driving drove me crazy. I was used to dealing with guys that drove their cars the way that they handled their women, with high speed and not afraid to take risks. I knew he couldn't handle a high octane, adventurous woman such as myself.

To top it all off, he always had the corniest lines when he tried to give me compliments. It was as though he watched every old mackin' movie from the '70s to develop his game.

Since I agreed to go out with him one time to dinner, he had been calling my phone off the hook. He was pressed, though he didn't even get as much as a good night kiss, let alone some pussy, after he took me to dinner at the Brass Elephant Restaurant. That was a one-time courtesy date for him and a free meal for me. To him, I was steak he was eager to take a bite out of, time and time again. If I had my way, he would be one starving brother.

Derrick's calls were starting to become more and more irritating. I decided that from now on, I just wouldn't answer them anymore. Since I got what I wanted from him, he had outlived his usefulness. Sooner or later, he would get the picture. If not, that was his problem, not mine.

Nick, another young playa I had strung out, was the caller on the other line. Nick was 21 years old, dark-skinned, with a body builder's chest and arms as big as tree trunks. He drove a brand spanking new Acura RL and his pockets stayed on swole. The fact that he worked magic with his tongue and knew how to lay the pipe just right gave him extra bonus points in my book.

We talked for a few minutes and set up plans to hook up some time during the holiday season. He had potential to be around for a while if he played his cards right.

I was grooving to the sounds of Nas's Illmatic album as I drove down the road. Even though the album was old school, the lyrics could still hold their own against most of the rappers in the game currently.

I made my way onto North Avenue and proceeded toward my house. When the CD ended, I turned on the radio to see what hot new tracks were in the station's rotation. When I tuned the radio to 92Q, I caught the tail end of the DJ dishing some dirt about a rapper getting arrested and facing life in jail. I didn't catch the rapper's name and I took it as just some more of the drama that came along with the music business.

About 10 minutes later, my cell phone went off. It was Latrell.

"Girl, do you believe that shit? They got your boy straight up this time. I don't know if he gonna beat this charge!" Latrell said.

"Latrell, what you gossiping about? Which one of these fools are you talking about?" I asked.

Since Scar and I had broken up, Latrell and I were on the prowl and taking no prisoners in running these cats' pockets in B'more. We ran game on so many dudes, Latrell could have been talking about several different guys that I had been kicking it with lately.

"You ain't heard the news? They've been talking about it on the radio all day. It was all over MTV and in the newspaper. Your boy, Scar, got arrested last night. He caught a rape charge. Plus, when they arrested him, they said they found a kilo of cocaine in the studio. Remember last week when I told you that Tank had told me Scar's whole crew got knocked off? Well, they trying to tie him into that, too. They saying that he was running a drug ring and using the studio as a front for his operation. That nigga ain't gonna see no daylight ever again when they finish with his ass," Latrell said.

"Get the fuck outta here! You gotta be lying. They gotta be making a mistake. I know Scar's a crazy nigga, but he ain't gonna rape nobody. He ain't got to, with all these bitches out here trying to give him some pussy," I responded, trying to sound shocked, as though this was news to me. Latrell was none the wiser.

"Yeah, well, they got his ass now. A black man caught with drugs and he a celebrity? Don't even mention the rape charge. Girl, he's done before he get to court. The press is gonna fry him and make him look guilty even if he ain't do it. He's getting time, plus she gonna get paid off of his ass. Shit, I wish that was me and not her. I could use that loot. If the nigga ain't rape me, I would damn sure make it look like he did," Latrell said.

"Yeah, that's the truth. I know your conniving ass would. His career is through before it even got a chance to get started. Fuck 'im. That's what he said about us. He ain't my man no more. Let some other ho deal with that headache. Yo, I'm outside your house right now. Come and open up the door," I responded.

Before I could finish parking the car, Latrell was at the front door to let me in. I went inside Latrell's house and the two of us retreated to her room to gossip some more. We took turns passing the blunt back and forth as we talked about Scar and finishing up our demo with the Smith Brothers. We were expecting a call from them sometime soon to see if they had any success in shopping our demo package for a record deal. Christmas was eight days away, and the year 2000 was right around the corner. Getting put on would be the perfect way to bring in the new millennium.

It seemed as though my plan to set up Scar had worked. Part of me felt a little guilt over him getting locked up, but that would fade in time, just like any other feelings I had for him. Shit, he tried to ruin my career over some nonsense, and now I had turned the tables on him. That's just the way the game went. He should've picked another bitch to fuck with. Besides, I told his ass that he better watch his back. He should've heeded my warning.

16

Scar

My arrest was all over the news. I had been trans-ferred from the Northwestern Police Department to the city jail. This was not the way I planned to spend my holidays. I expected to be up in some new pussy, smoking some killa weed out on a trop-ical island somewhere. Instead, I was trapped up in a tiny cell with another dude, with nothing to do but wonder how my life got to be so fucked up so fast. One minute I was on top of the world, and now I was at the bottom of the barrel, facing hard time.

City jail in Baltimore City was one of the worst places that a brother could be locked up. It was al-ways overcrowded, especially in the wintertime. That was when a lot of homeless cats would com-mit petty crimes just to get off the streets and have a warm place to rest their heads. The living condi-tions were almost unbearable, as the cells were run down, looking like something outta an old jail movie. In a lot of the cells, the toilets didn't work and if you took a shit, you had to smell the foul odor for days before it got fixed.

Being that it was so overcrowded and the inmates were packed on top of each other like sardines, there was nothing but tension brewing between the inmates and the CO's. Somebody was getting shanked, raped, or beat down on a daily basis. This was nothing new to me, as I had been locked up several times in my life, but I thought being locked down was a thing of the past.

I had spoken with Ace about the arrest and told him I was being set up. Given my track record, I knew Ace had a hard time believing my story. However, with the record company's financial help, he planned to get me the best attorneys available to help me beat the case.

I was still waiting for a bail hearing. Given the severity of the charges against me, my bail was likely to be in the $500,000 range, if not more. The money used for my defense and to pay my bail was gonna come outta my royalties. Unless my album was a mega success, any money I woulda made would now be paid directly to my defense team. I might not see another dime from Marquee Records.

Feeling depressed about my situation, I reached out to the main person I knew I could trust to have my back, my grandmother. Grandma Jones always had something positive to say about me, her favorite grandson, no matter how much hell I raised. I knew she was worried sick that she hadn't heard from me. When I got a chance to get to the phone, I gave her a call.

"Nathan, is that you? Boy, what you done got

yourself into? They're saying all these bad things about you all over the news. Please tell me that they ain't true," she said.

"Yeah, it's me, Mama. I swear to you, on my life, I didn't do what they say I did. I'm innocent. My lawyers are gonna make sure that my name is cleared," I said. I was trying to ease my grandmother's worries, even though I wasn't so sure how I was gonna get outta this situation.

"If you say it's so, I believe you, baby. Lord knows I ain't raise you to be no liar. I'ma have Reverend Paige say a prayer for you on Sunday. God is gonna make a way," she said.

Mama was a deeply religious woman. The only time she missed church was when her illnesses wouldn't allow her to get outta bed.

"I know he will, Mama. Have you been taking your medication? You know that you're all I got in this world. I'ma send Trevor over to take you to your doctor's appointment and to make sure that your bills get paid," I said.

"Yeah, I been taking my medicine. Don't worry about me, child. You're the one that needs to be worried. I need my baby home with me. My heart can't take seeing you and your father behind bars. I know that you done did some bad things in your life, but if God makes a way for you outta this mess, you better get down on your knees and swear to him that you gonna change your ways."

"I will, Mama. I will. I gotta get ready to go. I'll call you later in the week. I love you."

The CO's came around to do the evening count. I had to return to my cell.

"I love you, too, Nate."

I returned to my bunk to contemplate my fu-

ture. I felt like I was about to crack under pressure
for the first time in my life. In the streets, I never
allowed my emotions to show. However, given that
I was facing a long time behind bars and no one
would be there to take care of my mama, I wanted
to cry. Being locked up, though, that wasn't an option. I couldn't afford to show any signs of weak-
ness. All I could do now was wait for my bail hearing.
Then I would be back on the streets until my trial.
When I hit them streets, all hell was gonna break
loose.

17

Danita (D-Boogie)

I sat in my room wrapping up my Christmas gifts. This was a time of year that I looked forward to since I was a child. No matter how much my mother and I argued back and forth throughout the year, this was one holiday when we both enjoyed spending time together. About a week before Christmas, we would start hanging up the Christmas lights on the outside of the house, and place little reindeer and elf figurines up in the front windows. On the front, we hung a giant wreath with a picture of a black Santa Claus.

Around this time of the year, we would stay up all night to decorate the Christmas tree and drink eggnog. Underneath the tree, there were always so many gifts that they flowed out into the middle of the floor.

Ever since my parents had divorced, I had little

contact with my father. To make up for his absence, my mother would always spoil me by buying everything that I wanted for Christmas. She was trying to let me know that no matter what my father did or didn't do, I was always someone special to her. I loved her for that.

Not only had my father chosen not to remain in my life after the divorce, he remarried and started a new family. I had a little sister named Tamara who was 7 years old. I had never met her, nor did I know what she looked like.

I never understood why my father didn't try to stay in contact with me after the divorce. I spoke to him on a few occasions after the divorce, but our conversations were minimal, and I did most of the talking. Lately, when I called him, his wife would just say that he wasn't in and that she would tell him I called. However, he never returned any of my calls.

I had now made up my mind to stop reaching out to him. It was too painful to feel such rejection. We had such a good relationship before he and my mother split up. His absence from my life was something that troubled me deeply inside. In fact, it made me very distrustful of men. That was why, when I finally decided to open up my heart and trust Larry, his betrayal crushed me.

"Danita, hand me the star so that I can put it on the top of the tree," my mother said.

"Here you go, Ma. This tree looks off the hook. We did it up this year, don't you think?" I asked. I admired our artistry in hanging the bulbs, candy canes and various other objects on the tree so beautifully.

"I don't know what 'off the hook' means, but

the tree sure looks good. What I tell you about using that ghetto slang around me?" my mother asked. Even though my mother was in her early forties, she acted like an old woman sometimes.

"Ma, 'off the hook' means that it looks nice. You act like y'all ain't have no slang that you used when you was my age. Tell her, Mo," I said to my stepfather, Maurice.

A tall, fair-skinned man with brown eyes and fine hair, Maurice was six years younger than my mother. He was an air conditioning and heating system repairman. They met one day when he answered my mother's service call to fix our boiler. When he showed up at the front door, he was immediately attracted to my mother. Even though she dressed conservatively, her friendly smile and curvaceous figure were enough to get his attention.

My mother was also attracted to him instantly, but tried to deny it. After several unsuccessful attempts to get her to go out on a date with him, she finally gave in. They had been an item ever since.

Maurice had become like a father to me since he married my mother when I was thirteen. In fact, he adopted me as his own daughter and I took on his last name. Maurice was somebody I could talk to about things my mother didn't understand because she was so deeply religious and always seemed to be so judgmental. I would talk to him often about my relationship with Larry or my music career. He was always supportive of me in whatever I did.

"Nita, you know your mother ain't hip like me. I try to school her. All she wanna listen to is that gospel music. I told her that's cool, but she needs to listen to a little Jay-Z or Mary J. Blige every now and then. God will understand," Maurice said.

"Both of y'all heathens need to be saved. I used to cut a mean rug in my day before I was born again. Lord, that seems like ages ago," my mother said. She appeared to be caught up in a memory from the past.

"We know, Ma. We know. You done told me the stories a thousand times about how you were the prom queen and how all the men used to line up just to get a dance with you," I said.

I looked at Maurice and we both started laughing. My mother had to join in on the laughter. This was the one time of the year she let her guard down and just had fun with her family.

My mother made her way over to the stereo and turned on a CD of Motown's greatest Christmas hits. She started dancing in time with the music. Maurice and I joined in, we all sang along with the Temptations, Supremes, Smokey Robinson, and the rest of the Motown legends.

"Now, this is real music right here. I don't know what that foolishness that y'all listen to is about!" my mother said as she continued to get her groove on.

Latrell and T had called me earlier to say they would be over later. They always came to my house for the holidays because they knew my mother could throw down in the kitchen. We always had a vast spread of food to choose from. They also liked the holiday spirit at my house because at Latrell's house, the scenery was totally different. There was no Christmas cheer in the Collins household. No colorful lights or Christmas ornaments were to be found anywhere around the residence. Her mother was always more concerned with coming up with some new scheme to get money, than spending quality time with her daughter. Her two brothers had been abusing drugs so long that the holidays would come and go and they would be none the wiser. All they were concerned about was getting that next high.

Latrell couldn't even remember the last time her mother bought her a Christmas gift. She told me that her mother would always say Christmas was nothing but the white man's way of getting rich off the poor. Nonetheless, every year, Latrell would always buy her mother some kind of gift, with a card attached, and slide it under her bedroom door. Her mother would just give her a blank thank you in return and go on about her regular business.

The reason Takeisha spent a lot of time at my house for Christmas was because of her father's religious beliefs. She told me that when she was a little child, her house always had a Christmas tree, decorated in style, and she was ravished with an abundance of gifts. However, since he became a Muslim, Rashid didn't celebrate Christmas any longer. He would tell Takeisha it was pagan holiday that had nothing to do with the birth of Jesus Christ. Despite what her father believed, she still wanted to celebrate Christmas. She was always welcome at our home.

It was around 8:00 p.m. when Latrell and Takeisha finally arrived at my house with gifts in hand. We always exchanged gifts with each other, and Latrell and Takeisha also bought presents for my mother and Maurice. We knew each other so well that we always got the perfect gifts.

When they arrived, they heard the Christmas music playing in the background. My mother answered the door.

"Hey, girls, y'all look nice. Come on in here and get yourselves something to eat," she said.

Latrell and Takeisha placed their gifts under the Christmas tree along with the others. They made their way into the dining room area, where the table was covered with every kinda soul food you could imagine. There was fried chicken, baked chicken, macaroni and cheese, collard greens, candied yams, lasagna, beef spare ribs, string beans, turkey, dressing, and so many other dishes. My mother had also baked her famous sweet potato and apple pies and made homemade lemonade and iced tea to drink.

"Mrs. Robinson, you tore it up in the kitchen. Who's gonna eat all of this food?" Takeisha asked.

"We are, child. Whatever we don't eat tonight is gonna be leftovers for the week. Let's join hands now so that we can say a prayer to bless this food," she responded.

We all joined hands and bowed our heads. My mother said a prayer, thanking God for blessing her and her family, including Latrell and Takeisha, with another healthy year of life. When she was finished, we all said "Amen" and headed for the table where the food was located.

"Man, I don't know where to start. I'm starving like Marvin!" Latrell said.

Her hunger was probably fed by the blunt she and Takeisha had smoked before they came over. By their facial expressions, I could tell that they were lifted. I shot them an angry look because they had blazed up without me.

"Well, eat all you want. That's what I cooked it for. Danita, you need to eat more, too. You need some meat on them bones, girl," my mother said. She was always chiding me about my petite frame.

"I happen to like my slim figure, mother dear. *Excuse you!*" I responded. I knew I could get away with that smart remark because it was Christmas. Any other time, I would never be so sarcastic with my mother.

"Leave the girl alone, Donna. If she wanna be slim, then let her. It's her body," Maurice interjected.

"That's right. Tell her, Mo!" I said, cheering him on for having my back.

We sat down at the dining room table and chowed down. Latrell and Takeisha were having a serious case of the munchies. They almost ate an entire sweet potato pie themselves.

Maurice stuffed himself as well. When he was finished eating, he retreated to his favorite chair in the living room to watch television. His belly hung over his belt from eating so much food.

While my mother was in the kitchen washing dishes and cleaning up, we went into my room to talk.

"So, what y'all wanna do now?" I asked.

"I don't know about y'all, but I got some gifts to go get. Tank was supposed to be buying me this outfit that I saw at the mall. Petey was supposed to be getting me a leather coat. I know Mike said that he got some money for me," Latrell said.

She had her men trained. They knew what she

liked and she knew how to work them to get what she wanted. That girl was a player for life.

"Yeah, I gotta do the same," Takeisha said.

"Y'all go ahead and do what you gotta do. I'ma chill right here. Y'all just better make sure y'all are here tomorrow so that we can open these gifts," I responded.

"You got that. Call me if you need me," Takeisha said.

After they left, I lay in my bed and thought about Larry. I missed him so much. We used to have so much fun together. Every now and then, thoughts of him still brought tears to my eyes.

After I thought about how my girls were out having fun with the men in their lives, part of me felt jealous because I was home alone. However, I was too afraid to open myself up to be hurt again. Part of me admired my girls for the way they could shrug a dude off and not get all caught up in love like me. I wished I was strong like them.

18

Takeisha (T-Love)

It was nearing the end of January of the year 2000. We had heard no good news about our chances of getting a record deal. I spoke with Joe Smith, from Smith Brothers Entertainment, on several occasions, and he gave me the blow by blow as to what was going on with shopping our demo.

Joe told me that some of the companies they played the demo for gave them lukewarm responses to the tracks, but made no offers of a recording contract. Other companies just weren't interested, and didn't see the likelihood of a female gangsta rap group succeeding. They were told that the public would take the KS Crew as a novelty act and nothing more. Nonetheless, he still believed in our project and would continue to pursue a record deal for us. That made us keep a flicker of hope alive. One day, we would be successful.

What hurt the KS Crew even more than our explicit lyrics was the fact that we were from Baltimore. The city had a reputation of not producing any major rap stars since hip-hop became a part of the mainstream culture. Outside of the bidding war over Scar, whose career hung in the balance, nobody in the industry had checked for any MCs to come outta B'more. On the East Coast, if you weren't from New York or Philly, you got no love from record executives. The rap game had become very tribal, and if you weren't down with a clique from your town, then your chances of getting on were slim to none. The way the rules were becoming, you had to put out an independent CD and sell thousands of copies in the streets to get recognized by the major labels. If you didn't have any startup money, then putting out a CD of your own was out of the question. Your success hung on a wing and a prayer that somebody famous might decide to put you down with his team.

School was back in session from the winter break, and we resumed taking our classes at Howard University. We were beginning to think that our music career wasn't meant to be. Frustration was starting to set in, but Danita and I were keeping up with our studies. Latrell was rapidly starting to lose interest in attending college. She began to skip classes more frequently. She spent most of her time hanging out on campus, getting high. She made it to all the parties before she made it to her classes. When we arrived at school, we all went our separate ways.

We were concerned about Latrell and decided it was time to confront her about our feelings. One Tuesday, Danita and I had just left our last classes when we ran into Latrell on campus. She was hanging out with this Jamaican balla named Sterling. He was a student at the school, but he also was the man to see if you wanted to buy weed on the yard. His family was high up on the food chain when it came to importing marijuana into the country. He had good smoke and lots of money. It was only natural that even on a college campus, Latrell would gravitate toward the movers and the shakers.

"I thought you said your ass was gonna go to class today? What happened?" I asked.

"No doubt. Mi understand. Mi a go let you lovely ladies do ya ting. Trelly, hit me on my cell phone later. We can get together and twist a few. I wanna see you all at the party I'm giving dis weekend. You all get the VIP treatment, all night," Sterling said.

Sterling looked like Wyclef Jean, with his smooth, charcoal-black skin. He had dreads that hung down to his shoulders and the body of an African warrior. He was fine, and I got lost in his eyes for a minute before I regained my composure. I almost couldn't blame Latrell for ditching class to get with his sexy behind.

"Just tell us when and where and we'll be there," I said.

Sterling gave Latrell a hug and kissed her gently on her lips as he left the three of us alone to talk.

"Damn, that nigga is sexy. I'ma have to turn his ass out. So, what's up? What, you wanna lecture me about not going to class? If so, don't even waste your breath 'cause I ain't trying to hear it," Latrell said.

"Why you acting so ignorant, yo? All you do now is smoke trees and bullshit around. You wasting a lot of money that somebody else could use that really wanna get an education," I said angrily.

"Yeah, well that's my business. Don't act all high and mighty with me, girlfriend. Y'all both like to get fucked up right along with me," Latrell said.

"True dat. But we handle our business first. This partying mess isn't gonna last forever. We all need to take advantage of this opportunity to get an education to fall back on, just in case this music thing don't work out. Latrell, we're supposed to be a team. Right now you acting like the weakest link on the chain," Danita said.

"Well, if I—*I* mean *we* don't get a record deal, fuck this school bullshit. I'm just trying to keep my promise that I made to T's father for looking out. Besides, we coulda had a deal already if it wasn't for our good friend here fucking things up," Latrell shot back.

"Fuck you. I'ma act like I didn't even hear that nonsense you just said. I know it's the weed talking for you. Just be lucky that you my girl. Anybody else and I woulda been all over your ass," I responded.

I couldn't believe that Latrell threw me such a cheap shot about my breakup with Scar. She musta wanted me to whip her ass. If she said one more smart thing to me, I would give her just what she wanted.

"Come on, y'all. We're supposed to be family, remember? Let's squash this and go get something to eat," Danita said.

"A'ight, D. Where you wanna go? Ask your *friend* if she's coming along with us," I said.

"Ask me yourself, fool. Let's go to Bennigan's out at Security Mall when we get back in town," Latrell said.

She was acting as though nothing happened

and she didn't just piss me off, but Latrell was still my girl. I knew that when things got rough, she would have my back.

I decided to let the situation ride, but I didn't know how much more of Latrell's antics I could take. We were right to pull her coat to the fact that she was messing up big time, because that's what friends do for each other. However, her pride wouldn't let her admit it. We made our way to my car and got on the road, heading back to Baltimore. The peace between us was restored for now. Who knew what the future held?

19

Scar

Since making bail, I hit the streets on a rampage. I was on a mission to find Rock to put his ass to sleep for good. I knew he had to have something to do with this whole demonstration. I searched the city high and low for him, with no success. I put the word on the street that I was looking for Rock and even went so far as to put a $25,000 bounty on his head. My search turned up nothing. That nigga was ghost. Even Rock's mother had left town. I was back to square one.

I knew Rachel was in on the setup as well, but I couldn't figure out how her and Rock were connected. I tried to call her, but both her house and cell numbers were disconnected. I went past her house and her landlord told me she moved and left no forwarding information. I didn't know her that well, so I had no clue how to locate her family to try to intimidate them into giving up her where-abouts. However, I knew that she would have to show up for my trial. More than likely, the police had her shacked up in some seedy motel under 24-hour police protection. Someway, somehow, I would have to get to her before she testified against me. If she put on a show in court anything like the one she put on for the police the day I got arrested, my ass was grass.

Trevor held me down while I went through my battle with the law. While I was locked up, he took care of my grandmother and made sure she got everything she needed. Trevor was my road dawg 'til the end. He was a street nigga to the heart and lived by a code of honor. He loved to be out in the grind, on the corner, getting money. In fact, he had set up shop on the low, out in D.C., to keep the money flowing. To him, I was his brother and he had to have my back at this crucial time.

The two of us had to put our heads together to figure out how to get me outta this jam. The police tried to bring him a move, but Trevor's family ties put an end to that. His father, Bishop Harper, was a wealthy real estate developer with a lot of high profile connections in political circles. He used his influence to deflect the police's attention away from Trevor.

Since I came home, I spent as much time as pos-sible with mama. She was happy to have her baby back with her. I stayed up late nights with her, watching repeat episodes of *Sanford & Son* and *Good Times*, her two favorite television shows. We laughed together like we hadn't done in a good while. I enjoyed the time I spent with her as well. It gave me a chance to block out all of the craziness in my life, even if it was only temporary. Making her smile was the one thing that made everything else around me seem irrelevant.

Marquee Records was supportive of me throughout my whole ordeal so far. They scheduled a press conference so I could profess my innocence of all charges. They put together an all-out media blitz to portray me as a victim of an organized plot. I did interviews on BET and MTV to tell as much of my side of the story as I could without harming my cases in court. They put forth the position that I was a product of the ghetto who took my disenfranchised beginning and turned it into an American success story. They honed in on my lack of guidance and direction as a child, claiming they were the primary reasons I got into so much trouble as a kid. It was also introduced how I took care of my sickly grandmother. It was their intention to bring forth to the public my sensitive, human side to offset the negative press that portrayed me as a monster.

My lawyers depicted Rachel as a lying gold digger who fabricated the whole rape story in an effort to extort money from me. They planned to introduce several witnesses who could testify to her conniving ways. My lawyers claimed this was a case of her word against mine, and they were sure I would be vindicated in court.

In reality, they might have had a good chance to get the drug charges dismissed, but the rape charge was another story. Ever since Tupac got convicted of sexual assault and O.J. Simpson went to trial, it was open season in America on any black man involved in a domestic assault case. I would need a miracle to make the rape charge go away.

The house that I had my studio in had been seized by the police after my arrest. The record company arranged it so that I would still be able to finish recording the final tracks for my album while I awaited my trial. They booked a block of studio time at Omega Recording Studio in Rockville, Maryland, where I put the finishing touches on my album. The album was due to be released in May, around the same time my trial was to begin. They planned to capitalize on the publicity that my arrest generated to hype up record sales. We all hoped I did the type of phenomenal numbers that Snoop Dogg did with his debut album while he was on trial for murder.

With nothing else positive in my life at the time, I rededicated myself to my music. It took me about three weeks to finalize the track list for the album, then the master tapes were sent off to the Hit Factory in New York for the final mixes. The vocals I laid down on the last tracks for the album were by far more fierce and provocative than my prior work. I was letting out my rage about my legal troubles in my lyrics. Every thug nigga in America could relate to the pain and frustration I expressed in my songs about police brutality and racial profiling. I dropped lessons on the game out in the streets. They came from my soul and could only be understood by a true hustla that came from where I came from, the same world I did. This album was gonna be a bonafide classic, sure to etch me a place in history. I put my life on that.

20

Latrell (Luscious) and Takeisha (T-Love)

Latrell was sitting in the front seat of Ricardo's fresh-off-the-showroom-floor Infiniti Q45, bopping her head to the sounds of Outkast. Takeisha sat in the back, still not believing what she had agreed to do that night.

Latrell had met Ricardo one day when she was leaving the hair salon after getting her wig done at some poor fools' expense. She was immediately impressed with the way Ricardo carried himself. Outside of his height and cut-up physique, she noticed that he was bowlegged when he walked. There was something about a bowlegged man that turned her on. She was also digging his gear, as his ENYCE denim jeans set fit his body just right.

She was hypnotized by the smell of the Dolce & Gabana cologne he was wearing. He had a platinum link chain hanging from his neck with a princess-

cut diamond Jesus piece dangling on it. The blin-
gin' pinkie ring and three carat diamond stud he
wore in his left ear caught her eye and got her
mind to plotting. When Latrell got a glimpse of all
the ice he was wearing and estimated its value, she
gave him the green light that it was OK for him to
holla. In other words, his money was long enough
for her to allow him into her world for a minute.

Ricardo was from South Jamaica in Queens, New
York. He ran with a crew called the Hard Knock Life
Boys that hustled off of Mura Street in East Baltimore. He had relocated to Baltimore three years
ago because he saw the money-earning potential
here.

Since the mid '80s, there had been a long-standing tradition for uptown hustlas to come down
south to cities like B'more or somewhere in D.C.
or Virginia and set up shop. They knew they could
make more money selling cocaine in these slower
towns. New York cats would join forces with the
local hustlas and they all got rich together, or if the
locals resisted, they would take over the dealers'
drug strips by force. Many violent turf wars had
been fought in Baltimore between B'more niggas
and New York ballas for control of the drug trade.
To this day, there were still long-standing beefs between New York crews and Baltimore crews over
drug territory.

Ricardo had come out on top in this drug war,
and Latrell was seeing dollar signs as she looked at
him. They had just come back from dinner at Della
Notte in Little Italy. All throughout their meal, Ricardo eyed Latrell and Takeisha with nothing but
sleazy, sexual thoughts. It was written all over his
face.

As they drove down the road, Ricardo ran his hand along Latrell's thighs. Seeing that she wasn't resisting, he proceeded to work his way up her skirt until he had two fingers inside of her thong. Latrell parted her legs to make it easier for him to slide his fingers inside her throbbing pussy. Her thong was wet before he had ever touched her. This wasn't just about trying to work a nigga for some loot. Ricardo was sexy, and Latrell was eager to get a chance to pin his ass down and have her way with his manhood. This was gonna be his lucky night, and one neither of them would ever forget.

Takeisha would not forget the night either. She was initially uncomfortable with the idea of doing a threesome. Her and Latrell had done some scandalous shit together throughout the years, but they had never gone this far. Having sex with her best friend was something she had never imagined in her wildest dreams. However, when Latrell told her Ricardo would pay them five grand apiece, she had to jump at the opportunity. As much as they both loved money, this was too easy to pass up.

They both agreed it was a one-time thing, a secret they would take to the grave. They wouldn't even tell their girl, Danita. Takeisha needed to be high outta her mind to get through the night and fight her conscience telling her not to go through with it. In the morning, she would be five grand richer, she kept telling herself. Since neither one of them had a regular job and their rap career was in limbo, the money would definitely come in handy.

To Latrell, this was business as usual. Back in high school, she used to do private strip parties for a guy named Moochie. He ran a couple of after-hours spots across the city and he had line of young girls he hired to do sex shows for his clients. Even though she was only 15 at the time and Moochie was in his mid 30s, it wasn't hard for her to have him wrapped around her finger. She quickly became his top girl, earning anywhere between $500 and a grand a show. That money was just for her to dance. If a guy wanted to fuck, the price doubled. Seeing that she was built like a brick house, many playas were willing to kick out the loot to get a chance to tap that healthy ass from the back. Her shows were always freaky and uninhibited.

On several occasions, Latrell was approached at one of Moochie's parties by a dude, with his girl by his side, asking her to do some extra freaky shit with the two of them. If the money was right, Latrell was down for it. The fact that she was sexually open made it even easier. There was no shame to her game. It wasn't that she was into girls and the bisexual thing, but she did it for the love of the dough. If she happened to get turned on and had a good time along the way, then so be it. If not, she at least had a wad of cash to show for the night.

Takeisha and Danita knew that she did strip shows for Moochie, but they never knew the whole deal. Latrell never told her girls all of her freaky stories. Some things she chose to keep to herself. Well, tonight, the cat would be let outta the bag.

It was about 10 p.m. when they arrived at Ricardo's estate in the Owings Mills New Town section of Baltimore County. The two bottles of Moet that the three of them shared over dinner had them all twisted as they staggered toward the front door. When he turned on the lights, Latrell and Takeisha were awestruck by the immaculate house.

The shiny marble floors and elegant décor had them at a loss for words.

Latrell and Takeisha had hit the jackpot with this one. They had to make sure that he was satisfied for the money he was spending tonight and for the money they planned to trick him outta later on. After giving them a tour, Ricardo led them up the spiraling steps toward his bedroom.

Ricardo opened the double doors to his bedroom, and it was as though they had walked into the Garden of Eden. His bedroom was large enough to be a studio apartment by itself. The lights were dimmed just enough for them to navigate through the room.

He lit the fireplace to set the mood. There was a bearskin rug neatly laid out in front of it. Next, he lit the Good Life scented candles stationed around the room to give it an exotic aroma. He went downstairs to the kitchen and came back with a delightful treat. In one hand, he had a tray of different fruit with whipped cream on the side. In the other, he had a bottle of champagne chilled in a bucket of ice. He placed the spread on the nightstand next to the bed. He set up his CD changer to play an assortment of slow jams to set the mood right.

His king-sized bed was so plush and relaxing when Latrell sat on it that she almost wanted to have an orgasm in his silk sheets. They felt so soft up against her skin. Ricardo joined them on the bed.

"Y'all trying ta smoke?" he asked, pulling out a neatly rolled Dutchmaster and lighting it. He took two long tokes and closed his eyes to let the sweet taste of the bud take its effect.

"Hell yeah, nigga. Pass that shit over here. Don't hog it all to yourself!" Latrell said. She took the blunt from Ricardo and took a few hits then passed it to Takeisha, who did the same.

All three of them were feeling the effects of the weed as they blazed two more blunts. All the while, Ricardo got hornier as he playfully fondled both of them. They took turns feeding each other grapes, pineapple slices and chocolate-covered strawberries. The sexual tension in the room was so thick you could cut it with a knife.

"A'ight, so how we gonna do this? A nigga ready to be true ta set this party off. You know what I'm saying? My li'l friend is ready to get busy!" Ricardo said.

He had taken off all of his clothes, except for his boxers and a wife beater. He grabbed his hard dick to let them know it was time for the show to start.

"Slow down, baby. Be patient. Let me handle mine. I got this," Latrell said confidently.

Latrell motioned for Ricardo to join them back on the bed. She got up and began to take off her clothes. Latrell got on top of Ricardo and began straddling his rock solid member as it poked through his boxers. Every time she thrust her hips, he got more excited. The only thing that stopped his dick from sliding into her pussy raw was her thong. Ricardo playfully spanked her backside with both hands.

Latrell motioned to Takeisha to take off her clothes and get comfortable. Takeisha got undressed, except for her thong, and threw her clothes to the floor. All of the alcohol and weed had Takeisha open and down to do the damn thing. Any doubts she had went out the window. Seeing Ricardo's sexy naked body had her ready to get her swerve on.

Ricardo's eyes almost popped outta his head when he saw Takeisha's dark nipples standing at full attention. He sucked on both of them, swirling his tongue around as he licked them like a lollipop.

Takeisha took off her thong and sat her cleanly shaven pussy on his face, giving him a mouthful of her juicy private area. The way he sucked on her clit had her cummin' in no time. Her body was on fire.

Latrell was in between Ricardo's legs, sucking him off to the point of submission. She was a little jealous of the pleasure he gave Takeisha orally. She wanted to feel his tongue in between her thighs as well. His moaning and groaning gave her the sign of approval to keep doing what she was doing.

More ass and titties than he knew what to do with surrounded Ricardo. Nonetheless, he was willing to die trying to find out how to handle it all. If this was a dream, he didn't give a damn if he never woke up!

"That's right, shorty. Handle that shit! Slow down. You about to make me cum up in this motherfucker. Oh, shit!" Ricardo said.

He took a breather from between Takeisha's thighs and pushed Latrell away for a second so he could regain his composure.

"I'm ready ta ride this big motherfucker now, nigga!" Latrell said.

She pulled out a condom and slid it on his dick slowly. Once it was on properly, she mounted him and began to ride him like it was nobody's business. She lifted the bottle of champagne and poured some on Ricardo's chest, then licked it off him slowly, enjoying the fruity taste.

Takeisha had switched positions on top of Ricardo and turned to face Latrell while he ate her out. They were both so turned on by Ricardo that they found themselves locked into a wet tongue kiss. It felt so good that they wanted to explore each other further. Latrell's tongue slid out of Takeisha's mouth and found its way down to her neck.

Takeisha balanced herself against the wall while Latrell began to lick her firm breasts. With delicate care, she massaged them. Takeisha's body jerked violently. She was overcome with a warm feeling. No man had ever made her cum by just sucking on her breasts. This feeling was totally new to her. It let her know Latrell wasn't a rookie. She knew what she was doing.

While she was pleasing Takeisha's body, she never missed a beat in riding the shit outta Ricardo's dick. He let loose a load of cum so big it almost spilled out the sides of the condom.

"That's what I'm talking about. Hell yeah! A'ight, let's flip the script. I wanna see y'all do your thing with each other while I watch," Ricardo said.

Takeisha raised up from her squatting position on Ricardo's face and lay across the bed. Her legs were tired. Latrell climbed off of Ricardo and made her way over to the center of the bed with Takeisha. Ricardo went to the sofa, which was positioned at the perfect angle to get a view of the show they were about to put on.

Without hesitation, Latrell instructed Takeisha to lie on her stomach in the middle of the bed. She retrieved the bottle of cherry-flavored warming massage oil Ricardo had stationed on the nightstand by the bed.

Latrell rubbed the oil into Takeisha's satiny smooth skin. Each stroke of her hand sent a chill up Takeisha's spine. The warmth from the oil got her even hotter as Latrell teased her body with tantalizing kisses.

She flipped Takeisha over and did more of the same as she made her way down toward her overly excited clit. With every lick from Latrell's tongue, Takeisha let out screams of joy like she never had before. Her sexual juices had the sheets so moist that they soaked through to the mattress cover.

Feeling sexually fulfilled, it was time for Takeisha to return the favor. Since it was her first time being with a woman, it took her a minute to get the hang of the cunnilingus thing. However, she was a fast learner. When she was licking the right spots, Latrell let her know by yelling at the top of her lungs and grabbing onto the sheets. The muscles tensed up in Latrell's thighs as she wrapped them around Takeisha's neck. Before long, Takeisha had her cummin' up a storm.

She sprayed whipped cream on Latrell's thighs and the outer layers of her pussy lips. The taste of the whipped cream mixed with Latrell's body fluids soothed the back of her throat as she swallowed every drop.

Ricardo had worked his deflated dick back to erection as he watched them do their thing. He made his way back over to the bed, greeted by the sight of Takeisha's bodacious ass staring directly at him.

He slid inside of her with ease. As he proceeded to pound on her pussy, he watched her ass shake in tune with his body rhythm. They were right on beat with the music playing in the background. He stepped his game up another level when his favorite slow jam, "Come Inside" by Intro, came on.

Ricardo fucked Takeisha doggy-style for about 25 minutes. He grabbed her waist to get a firmer grip. Her pussy was so wet that his dick kept sliding out.

Latrell was in her own zone, while one of her best friends took her into uncharted territories of sexual pleasure. Their relationship would never be the same after tonight.

After another five minutes of getting his, Ricardo came for a second time. He collapsed onto the bed in exhaustion. They all fell asleep in the king-sized bed.

The next morning was another story. Takeisha couldn't believe she actually went through with the whole thing. She couldn't front, though, because she loved every minute of it. Latrell did as well. After they got dressed and were about to leave, Ricardo paid them the money he agreed upon for fulfilling his fantasy.

There were very few words spoken between the three of them. The girls silently glanced in each other's direction with smirks on their faces. They knew they had crossed the boundaries of friendship and things would never be the same.

21

Scar's Day In Court

I sat in the courtroom motionless as I listened to the day's legal proceedings. I was dressed in a conservative Italian suit that my lawyer, Murray Reisenberg, picked out for me.

I was optimistic about the way things were going so far. The tide appeared to be turning in my favor. I started to feel that I might be able to beat all of the charges against me. In the last month or so, I had received a few blessings in disguise that could only have come from above.

All of the members of my crew who got knocked took their charges like men and accepted their time as it was handed down. Not one of them mentioned my name, regardless of the pressure applied by the DA or the deals that were offered. As a result, the DA was unable to establish a connection between me and the countless raids they had made on my stash houses. As for the drugs that were found in the studio, I received even more good fortune.

My attorneys came up with a brilliant idea to make the drug case disappear. It was a costly plan, but it was surely effective. My lawyers worked it out with the DA and the police departments for two of my loyal workers who weren't locked up to become informants, helping them crack other drug rings in the city. In exchange, the charges against me would be dropped.

Each of the informants would be paid $50,000, courtesy of me, of course. I coerced Jerome and Reese, two of my young disciples, into doing the job. They both were 16 years old and worshiped the ground I walked on. When I told them how much money I would pay them and they actually saw it in cash, there was no way they could turn me down. Besides, with the competition outta the way serving long prison sentences, it would leave them more room to expand their territory on the streets of Baltimore and to make money. It was a win-win situation for them all the way around.

This typa arrangement went on all the time in law enforcement circles where they used street level dealers to set up other drug dealers, helping them increase their arrest rates. The police in every major city and the DEA had longstanding, mutually beneficial working relationships with dealers on the streets. It helped them appear as though they were doing their jobs effectively. They wanted the public to think that the war on drugs was producing results. However, a fool could see through the bullshit and know that was a lie.

The plan worked as expected. The police were

able to use the information they gathered from Reese and Jerome to enact several successful covert sting operations. They arrested leading members of several drug crews in East and West Baltimore. Hundreds of street level dealers were also taken into custody and were sure to serve prison time. The police looked proud on the television as they displayed the drugs, money, and guns seized in their arrests. They kept their end of the bargain with me and agreed to dismiss the drug charges I faced.

With the drug case outta the way, I could now focus on the rape charge. The rape trial had been going rather slowly. There was a wide array of expert witnesses who testified for the State, as well as those that testified on my behalf. My defense team's cross-examination tactics countered most of the evidence that the DA, Barry Stevenson, presented to forward his claim that Rachel was raped. Reisenberg was an expert at breaking down a witness on the stand to create a reasonable doubt in the eyes of a jury. That was his specialty, and he did it with authority and unbreakable confidence. Sometimes, he was so good that he even made witnesses question the truthfulness of their own testimony.

The jury heard testimony from several defense witnesses, including friends of Rachel, who testified about her promiscuous lifestyle and her penchant for the finer things in life. They heard evidence that painted her as a gold digger who would do anything to anybody for money. A few of her ex-boyfriends gave their accounts of how she had traded sex for cash throughout their relationships. Their testimony was especially damaging to her credibility.

The private investigator, William Dent, hired by

Reisenberg, was able to uncover a host of information about Rachel and her background. Dent discovered that she was originally from Virginia and had moved to Baltimore after her mother died in a car accident three years ago. She had a younger sister who still lived in Richmond, Virginia. Her sister, Mischa, worked as a cashier in a local supermarket. Dent found out that Rachel had served 10 months in juvenile detention for theft as a teenager. Rachel had no work history, other than being a paid escort at a private agency, called Chocolate City Beauties, in Washington, D.C.

The jury was being swayed in my favor because Reisenberg was able to call into question Rachel's checkered past. However, that all changed when Rachel took the stand. She was cooler than a fan as she told her twisted account of the night the alleged rape took place. Not even Reisneberg could break her down with all his years as a trial attorney.

I tried to fight back my anger as she told her bullshit story to the jury. Rachel was in rare form. She gave a performance worthy of an Oscar, going on and on, telling the jury how I had manipulated her into coming to my studio the night of the attack by telling her I could to make her a star. She played the naïve, star-struck female role to the hilt.

She went further with her fiasco by describing how I forced myself upon her when we got to the studio. She said we had never had sex before that night, which was a lie. However, I had no proof to back up the fact that I had been screwing her since the first night we met.

On all our previous dates, she said that I was a perfect gentleman, and she had no intentions of having sex with me the night of the attack. When I attempted to make sexual advances towards her, she claimed she resisted me. It was at that point that she said I pinned her down and forced her to have sex with me, raping her several more times throughout the night. She said that I wouldn't let her leave and I tied her up so she couldn't get away while I slept.

Rachel let the tears flow, and had to be interrupted several times during her testimony to regain her composure. I could tell that the jury was moved by her story. They were buying into the nonsense. It's something about a woman crying her heart out that sways a jury almost every time.

When Reisenberg tried to attack her money-hungry ways in her past relationships and her stint in juvenile hall, Rachel turned the tables back on him. She admitted to doing all of the things she was accused of doing in her past, but said she did them to survive. She proceeded to tell the jury about how her father and her uncle used to molest her as a child, and she ran away from home to escape the abuse. She said that she didn't move back home with her mother until after her father was sent to prison for twenty years for assaulting a police officer. He damn near beat the cop to death one night when he was being arrested for being drunk in public outside of a local bar.

She described her childhood growing up on welfare, and how she resorted to shoplifting to get food to help her mother feed the family. All of this part of her story was true, according to what William Dent uncovered in his investigation.

After hearing about her harsh upbringing, the jury was eating outta the palms of her hands. I knew I was going to jail, and resigned myself to my fate. It took the jury eight hours to come back with a guilty verdict. When it was time for me to receive my sentence, the judge gave me to 7 1/2 – 15 years for the trumped up rape charge. Rachel was in court to hear the sentence.

My music career was over. After the jury read the verdict, I couldn't hold in my anger any longer. When the judge asked me if I wanted to make a statement before he handed down his sentence, every bit of fury I felt came out at once.

"This is some bullshit. This bitch is lying. Y'all let this no good whore take away my freedom! Fuck this court! Fuck you, judge! Fuck you, jury! Fuck you, prosecutor! All of y'all can kiss my ass! Rachel, if it's the last thing I do, I'ma get ya ass!" I yelled. I threw my chair in Rachel's direction. It barely missed her. I had to be restrained by several bailiffs. If I got my hands on her, I woulda strangled the life outta her. They carted my ass off to jail.

To add insult to injury, my grandmother passed away during the course of my trial. She suffered a massive heart attack at home one night. A friend from church who happened to be visiting, rushed her to the hospital. The doctors could do nothing to revive her.

My grandmother's was death a blow that devastated me. The closest person to me in this world was now gone. Somehow, I managed to summon up the strength to make it through the trial. All of my years out in the streets had made me thick-skinned and able to deal with extreme adversity, unlike the average individual.

The one good thing that happened outta all of this madness was that my album was a smashing success. The press that ensued from the trial made me a household name. In hip-hop, controversy always sells. Everybody always wanted to know more about a star when he either died or faced jail time. According to Soundscan, I sold over 700,000 copies of the disc in the first week. I held down the number one album spot on the charts for seven straight weeks.

While out on bail, I shot three videos for my first three singles. They were all in regular rotation on MTV, BET, and VH1. "Straight Gangsta", my first single, reached the top spot on the Billboard Rap charts. My record sales would easily top the 3.5 million mark by the end of the year at the rate that they sold. However, with all of the revenue that I generated with my music, the ones who benefited the most were the executives at Marquee Records. When I added my legal expenses and the money Rachel was gonna get in her civil suit, my resources were almost tapped out. I would receive some royalties, but not what I expected before all of this mess.

Luckily, I still had money stashed away from hustlin' that would be there when I got outta jail. I had stashed my money in a safe place, where I knew no one could find it. I had over 300 grand put away. The only person who knew about my secret stash was Trevor.

News reporters stormed the courthouse steps and cameras flashed everywhere as I was escorted from the building. I was off to my new home at Patuxent Institution in Jessup. Hundreds of my fans were out in front of the courthouse to show their support. Packs of my female admirers held up large signs that said *Free Scar* and *The Bitch is*

Lying! He Ain't Do It! Even some of the local hustlas were there to show their support, because with all of the pitfalls that a brother confronted on a daily basis out in the streets, the only way the cops could bring me down was by using a lying-ass trick.

Countless numbers of my rap peers spoke out on my case. Some talked about how I was set up by the government because they were scared to see another young, black male rise up outta the hood and do something positive with his life.

Some saw my fate as another tragedy in the hip-hop world that would add fuel to the fire of the debate over the negative images associated with the art form. Feminist advocate groups were glad to see me go to jail. They saw my incarceration as a victory in their war against the alleged degradation of women in rap videos. I was the topic of the moment in the hip-hop industry. However, like all hot headlines, I would soon fade away into oblivion, just another fallen star in the world of fame and fortune. I swore once again that if I ever got outta jail, I would pay Rock and Rachel back for setting me up.

22

Takeisha (T-Love)

"**D**addy!" I yelled at the top of my lungs.

Rashid was in the basement, where the walls were lined with portraits of The Backsliders and some of the top musical stars of their day. My father looked back fondly over his musical career every time he glanced at pictures he took with stars such as The Gap Band, Brothers Johnson, Mtume, and Evelyn "Champagne" King. Framed copies of the group's gold albums and singles were also on display. He hoped to one day add some of my accomplishments in the musical business to his wall of fame.

Even though his days of performing to sold out audiences were over, my father still loved to pull out his drumsticks and keep his skills sharp. Playing the drums was also his way of unwinding after a hard day at work or handling business at the mosque on Garrison Boulevard. He enjoyed coming home and kicking back as he listened to his collection of old Parliament Funkadelic and Earth, Wind and Fire records. He loved to play along with their songs as they pumped outta the speakers. It was also normal to hear him playing classic tracks from the early '80s and Studio 54 disco days.

I knew that when he was in the basement playing his collection of greatest hits, it meant he wanted to be alone. However, today was a special day, and I had news to tell him that just couldn't wait.

"Daddy, we did it! We did it!" I yelled in excitement.

"Did what, baby girl? What done got you all excited?" he asked, putting his drumsticks to the side and turning down the volume on the stereo.

"We got a record deal! I just got off the phone with Joe, from the Smith Brothers, and he gave me some good news. He found a record company that wants to sign us to a recording contract!"

"Are you serious? That's good, Ki! Tell me exactly what he said."

Rashid was eager to hear all about the deal being offered. I knew he would be cautious because he didn't want me to jump the gun. He would tell me all the time from his experiences that nothing was etched in stone in the music business until you had a signed contract. Sometimes, even then, the record company could still screw you over.

"Well, the Smith Brothers want us to sign a production deal with their company to present us officially as their artists. Once that's taken care of, we're gonna be the first group they put out on their label. They got a partnership set up with a company called Cash Rules Records for distribution. The guy that runs the company, Samson, is from Baltimore. Ain't that a trip?" I said.

"Sounds good so far. When is this deal supposed to take place?" he asked.

"Well, we're supposed to fly to New York on Monday to meet with Samson and go over the specific details of the deal. That's where the company's main office is located. I want you to come with us to make sure everything is legit," I replied.

"Oh, you know I was gonna say that anyway. I can't have anybody tryin' ta take advantage of my baby girl. We gotta hire a lawyer to look this paperwork over. I'm so proud of you, Keisha. Your mother would be so proud of you too," Rashid said.

"Daddy, don't spoil the moment for me," I said. The mention of my mother brought back bad feelings from the past.

"Okay, baby girl. One day you're gonna have to make peace with your feelings of resentment toward your mother. You can't go through life holding grudges. It's not good for your mind, body, or soul."

"I know, I know. I love you so much, Daddy. You know you my hero, right?" I said.

"I love you too. Right now, you're my hero. You saw what you wanted outta life and you went for it. Have you told Danita and Latrell yet?" he asked.

"Yeah, they're on their way over now. I told them you were gonna take us out to celebrate," I replied.

"Oh, did you really? You must think you got your old man wrapped around your finger, huh? You lucky that you do or I would tell you a thing or two right now. So, where do you soon-to-be superstars wanna go?" he asked.

"Let's go to The Outback. I got a taste for some steak," I replied.

"If that's what you want, then so be it."

A few minutes later, Latrell and Danita were at the front door. We were all on our way out to celebrate. It was on and poppin' now!

23

First Meeting with Samson at the office of Cash Rules Records

Samson Miles had an imposing physical presence. He stood 6' 4" tall and weighed almost 300 pounds, all of it solid muscle. He could easily be mistaken for Suge Knight, the incarcerated CEO of Death Row Records, except for the fact that he was dark-skinned. They were both bald-headed and wore a full beard for that distinguished look. Since Suge Knight was locked up, Samson had developed a reputation as the Second Coming, with his roughhouse tactics and business savvy. This large black man, who traveled with an entourage of his homeboys from the streets, intimidated heads of other record companies.

Samson had come a long way from his days hustlin' on the streets of Baltimore. In the late 1980s and early 1990s, he ran one of the most hardcore drug gangs the city had ever seen. They were called the Ruthless Disciples, and no name was more fitting to describe their operation. Rival drug crews were afraid to cross their path because they knew it would mean a neverending bloody street war. Samson was infamous for his excessively violent means of exacting revenge on anyone who stepped on his toes.

It had been long rumored in police circles that he had his best friend, Kevin Wilkes, killed for making a pass at one of his female associates without his permission. Samson was alleged to be that ruthless. Kevin was found dismembered, his head, arms, and legs cut off and stuffed in several Glad trash bags. No one was ever arrested for the murder.

Despite being a public menace for so many years, the police were never able to charge Samson with any crimes. Any alleged witnesses would be too afraid to testify for fear of the repercussions. He was one of the few cats who could honestly say that crime did pay because he walked away from the drug game a rich man with no criminal record. He knew that eventually his luck would run out, so he had to find a legal way to make his money expand.

A shrewd businessman, Samson quickly saw the money-making potential in rap music when he met a young MC from New York who called himself Treacherous. He used to hustle for one of Samson's crews in Baltimore. One of Samson's lieutenants, Andre, brought Treacherous to his attention because he used to draw crowds on the corner when he would be freestylin' on the block.

When he heard Treacherous's rhyme, Samson's mind went into overdrive. He began to think about the money he could make off of him. He didn't know much about the music business, but he had enough friends in the industry to give him a crash course on the rules of the game.

Samson was known to be the man to see when you wanted to have a good time. He would throw some of the livest after-parties for the biggest names in hip-hop. With a load of money to spend and the appropriate industry resources at his disposal, he quickly signed Treacherous to a contract and got to work at forming a record label. This marked the birth of Cash Rules Records.

Samson decided to relocate to New York City, where all of the action in the music business took place on the East Coast. He needed to be in the right spot to rub shoulders with the movers and the shakers in the field. Just like he handled his business in the streets, it didn't take him long to make a name for himself among the top executives. He crashed several industry parties, with his large entourage in tow, and let it be known that Cash Rules Records was gonna be a force to be reckoned with in the rap world.

He traveled around town in stretch limos to his various business meetings. He took out full-page ads in all of the top rap magazines, like the *Source* and *XXL*, announcing the release of Treacherous's debut album, entitled *Only For Da Hood*. Anything he did, Samson believed in sparing no expense to make his mark in the game. Treacherous's album did respectable numbers, going gold and spawning two hit singles.

Samson also signed a group outta New Jersey, The Assassins. They were five young cats from Newark who brought back memories of Onyx in their heyday, with all of the energy that their live performance gave off. Each of the group's members had a unique rhyme style, but when they came together on a track, the chemistry was undeniable. Their album, *Faces of Death*, did even better than Treacherous's debut, selling over 750,000 copies. They had also done guest appearances on singles for artists like Joe, Brandy, and Case.

Samson's office was set up in a noble fashion, fit only for a king. He had framed portraits of John Gotti, Al Capone, and Scarface hanging on his walls. Right alongside those portraits, he had pictures of himself with some of the most notorious young gangsters that he came up with on the streets of Baltimore and other cities like Philly, Los Angeles, and Detroit. He had a wall-length aquarium in his office, filled with a wide array of exotic fish imported from Mexico. He had a super-sized leather sofa that folded out into a king-sized bed for use when he engaged in extracurricular activities with his secretary or some other young groupie of his choice. Behind his glossy burlwood desk, he could be found seated in his butter-soft leather executive chair, playing the role of a powerful CEO to the fullest extent.

As he sat behind his desk waiting for his appointment with the KS Crew, he puffed on a sweet-tasting expensive cigar. He glanced through the group's portfolio and was captivated by a photo of Takeisha. All three of the girls were fine, but there was something about her that stood out. She gave off a presence of power that instantly had him mesmerized. Samson liked his women to be the sassy, take-no-shit type that many people would classify as a bitch because of their drive and determination to be successful. He didn't care for a broad he could walk all over because that is exactly what he would do, walk all over her and disrespect her in every way imaginable.

Just looking at a photo of Takeisha, he sensed there was something special about her. Outside of her being his ticket to the big time, he definitely planned to get to know her better. He rarely found himself so curious about a woman. He always had several fine dime pieces at his beck and call, down to do whatever he wanted them to do.

As he was caught up in a daydream about tapping Takeisha's phat ass from the back, his secretary, Malonda, buzzed him.

"Mr. Miles, your 2:30 appointment is here."

Malonda was a fine, young honey. She had the cutest set of dimples to go along with her alluring hazel eyes. She had a big ass for such a petite frame, and her large breasts were a definite sign that she was a Similac baby. She had found herself bent over Samson's desk on numerous occasions, taking "dictation" of the freakiest order.

"A'ight. Send them in," Samson said.

Minutes later, the KS Crew walked in as the Smith Brothers and Rashid followed closely behind them. The KS Crew had already signed a production agreement earlier in the week with the Smith Brothers, and all that was left was to finalize the deal with Cash Rules Records.

Samson was reminded of how fine Takeisha was when she sat her sexy self in the seat directly in front of him. He came from behind his desk and gave all three of the Smith Brothers a pound as well as Rashid. He gave warm hugs to Latrell and Danita. When he reached Takeisha, he hugged her as well, but held on a little longer with a firmer grip as he cradled her voluptuous body in his enormous arms. His lingering embrace didn't go unnoticed by Rashid.

"Ladies, it's nice to meet all of you finally. Your pictures truly do you no justice. I've been wantin' to put y'all on my team since that time I saw y'all perform in Baltimore at the Ruff Ryders show. With your beauty and my money backing y'all, ain't no way we can lose. Y'all ready to get paid or what?" Samson asked enthusiastically. As hard and heartless as he was in the streets, he knew how to turn on the charm when it came to the ladies.

"You know it! It's nice to finally meet you also. We've heard a lot of good things about you and your company. We've been out here grinding for a minute. I'm glad you decided to give us this chance to do our thing. I promise you, speaking on behalf of the whole group, you're gonna get your money's worth. You won't be disappointed. This is my father, Rashid. I brought him along to hear what you have to offer us. I hope you don't mind," Takeisha said.

"Of course not. I would do the same thing for my daughter. I've done my research. You used to be in that group The Backsliders, right? I used to dig y'all music," Samson said.

"Yes, I was. I'm glad to hear that somebody remembers us," Rashid said. He observed Samson's every move carefully.

"Okay, let's get down to business. What I'm offering is simple. I'm willing to do whatever needs to be done so you leave outta here today with at least a verbal agreement that you wanna be a part of the Cash Rules family," Samson said.

"Sounds good so far. Keep going," Takeisha replied.

"I know my man, Joe, done told y'all the basics, but let me break things down for you. I wanna offer you a one million-dollar advance to show you that I'm for real about making you girls stars. As for royalties, you start at fourteen points for the first million copies sold. After that, you go up a point for every million sold, up to a maximum of eighteen points. Are you with me so far?" Samson asked.

"Hell yeah! I mean, we're with you," Takeisha said.

Joe had told them that the deal was sweet, but he didn't say that it was this major. After they heard the $1 million advance statement, all three of the girls went into a trance, daydreaming about what they could do with the money. Rashid was excited, too, but he didn't let it show. He wanted to hear the flip side of the story. He knew that with every record deal there was a downside.

"You'll have your own hair stylist, wardrobe designer, fashion consultant and personal assistant. I got a condo in Manhattan for you to stay in while we work on putting the album together. You can call that your new home. I plan to get the group in the studio as soon as possible. I wanna try to have your album out by January, for the first quarter of the year. That means we need to get cracking ASAP. That's about it. So, what's up, you ready to join me and get rich or what?" Samson asked. He reclined in his chair and awaited their response.

"I'm with it. Where do we sign?" Latrell responded.

"Not so fast, Mr. Miles. Your offer certainly sounds

generous. However, I'm gonna have to have my lawyer look everything over to make sure it's on the up and up. Can you give us a week to get back to you?" Rashid interjected.

"I have no problem with that at all. By all means, have your lawyer look the contract over. I promise you, no company is gonna give these girls the personal attention and promotion that we will," Samson replied, looking directly at Takeisha. He knew that if he hooked her, the deal was done. He could tell that she was the leader of the group. Her dominant personality made that evident.

"Glad to hear that. You'll be hearing from my attorney at the beginning of the week," Rashid replied.

"Now that we've got that business outta the way, let's have some fun. I'm gonna take you all out for a meal, show you around town a little, then get you back to the hotel. Ladies, are you ready to have a good time?" Samson asked.

The KS Crew didn't have to say a word. Their facial expressions and the pace at which they rose from their seats said enough. The Smith Brothers, who were virtually silent spectators throughout the whole meeting, followed behind them.

Samson asked Malonda to let the limo driver know they were on their way down to the lobby. He took them all out for a lavish night on the town and gave them a glimpse of the good life that was in store once the contract was signed.

After they returned to Baltimore the next day, Rashid got his lawyer to look over the paperwork. The lawyer took about five days to review it. Everything appeared to be in order. By the end of the week, all of the girls had signed off on the contract and it was sent via overnight mail to Samson. Going back to school in the fall wasn't even on their minds at this point. It was now official that the KS Crew was added to the Cash Rules artist roster. The girls had no idea how fast they were about to blow up.

24

Takeisha (T-Love)

Martin's West was the place to be. The banquet hall was packed to capacity and everybody was dressed to impress. All of Baltimore City's top ballas and finest ladies were in the house. The parking lot looked like a car show, with all of the Lexuses, Acuras, Benzes, and Beamers out there. I even saw a couple of Escalades and Navigators up in there.

All of the fellas were decked out in their platinum jewels like they were shooting a commercial for Jacob the Jeweler. I saw a couple of girls decked out in full-length fur coats and minks.

The KS Crew's coming out party, of course, was the reason for this grand occasion. Samson made sure that our celebration was nothing but the best since we were his top artists. Even though we lived in New York now, we wanted to have the party in B'more for our hometown fans.

Our album, *Beautiful But Deadly*, was released last month, and even Samson was surprised at the numbers we did. We sold over one million copies of the album in four days. The next week, we sold another 800,000 units. Not even Jay Z, Pac or Biggie moved units like we did. Record stores were having a hard time keeping the album on the shelves.

There was talk in the industry that our album was on course to possibly be the biggest seller of 2001, and it was only February. Our shit was on fire. Lil' Kim, Foxy Brown, and any of them other broads in the game had nothin' on us. In less than seven months, Samson had kept his word and made us superstars.

Since Scar's album went multi-platinum the year before and we followed that up with our album on course to do the same, record label heads were now checking for the rap scene in Baltimore. I was sure that a few other local acts would be getting deals soon.

Scar had written me several letters since he was locked up, telling me how he was sorry that things went down between us the way they did. He said that his time in jail gave him a chance to look back over his mistakes in life. Marquee Records terminated his contract after his conviction and after they paid out the $500,000 settlement to Rachel for her civil suit. There was some kinda clause in his contract where they could void his contract if he was convicted of a felony.

Even though I felt guilty about being responsible for his demise, I never responded to any of his letters. He was part of a past I was eager to leave behind. He had his chance and he fucked it up. I wouldn't make the same mistake with mine.

I think our album did so well for several reasons. First of all, Samson did a massive marketing campaign everywhere to make us known before our album hit the stores. He got us appearances on *Rap City*, MTV, and every local rap video channel in every major city across the country. He made sure our faces were seen in every venue we needed to get the public's attention. We did free concerts in several underground clubs to create a buzz in the streets for our sound. Everywhere we went, the crowd was feeling us. We did a guest appearance on a remix single for the singer Monica, and it was in heavy rotation on the radio. Damn, a nigga done came up, for real!

Another reason I think we were successful and received so well was our looks and style. It was easy for us to get the female rap fans to buy our shit. All we had to do was dress in the latest designer gear they had never seen before, and they would be clamoring to figure out where we got it from to cop it for themselves. Plus, in our songs, we talked about shit that any female in the hood went through with niggas, from baby mama drama to your nigga getting locked up and leaving you behind to carry his weight. That was all it took to get the broads hooked on our sound.

However, hooking the fellas was another ballgame. I mean, they could see that we were some pretty-ass eye candy for them to look at, but that type of support don't last long. Brothers would watch your videos and buy your album if you had some skimpy clothes on just to fantasize about fucking you one day. However, that type of fan don't last long because once the next bitch come along with a phatter ass, you can be replaced faster than you can change outfits between songs.

We were able to hook the dudes because our rhymes were hardcore. They had never heard females flow the way we did. Our shit was straight gutter, but hood classy. We kept it gangsta but still were able to flaunt our sex appeal. We could easily hold our own against the males in the game.

The final reason I think we were so well received was the fans were looking for something new in the rap game. Outside of the established artists like Jay Z, Nas, DMX, Dr. Dre or Scarface, there was no new flava that came out to hold their attention. All the artists that record labels were bringing out were trying to imitate the stars in the game and brought nothing original to the table. It was like these record executives saw the formula the rap superstars used to get on, and they tried to make a carbon copy of them with their newly signed acts. We, on the other hand, brought our own unique style of hip-hop with a B'more flair. The world had no choice but to show us love.

The party was to celebrate our success and to celebrate the thrusting of Cash Rules Records into the forefront of the music industry. Of course, the whole Cash Rules family was there. Treacherous and The Assassins had to represent for us.

Our success had the industry buzzing and expecting big things from the label in the near future. Samson had signed a couple of other acts he planned to bring out this year. In fact, we did a feature on the new single for a three-member R&B group, Menage, that Samson planned to bring out this summer. The track, called "Damsels In Distress", was a sure 'nuff hit waiting to happen.

"A'ight, can I get everybody's attention? I wanna propose a toast right now," Samson said. He held a bottle of Cristal in his hand. He was having a ball getting his drink on as he wobbled to the stage.

"Baltimore, this event tonight is in honor of the KS Crew. When I first saw these three young ladies, I knew they were gonna blow up. Not only did they blow up, they let the world know that Baltimore got some real MCs in this motherfucking town. Is that right?" Samson asked the crowd. They replied with a thunderous applause.

"Since this is their night, it is only right that I propose a toast to these ladies at this time. The Cristal is on me tonight. I want everybody up in here to have a good-ass time on me, you know what I'm saying? Without further delay, I wanna bring out the guests of honor and then we can all tip our glasses and get our drink on. Ladies, get y'all fine asses up here and everybody show some love for Baltimore's own, T-Love and the KS Crew," Samson yelled.

As I made my way to the stage, I was surprised that Samson singled me out and mentioned my name as though I was more than just another member of the group. I mean, I was the leader of the group, but we all shared equally in making us a success.

It might have been a mistake on his part because he was drinking, so I decided to pay it no mind. Danita did the same, but I could tell that Latrell was a little pissed. Her facial expression showed that she wasn't at all happy about what he did. Nonetheless, when we reached the front of the stage area, the whole crowd just went bananas. We shared a toast with Samson and the whole crowd. This was our city and we had the keys to this motherfucker. Nothing could stop us now. The spotlight was something I could definitely grow used to, fa sho'!

After our little celebration, we all hit the dance floor to get our party on. We weren't worried about mingling with the crowd because Samson and his boys had security tight. A lot of our friends from junior and senior high school came out to show us support. Even bitches that couldn't stand us in school were there and had to give us our props. We were the toast of the town.

I saw a couple of dudes I used to mess with, and they were clawing through the crowd to get a chance to holla at me. I made it my business to avoid certain individuals like Derrick and his crew of 'bamas. I spotted him from a distance and went in the other direction. Since this was a new day, it was time for me to start messing with a new crop of niggas. Them old cats I used to work for their money were no longer needed. I had loot of my own now. I was out to get my hooks into one of these industry playas with status.

As the night wore on, we were having so much fun. We danced until our feet were sore. The Assassins and Menage did a brief performance in dedication to us for our success. Some of the other new acts on the label also got a chance to shine. Silk, a singer that Samson signed from Columbus, Ohio, sounded and looked like a young Johnny Gill. He sang the hook on our next single, "Forever Yours." He was fine, and I had my eyes on him for a later date.

I was walking toward the bathroom when I felt a

cold hand touch my shoulder. I was startled when I turned around and saw Ricardo. I hadn't seen his ass in person since the night of our little kinky party with Latrell. He had called me several times after that night, but I never got back to him. Latrell told me that she hooked up with him a couple more times, but he was somebody I was surely trying to forget.

"What's up, shorty? I see you all big time now. Miss Superstar," he said. He had a devilish grin on his face. I should have known he was up to something.

"Hey, Ricardo. How you been?" I asked. Truthfully, I really didn't give a damn.

"Oh, now you can speak to a nigga. Give a nigga some pussy and then start actin' all anti and shit, not returning my calls. What's up with that?" he asked.

"Whatever, man. We had fun that night. You got yours and we got what we wanted. Let's leave it at that," I shot back.

"Maybe I don't wanna leave it at that. I might wanna tap that phat ass again. If you know like I know, you better play ball with a nigga and give me what I want," he said. He reached out to try to grab my ass, but I slapped it away.

"Why the fuck would I do that?" I asked. I was trying to entertain his dumb behind for a minute. I figured he was talking outta the side of his neck because of all the liquor he had to drink.

"If you don't want the video tape of our little party getting out to the public, you better act like you know," he responded.

"What video tape?" I asked. He didn't appear to be joking.

"I got it at the crib. You should stop by one day and watch it. I'm sure it's gonna be worth a hunk of change to you and your girl since y'all all famous and shit. I know you don't want your daddy to see his daughter in no porno movie, do you?" he asked.

I was hoping that this son of a bitch didn't actually tape us all fucking. It had never crossed my mind that he had a hidden camera in the room. All I thought about was the five grand that I made that night. This could not be happening to me now, after things had gone so smoothly for us. Niggas always gotta try to fuck things up.

"Hell nah. I wanna see it for myself. Write your number down and I'ma holla at you," I replied, trying to stay as calm as possible.

"That's what I'm talking about. I can see myself selling it to you for half a mil cash. You and your girl should be able to come up with that between the two of y'all. The two of you work together well, as I recall. Here you go," he said, handing me his number. He calmly walked away like a man who had the winning lotto ticket for the $100 million jackpot.

I couldn't wait to tell Latrell about Ricardo's ass. When I found her in the crowd, I pulled her to the side so we could talk in private.

"What's up?" she asked.

"Girl, you know I just saw that fool Ricardo. He claims that he got a video tape of the night we spent with him. Did you know anything about that?" I asked.

"Oh, girl, don't trip over that nigga. He told me that he was taping us. He's a freak like that. He wanted to keep a memory of us to jerk off to. I watched it with him a coupla times. Come on, T, the nigga did pay us five grand," she said.

"You mean to tell me you ain't tell me that we were being taped? Damn, Latrell, how stupid could you be? I woulda never did that shit if I knew that was the deal. That's some fucked up shit right there," I said.

"What's the big deal?" she asked.

"The big deal is that ya boy just told me he wants five hundred grand from us to keep quiet about the tape, stupid ass!" I said.

"He wants how much money?" she asked in disbelief.

"You heard me. We gotta figure out what the fuck we're gonna do about this. I done came too far to let some shit from my past ruin my career," I said.

"No doubt. We gotta come up with a way to handle this nigga. He ain't fucking up my shit either. I'm sorry, T. I didn't think things would turn out like this," she said.

"Yeah, I know. I can't worry about that now. What's done is done," I said.

Latrell was right. More often that not she didn't think before she acted. I was just as guilty because I went along with her in that hare-brained scheme. Ricardo had to be dealt with soon. If we waited around, he might ruin our careers. I knew the right person to help me get outta this situation. I just wasn't sure how much it would cost me.

25

Danita (D-Boogie)

My mind was telling me no, but my body was having a hard time resisting his advances. Silk was turning me on in ways that I hadn't felt in a while. His touch warmed my soul and his muscular arms made me feel so secure when he held me. I had been trying to convince myself that I didn't need a man, but he had worn all my defenses down. Silk was the right nickname for him, because he was as smooth as could be.

Since he had joined the Cash Rules family, Silk and I had become mad cool. We shared a lot of things in common. For one, being a songwriter himself, he shared my love of poetry and spoken word. Takeisha and Latrell weren't much into the poetry scene as far as going to poetry sets, so I did my thing without them. When I found out that Silk was into poetry as much as I was, I found somebody to go with me. We hit all of the hot poetry lounges in Baltimore, New York and New Jersey whenever we got some free time. I made it clear to him that I wasn't looking for a man, and he said that he understood.

On the real, I was only lying to myself. From the first time saw him, I felt a spark between us. I could tell he felt it too. Silk, whose real name was Andre Rogers, was a sexy chocolate brotha who was very easy on the eyes. He was a true pretty boy in every sense of the phrase. He kept his hair close and freshly cut. His dark chocolate skin tone matched well with mine, and I was fascinated with his innocent smile. He had the softest hands, and I noticed that he kept them manicured. Some girls thought a guy was soft if he got his nails manicured, but I thought it was the sign of a man with class and good hygiene. Shit, I didn't want a man with dirt all up under his nails touching all over my precious body.

Silk and I agreed to work together to write a few songs for his album. I had let him read some of my poetry, and he told me that he liked all of it. He suggested I take some of my poems and turn them into songs. He explained to me how I could make a fortune by writing songs for R&B artists. He would demonstrate by taking some of my more intimate and romantic poems and serenading me with my own words. The way he created melodies for my poetry and turned them into songs had me in awe. I had never considered being a songwriter, but now I would definitely give it more thought.

When we were together in the studio or at one of Samson's company parties, we always seemed to gravitate toward each other. My girls noticed this as well. Takeisha mentioned to me that at first she was interested in Silk, but after she saw how he would look at me, she killed the thought. She would always talk about me being lonely, and she believed we would make a good couple.

I, of course, tried to act like I didn't know what she was talking about. All the time I had put into isolating myself and my feelings from men had me frustrated inside and only increased my desire for Silk. A sistah was backed up for real and in need of a brotha that could blow my back out. However, my heart was still healing from the situation with Larry and all of the scars and unresolved issues from that situation.

Silk and I had become so cool that I confided in him about my relationship with Larry, and he did the same about his relationship with his ex, Tionna. They had a 4 year-old son, named Mikell, and she was making his life a living hell. Since he got his record deal, she was hounding him for money because she knew that he was about to blow up and become larger than life. I joked about her taking him down to child support to try to get her hands on his loot. On the real, that was very likely to happen.

I think the bond we developed as friends made me let my guard down for him so easily. This man had me open, and I hoped he wouldn't play with my heart.

Silk told me about how his childhood was, and our life stories were somewhat similar. His mother and father divorced when he was young, just like mine did. He also had no relationship with his father after the divorce. His father made no effort to be a part of his life and had also remarried, just like my father did. Silk said the absence of his father led him to look to the older drug dealers in his hood as his role models. He started hustling when he was 14 years old to help his mother pay bills. However, after he got arrested several times, he realized that the drug game wasn't for him.

Silk had a music teacher in high school who always talked to him about his ability to sing and encouraged him to focus more of his attention on music to keep him outta trouble in the streets. Silk took that advice to heart and joined the school choir. After graduating from high school, he got more serious about pursuing a career as an R&B singer. He knew he could hold a note as good as anybody he heard on the radio. Not only that, he had the looks and the charm to sway the ladies.

He hooked up with some local producers in Cleveland and made a demo tape of some songs he had written. He had saved up a sizable stash from hustling to pay for his studio sessions. After shopping his demo around for two years with no success, his demo managed to land at Cash Rules Records. One of Samson's assistants, Ray, heard the demo, liked it and brought it to Samson's attention. Samson listened to the demo and was feeling it as well. In no time, he had Silk on a flight to New York and signed to the label. Silk moved to New York to work on his album. The rest is history.

His relationship with his mother was as tight as could be. In fact, the first thing he did when he got his signing bonus from Cash Rules Records was buy his mother a house and car. His mother, Ramona Rivers, had worked hard all her life, doing domestic jobs to take care of him and his two younger brothers. Buying a house and a car for her was his way of showing appreciation for all of her sacrifices throughout the years. When he told me about his close bond with his mother, that only made me want him more.

We had just come back from dinner and the movies. I had finally reached a point in our friendship where I was comfortable going back to his place alone with him. It wasn't that I didn't trust him. I didn't trust myself. As horny as I was, I didn't wanna give him some pussy and get my feelings hurt again. However, Silk was a smooth talker and he appeared to be sincere. After all of our flirting back and forth over the last few months, we were finally gonna do the damn thing.

He slowly ran his strong hands down the small of my back, rubbing the coconut-scented massage oil into my skin. Every movement of his hands up and down my body had me feeling inexplicable and unadulterated horniness. His tongue stimulated the hairs on my back to stand up. When he swallowed my earlobes in his moist mouth, he whispered some ol' playa shit in my ear about how he hoped the rest of me tasted as delectable. I moaned sensuously in response. The smile on my face let him know I was enjoying his exploration of my body.

"Nita, I been waiting for this for a long time. You just don't know how bad I want your sexy ass," Silk said.

"Don't talk about it, just be about it then, nigga," I said.

"You ain't said nothing but a word, sweetness. Your every fantasy is my desire tonight. I wanna please you in every way."

He began to undress, slowly removing his Rocawear sweater and matching jeans. He looked like a chocolate-covered sundae that I was eager to sink my teeth into and devour. When he took off his wife beater and boxers, his naked body glistened in the moonlight. His dick was already hard as steel without me doing anything to motivate it.

He came back toward the bed and kissed me gently on the forehead. His tongue slowly made its way down to my breasts as he aroused my nipples with his love strokes. D'Angelo played in the background as my toes curled from the naughty feelings of erotic bliss that he gave to me.

After he got my juices flowing by licking the sweet cherry-flavored fluid that dripped from my pussy, I pulled him down on the bed and began to massage his manhood with my mouth. I opened my jaws wide to take as much of his hunk of manhood into my mouth as possible. I almost choked on it when it reached the back of my throat. He let out a loud grunt of submission to let me know that my up and down motion had him weak in the knees. Some good head would always make the most thugged-out nigga whine like a bitch. We got into a 69 position, and it was on and poppin'.

After orally pleasing each other, I climbed on top of him and straddled his dick. I rode him into the night as I tightened up the walls of my pussy to collapse around his dick in a vice grip. I wanted to feel the friction from every inch of him inside me. I exploded at least three times from the pleasure of the roller coaster ride I took him on. He came inside of me to make our union complete.

I let him rest for a few before I was ready for another dose of his lovin'. I began licking on his chest and along his rib cage, and he laughed because my hot kisses tickled. I got him to turn over on his stomach and rubbed his shoulders and lower back to make his muscles relax even more. He had the sexiest, perfectly round muscular ass, and it tasted just as appetizing when I ran my tongue across it with reckless abandon. He almost lost his mind when I started to lick the area between his balls and his asshole. It was something about that spot down there that made a man just lose it all.

After I tongue-whipped his ass for a while, he got behind me and fucked me doggy style like a man was supposed to do his woman. He fucked me like he owned my pussy. Every time he went in and out of me, he took a piece of my soul with him because I was definitely falling for this man. When he finally came again, my hot den of love was worn the hell out. I couldn't take any more.

As we lay up against each other in the sweat-drenched sheets, our ebony bodies were entangled in an inseparable love lock. It was as though we had become one with each other on all levels. Two drops of chocolate never looked so beautiful together.

We would make the most beautiful babies together, I thought. This man had to be the one I had been searching for to be in my life. Lying next to him, I felt at home. I decided to myself that night that Silk was gonna be my new man.

26

Latrell (Luscious)

In the past couple of months, I experienced the fame and fortune of being a rap star, and it was outta this world. We were rubbing elbows with the who's who of the entertainment industry, and I must admit that I fit right in. I made myself a regular at every industry party I could squeeze into my busy schedule of studio sessions and sold out concerts. I had never before seen the amount of money we made, and it was giving me a natural high. Fuck smoking blunts, seeing six figures in my bank account got me lifted on another level. The money was making me hiiiigh!

Being a member of the hottest rap group in the country also made me the center of attention whenever I went out in public. I was mobbed by the paparazzi, snapping pictures when I went to the mall or just to hang out. Being a star didn't hurt my social life, either. All of the finest rappers, actors, singers, and executives were sweating me whenever I went out to the club. I had the pick of the litter of the sexiest niggas in the business to choose from. Believe me, I had more than enough fun playing the field.

One of the first celebrity niggas I fucked was the rapper Sincere. He was from Brooklyn and he spit conscious lyrics with a street vibe. He was signed to Cipher Sounds Records and had a couple hot singles that got play on the radio. He resembled Allen Iverson with his neatly done cornrows. He was a Five Percenter and tried to convince me to become a member of The Gods and Earths Nation. However, the only member I was interested in getting to know was the long snake that swung between his legs.

Sincere wore my backside out when I gave him a chance to hit this. That nigga could fuck all night. We messed around for about two months before I sent him on his way.

The next cat I added to my list was the R&B singer Raheem. This was one of my most forgettable experiences. Raheem had a voice like Luther with a touch of Brian McKnight. He had all of the ladies on his dick, wanting to break his ass off something real proper. If they only knew what I knew, they wouldn't waste their time. Behind closed doors, Raheem was hardly the mack that everybody thought that he was. He had a nice-sized dick, but he didn't know what to do with it. He was inside of me for like two minutes before he busted a nut. I didn't even get a chance to blink my eyes before he was done. Oh, and his head game was totally wack. A nigga that couldn't even eat pussy good wasn't worth a damn to me.

I dismissed his ass without a second thought. He made me promise that I wouldn't tell anybody about our encounter. For my own sake, not his, that would be our little secret.

I had several more fantasy niggas in the industry that I sexed up, and even more that I planned to get with in the future. All in all, this celebrity thing agreed with me. I moved outta the condo that Samson rented for us and got my own studio in Greenwich Village. I needed my own space to spread my wings. I also bought myself a powder blue Jaguar to floss in and flaunt my superstar status.

My wardrobe was over the top, and both of my walk-in closets were filled to capacity with designer gear and shoes. It felt good to be able to go into any store I wanted and purchase everything on my list. Notice I said purchase because in the past, all my high-end gear either came from one of my mother's boosting sprees or from some unsuspecting sucka that I finessed outta his cheddar.

With my newfound riches, of course, I had to take care of my needy-ass family. I bought my mother a three-year-old convertible Beamer to cruise around town in. I set her up a bank account with twenty grand in it to live off for a while until our royalties were paid out at the end of the year. I gave my brothers five grand apiece. I knew their money would be gone less than a month. The drug man would get every penny of it. I didn't care, because they were free to do what they wanted with the money.

The best part of all of our success was that we

got a chance to travel all over the world and see new things. We did a show in every major city in America to a packed audience and ripped it. Samson arranged for us to do a ten-city tour in Europe and to perform in countries such as Japan, Australia, and Jamaica. Everywhere we went, we drove the crowd crazy. The KS Crew was the shit, and we had the world at our feet.

We had a studio session with the Smith Brothers to do a remix for the single, "Gangstress." The song had been getting mad radio play, and Samson wanted us to milk the success for all it was worth.

I had to admit that the remix track they laid down was hotter than the original. After they had so much success working with us, the Smith Brothers had become the most sought-after producers in the game. They were called in to produce tracks for the likes of Mary J. Blige, Lil' Kim, Whitney Houston, and even LL Cool J.

"Yo, are y'all ready to get started?" Joe asked us.

"Hell yeah. I'm ready," Takeisha said.

Takeisha and I were on time for the studio session. In the past, I was the one who was always late. We were waiting on Danita to arrive. She was probably out with Silk somewhere. Since she started to get some dick on the regular, that girl didn't know how to act. She started to slack off in handling her business as far as the group was concerned. She was constantly late for our appointments, and she didn't seem to care. That was so unlike her, because D had always been the one to be on time and on point with all of her shit.

Had I done the things she did, T would have been all over me about fucking up the group chemistry. However, since it was Danita, she never said a word. She let her get away with murder. She was the leader in the group, but that didn't make it right for her to treat us differently. Her double standard started to get on my nerves.

"Bet. Since D ain't here, y'all can lay down y'all verses first. Then we can get to work on the hook. By that time, she should be here. She called to say that she was caught in traffic," Elliott said.

Caught in traffic, my ass. That bitch was probably caught up with Silk's dick in her mouth. Nonetheless, I laid my vocals down first. I got it right on the first take.

Takeisha went in the booth after me and did her thing. By the time we were finished recording our verses, Danita showed up with Silk by her side. She was all giggly-acting and whatnot, but I was hardly in a laughing mood.

"It's about time you showed up," I said. I wasn't letting this bitch get away with this shit without speaking my piece.

"Chill out, girl. I'm sorry I'm late. It ain't like you ain't missed a recording session before. Ain't that right, T?" Danita said. Takeisha nodded her head in agreement. This heifer was getting bold to talk to me like that. T might give me a run for my money, but Danita knew that I could kick her ass with no problem. She now irked my nerves as well.

"Enough of the BS. Let's get to work so we can finish this track. Samson got us on a tight schedule. D, go do your thing, ma," Charles said.

Without a second thought, she took off her coat and went into the vocal booth. It took her like ten takes to get her verse right. She was stumbling over her words and had to read from her rhyme book. She used to be able to flow off the dome.

The Smith Brothers appeared frustrated with her fuck-ups, having to do take after take. When she finally got it right, all three of us went into the booth to lay down the hook. It came out perfect with no flaws. When the three us put our heads together and were focused, our chemistry was undeniably tight.

As we were listening to the track play in the studio as it was being mixed down, Samson called.

"Latrell and Takeisha, Samson wanna meet with y'all about something. He said that he was sending a car to come and get y'all in twenty minutes," Joe said.

"He ain't ask for me?" Danita asked.

"No, he just said Latrell and Takeisha," Joe replied.

"Did he say what it was about?" I asked.

"No, he just said be ready when the driver gets here. He said it was important," Joe responded.

I was confused about why Samson wanted to see us all of sudden and why it was so important. Takeisha didn't seem to be as mystified as I was. Something had to be up. I would find out soon enough.

Danita and Silk made a quick exit from the studio. The Smith Brothers stayed in the studio to do what they do to make our record a hit. Right on time, the limo driver arrived to take us to our meeting with Samson. Only God knew what was going on. All I knew was that I had a funny feeling that something wasn't right.

27

Takeisha (T-Love)

As Latrell and I rode in the Lincoln Town Car, we didn't speak much. She didn't know that I told Samson about the situation, so she was still in the dark about why we were going to meet with him.

I knew some shit was about to go down. Just the thought of the tape getting into the wrong hands had me at my wit's end. If Samson took care of Ricardo's punk ass for me, I would be eternally indebted to him.

He called me earlier and told me he had something special for me later on. This had to be what he was talking about.

I wasn't really into older guys, but Samson was different. He was a powerful man. When he told somebody to do something, they usually did it. When he said that he was gonna make something happen, nine times outta ten, he made it happen. The one time that it didn't happen, it was because it was humanly impossible. Whenever he walked into a room, everybody took notice. He just had an aura of invincibility and nobility that drew me to him. Plus, he was a straight gangsta nigga that handled his business.

I knew he was more than twice my age, but I didn't care. I noticed how he flirted with me on the DL that first time we officially met in his office. From that point on, he made a lot of veiled sexual comments toward me when we were in the studio recording our first album or alone in his office. I played along with him. More than a couple of times, I caught him watching my ass when I walked by.

Eventually, I decided to give him just what he wanted. I just hoped he could handle all this woman here. I knew I was young in years, but I knew how to work with what my momma gave me.

Being realistic, I knew I wasn't gonna have a long-term relationship with him. I knew he was a playa and had his choice in women. I was just out to have some fun and experience something new. I also saw an opportunity to advance my career. A cat with paper long like Samson was always good to have around. I wanted to wrap him around my finger and make him my slave. Giving him some bomb-ass punany was a way to make that happen with a little more ease.

It happened one night when we were alone. We had just left the studio and he invited me out to dinner with him. He said he had to stop by his office to get something, and asked me to go up there with him. When we got to his office, we started talking and wound up having a few drinks. He turned some old school Teddy Pendergrass on the CD player and dimmed the lights.

"So, T, what's up? Ain't no need for us to play no more games. Let's get right to the point. You know I been checking out your fine ass since we first met. So, where's that special nigga in your life?" Samson asked me.

"I don't have anybody special. I like to keep my options open," I said. I was making sure I wasn't revealing too much too soon.

"Options are a beautiful thing in both business and romance, ya know?" he replied.

"True dat, true dat. So what you saying, Samson? You trying to kick it with me?" I asked. The Hennessy had me talking cash shit. I wanted to beat him to the punch to take control of the situation. I knew that as a powerful man, he was used to calling the shots. Being aggressive, I threw him off guard and turned the tables in my favor.

"Hell yeah, as long as you can keep business and pleasure separate. This'll be our little secret. Nobody else has to know. An open relationship typa situation. You seem like you can handle that," he replied.

"I can show you better than I can tell you," I said. From that point, he had no idea what he was in store for.

I walked over behind his desk and sat in his lap. The bulge in his pants instantly impressed me. Most guys his size usually had small dicks, but not this brother. Samson was packing some serious heat. From what I could feel, he could go at least eight inches deep. I took his drink outta his hand and began massaging his sexy, bald head. I licked his forehead with my curious, hot tongue, then made my way down to his ears and began nibbling on his earlobes forcefully.

"Damn, shorty, that shit feel good as a mother-fucker!" he yelled out.

"Oh, I'm just getting started with you. You might be the CEO of Cash Rules, but I'm in charge to-night," I said.

I slid off my shoes and unzipped my jeans, let-ting my pants fall to the floor to reveal my pink thong. Samson reached out to try and take off my top, but I pushed his hands away.

"I told you this is my show. It's my way or no way," I scolded him. He threw his hands up. I was the boss tonight.

I lifted my shirt over my head to reveal my firm breasts. I didn't have a bra on because I figured that something was gonna go down between us, and I was prepared for easy access. I got down on my knees and told him to drop his pants. When he complied with my wishes, I put my head between his legs and began to make love to his dick with my mouth.

He grabbed hold of the arms on the chair to hold his balance. I had him about to lose control. I started sucking him faster and faster until he said he was about to come. That was when I pulled away from him and sat up on the desk.

I spread my legs across Samson's broad shoul-ders and invited him to taste me. He leaned for-ward and within seconds, his head was buried in my coochie hairs. He probed the walls of my pussy with his tongue and two fingers. I leaned my head back on the desk and enjoyed the moment. My legs began to shake from the tingling sensation that Samson gave to me. For an old head, he knew how to handle his business!

Samson got up from his chair, put on a condom, and inserted his hard dick inside of me. He filled my insides with joy as my natural moisture made his journey a wet and wild one. He was pounding on me and I was loving the feeling he gave to me. I raised myself up off of the desk and told him to lean back in his chair because I wanted to ride his dick for a minute. We did that to death until he said he wanted to hit it from the back, my favorite position.

I turned around and bent over so my ass was up in the air and my face was buried in the papers spread out on his desk. Samson got behind me and went to work. Sweat started to pour from his forehead and all over his back as he thrust in and out of me.

"Give me that dick, Daddy! Fuck this pussy!"

"You like that? Huh? You like that?"

"Yes, Samson. Yes, I love that shit! I'm cummin'!"

I let off a big load of cum all over his dick. Minutes later, Samson did the same.

We chilled for a minute before we got dressed, then we sat up in his office to chit-chat and smoke a blunt. I must admit that Samson was cooler than I thought he was after we talked for a while. Since that night, we had many more romps in the sack. It wasn't always about the sex, though, because sometimes we would just go to dinner or back to his estate in the Hamptons to relax.

Samson told me that I should never be afraid to come to him if I had any problems or needed his

help. He said his door was always open to me or
the rest of the group. I decided to take him up on
his offer when I couldn't resolve the issue with Ricardo and the videotape.

After I went to Ricardo's house in B'more to verify that he had the tape, I knew we were in trouble.
When I told Samson about Ricardo trying to blackmail us, he told me to relax, he would take care of
the matter as soon as possible.

I gave him all the info I had on Ricardo as far as
where he lived and hung out. He said we were all
family and he didn't take too kindly to someone
trying to harm his family.

I also told him about what Rock, Rachel, and I
did to set Scar up to go to jail. Samson had me feeling relaxed enough to confide my deepest, darkest
secret. I also wanted his input to make sure that I
was in the clear. With his street smarts, Samson was
the best person to tell me how to make sure that
shit didn't come back to haunt me. He told me not
to sweat the matter because even if Rachel did decide to ever talk to the police, it was her word
against mine. It would be hard for her to prove
that I was connected to the situation.

When we reached Samson's office, we were
greeted at the door by Lem, Samson's personal bodyguard. Lem wasn't no joke. Samson was a big man,
but Lem was bigger at 6' 8" tall and 350 pounds of
brute force. He led us into Samson's office, where
I saw Ricardo tied down to a chair in the middle of
the floor. His face was all beat up and bloodied.
Samson stood in front of him with a sinister look
on his face.

"Come on in, ladies. Have a seat. Our friend here

has something to say to y'all. Talk, motherfucker," he said. He removed the handkerchief that covered Ricardo's mouth.

"I'm sorry that I tried to blackmail y'all. Please accept my apology. You can have the tape. I don't even want the money. I just wanna live. Please forgive me! I'm begging you, I don't wanna die!" Ricardo said.

Samson enjoyed torturing Ricardo. He had a pair of pliers in his hand that he clamped around Ricardo's testicles. Ricardo yelled out in obvious pain. Latrell started to laugh as well. It was as though she enjoyed this as much as Samson did. I had seen some crazy shit before, but this was over the top. I heard stories about Samson and how he violent he was, but to see him put in work was an eye-opener.

"Shut up, nigga! This is what happens to a motherfucker when he fucks with one of my family. You tried to blackmail my girls with this tape here. Now you about to meet your maker, bitch!" Samson said.

He took the tape and threw it in our direction. Latrell was able to catch it. Samson began to mercilessly beat the shit outta Ricardo.

"Good looking out, Samson. Beat that nigga's ass. He deserves it for trying to play us out like that," Latrell said.

"Samson, no! Don't kill him, please!" I yelled. I wanted Ricardo to pay for what he tried to do to us, but I didn't want him to die. I should have known that Samson was the typa nigga that played for keeps.

"T, this pussy-ass bitch has gotta go. If we let 'im him live, he going straight to the police. This weak-ass nigga ain't got no heart. I ain't going to jail for no shit like this. I told you I was gonna handle this for you, didn't I? That's why I brought y'all here. I wanted you to see for yourself how I get down so you know that I got ya back," Samson said with a mean scowl on his face.

I started to plead for Ricardo's life again, but I knew it was useless. I just nodded my head in agreement and Samson proceeded to pound on Ricardo. Blood was everywhere and Ricardo was helpless to fight back.

After Samson had finished beating on him for what seemed like forever, Ricardo's body was lifeless, slumped over in the chair. Samson made a phone call to some of his boys to come and clean up the mess. He went into the bathroom to wash up and change his blood-stained shirt.

When his boys arrived, he motioned for us to follow him. We exited the building and made our way toward his limo. Inside, he tried to explain to us what just went down.

"I know that what just happened might've threw y'all off for a second, but it's some things that you gotta understand. When you dealing with street niggas on any level and it's beef involved, you gotta be down to take somebody's life before they take yours. Ricardo was the kinda cat that needed to be dealt with. He had other copies of the tape and if you would've paid him the money, he would've just tried to blackmail y'all again with the other copies. Don't worry about that, though, because I destroyed those copies already. The copy you have is the only one left.

"If you really look at it, I did y'all a favor getting rid of that fool. Now he can't tell nobody shit. His body will never be found. As far as the two of you are concerned, this night never happened," he said.

"I know that's right. You good peoples, Samson. Damn, T, you shoulda told me that Samson was gonna take care of us. Then I wouldn't have been stressing so much. Samson, I liked the way you had that nigga cryin' like a bitch! 'Oooh, I don't wanna die! Don't kill me!'" Latrell said, mocking Ricardo. This bitch was just as crazy as Samson.

Samson felt no guilt about beating Ricardo to death. He dropped us off at the condo that Danita and I now shared. Before we got out of the limo, he leaned over and kissed me on the cheek. When his lips touched my skin, I wanted to throw up. I was hardly feeling him at this point. I wanted to be as far away from him as possible. I knew he meant well, but to take somebody's life was another thing altogether. I needed a vacation to get my head together. It was time to go spend some time with Rashid.

Since the night Latrell and I saw Samson kill Ricardo in his office, things kinda went back to normal. I wasn't feeling as bad about the situation. Shit, Samson was right—that snake got what his ass deserved. I had decided that night would be just another secret I kept to myself. I would be damned if I was gonna open my mouth and send myself to jail over that foolishness. In fact, that night made me realize how much Samson cared about me. If he would kill a motherfucker to protect my ass, then he was a nigga I wanted to keep by my side, even if he wasn't gonna be my man.

It was about a month after the incident at Samson's office, on a Sunday morning, when Danita and I jumped into my Cadillac Escalade, headed toward Baltimore. The wind was blowing through my hair as I caught a mild breeze in the midst of the August humidity. We were bumping the sounds of Jay Z on the stereo as we were about to exit the New Jersey Turnpike. Once we got off of the turnpike, we knew it would only be another hour and some change before we reached our destination.

"Hey, T. You know Latrell is really getting off the hook lately. I mean it's mad rumors going around that she done fucked every nigga in the industry. She's making us look bad," Danita said.

"Yeah, I know. She is off the hook, but when has she not been off the hook? She's been that way all of her life," I responded.

"True, but this is business. I don't want everybody to think that we're easy like she is and whatnot. I'm trying be in this game for a minute. You feel me?"

"I feel you, girl. I'ma get Samson to say something to her. He'll know how to handle the situation."

"Speaking of Samson, what's up with the two of y'all? I know y'all must be getting tight now. You got the boss all caught up and whatnot," Danita said. Being so busy, we didn't talk as much as we used to about girl things.

"That's a good question. It ain't nothing serious between us. He's free to do his thing and I'm free to do mine. He's my homey-lover-friend," I said. We both had to laugh at my comment.

The time had passed faster than we thought, and before I knew it I saw the sign saying we were in Baltimore. I dropped Danita off at her mother's house and made my way to my father's. In no time, I was pulling up in the driveway of the new home that he recently bought for himself out in Randall-stown. It was equipped with five bedrooms, four bathrooms, an Olympic- sized swimming pool, and all of the finest amenities. I wanted to help him pay for it, but my father refused my assistance. He was too proud.

I got out of my truck and walked up the winding walkway toward the front door. I didn't tell my father that I was coming. I wanted to surprise him. He had given me the keys to the house to let myself in.

I saw my father sitting in the living room. He seemed somewhat startled to see me. He was usually the most relaxed man I knew, but he was jittery and appeared off balance. Nonetheless, he gave me a big hug because it had been a while since he last saw me. Next, he went out to the truck to get my bags out of the back seat.

"So, what brings you to town? You should have called me first," he said. I almost felt as though he didn't want me there. My father never acted that way with me. Something had to be up. We made our way into the house.

"Well, since I done become a superstar and all, I haven't been back to B'more in months. I needed a taste of home in my life. Besides, I got a taste for a cheese steak from Halal's up on Park Heights," I said.

As we were sharing a laugh, I noticed a woman coming down the stairs. She was wearing my father's bathrobe and appeared to be right at home. She had light brown skin with a pretty face and nice shape for a woman in her late 30s to early 40s. Now I saw why my father was a little jumpy when he came to the door. He was obviously getting his freak on. Let me find out my daddy done turned into a playa while I was gone!

"Who the heck is that?" I asked.

"Takeisha, this is Bernadette. Bernadette, this is my daughter, Takeisha. I'm so proud of my little girl," Rashid said.

"Nice to meet you, Bernadette," I said as I extended my hand to her. Really, I was checking her out to make sure she was fit to be with my pops. Time would tell it all.

I was a little disappointed that my father had kept Bernadette a secret from me. We usually told each other everything.

As I talked with her, I found out she was a legal secretary for a prestigious law firm in downtown Baltimore. They met one day when she came into my father's record store. Rashid told me they struck up a conversation and found out they had a lot in common. They began dating not long afterwards and were now an item.

It appeared as though she made him happy, so I couldn't complain about him having a girlfriend. It was just a little uneasy because I hadn't seen him with a woman since my mother left us.

We decided later that night to go out to dinner to spend some quality time together. We definitely had some catching up to do. We chose to go to Ruth's Chris Steakhouse to eat.

"So, what's been going on, Miss Lady? How is the music business treating my little girl?" Rashid asked.

"Everything is going lovely. Samson told us we

were gonna be nominated for a bunch of awards for the album. You know, the usual—The *Source*, a Grammy, American Music Awards . . . Your baby girl done blown up!" I replied.

"I'm not talking about the money or the fame aspect. I'm talking about how are you doing? I saw the rumors in the paper about you dating Samson. Is it true?"

"We hang out at times. It's nothing serious. I'm not the only one keeping secrets, ya know?" I had to throw that in the mix to let him know I was a grown woman with my own life now.

"Yeah, Bernadette is a special lady. I wanted to wait until the right time to tell you. I guess no time was better than the present, huh? As for you, just be careful, baby girl. Don't let your personal life interfere with business," he advised me.

"I got this, Daddy. Trust me. I'm not looking for a serious relationship. I'm too focused on my career."

"That's good. That's what I like to hear."

We ate our meals and engaged in small talk. When we were finished eating and stuffed to capacity, we made our way home. While my father went out to spend time with his new woman, I chilled in the house to get some much needed rest and relaxation. I had been running on fumes for the past few months and I needed to chill.

The next morning when I woke up, I decided I needed to go to the gym to work out. I had a membership at Bally's, but I rarely used it. Over the last few months, I had put on a few pounds and I needed to work them off.

I went to the Sports Authority to buy some gym gear then I was off to do a light workout. I chose to go to the Bally's on Route 40 because it was less crowded than the other ones, so there was less chance of me drawing any attention or fanfare.

When I got to the gym, I was greeted at the door by one of the fitness trainers. She was a young black girl, about my age, and she immediately recognized me. Her name was Kelli, and she was a big fan of the KS Crew. I begged her not to make a scene, and agreed to give her an autograph if she wouldn't. She complied with my request and led me into the main gym area to work out.

We started off with a light warm-up on the fitness bikes. Once that was done, we made our way over to the treadmill. The cardio exercise had me pumped and eager to hit the free weights. As we were walking toward the weight training section of the gym, I heard a male voice yell out my name. I turned around, but I didn't recognize the fine brother who was trying to get my attention.

"Takeisha Jenkins, you don't remember me? It's been a long time, but I could never forget your face. It's me, Travis Martin, from elementary school," he said.

I was shocked because Travis had really filled out. That cute little boy I had a crush on as a kid had blossomed into a bonafide stud. He had a body to die for. I could tell that he made good use of his gym membership. His legs and arms displayed a level of muscle definition that had me intrigued. I wondered if he was in good enough shape to handle a romp in the sack with a diva like me. I definitely planned to find out.

"Travis, what's up? Long time, no see. What you been up to?" I asked him as we hugged. Damn, it felt good to be in his arms.

"I'm trying to finish school. I go to the University of Baltimore. I graduated two years early from high school. I'm working on my law degree in entertainment law. I'll be finished in a year and a half. I heard about how you and your girls done blew up and became famous," he said.

"Yeah, we're doing our thing. I'm happy and all. I always knew you were the smart type. When you graduate, I might need your legal services," I said flirtatiously.

"Just ask and you got me. Well, if you're not busy, maybe we can do dinner while you're in town. That is if your boyfriend wouldn't mind," he inquired.

"I don't even have one of those. I have friends. That would be cool. Give me your number and I'll be in touch," I replied. I saved his number in my cell phone.

I didn't bother to ask if he had a girlfriend because that didn't matter to me. Even if he did, when I was done, she would be history.

I finished up my workout with Travis. He showed me how to use the weights properly and how many reps to do on each machine. The heat was rising between us. I had a thing for him so many years ago. I couldn't wait to see if he could bring the pain the way I liked it.

We went out a coupla times before I left town, and agreed to stay in touch. He said that he would make it his business to come to New York to hang out when his school schedule permitted him the time to do so.

When I returned to New York, I decided to move outta the condo Samson had leased for us when we first signed our deal. Danita must have felt the same way. She moved into Silk's house out in Long Island. I wanted my own space as well.

I hired a real estate agent and it took her about two months to find me a nice three-bedroom home in Jamaica Estates out in Queens. Once all of the financial loose ends were tied up, I moved into my new home.

This was my first time living out on my own, and I loved it. It felt good to be independent and rich. I hooked my crib up just the way I liked it. I hired an interior designer to assist me with the layout. She helped me pick out my furniture, as well as the hot artwork on display throughout the place.

I had just stepped outta the shower on this particular day when the phone rang. It was Samson. He picked the wrong time to call me. Travis came in the night before to hang out with me. Since we ran into each other in B'more, we had hooked up on several occasions. Sometimes I went to B'more to chill with him, and on other occasions, he came to New York to lounge at my crib. I liked his company, and he enjoyed spending time with me as well.

I usually only messed with thug niggas, but Travis was so fine, I made an exception for him. His personality and charm drew me in. Outside of that, the sex between us was pure fire. He knew how to satisfy my body in every way. We weren't a couple just yet, but our situation had some serious potential.

"What's up, girl? I got some good news for you. The KS Crew is scheduled to perform at *Street Flavor* magazine's Hip-Hop Awards show next week. Y'all have been nominated for the Best New Rap Artist, Best Female Rap Group, Hottest Rap Single, and Album of the Year awards. From what I get from my inside sources, y'all are a lock to win them all," he said.

"That's good. Can I call you back?"

"Damn, T, what's wrong with you, girl? I'm telling you this good news and you don't appear to be the least bit excited," Samson said.

"Nah, it ain't that. I'm pumped as shit that people are feeling us on that level. It's just that you caught me at a bad time. I was in the middle of something," I said.

"Oh, you must got a nigga up in there with you," he said.

"Yeah, it's something like that," I responded.

"That's all good. You know how we go. I ain't got no papers on you," he said.

"Yeah, I see your point. We are definitely gonna have to talk about this in more detail later," I said. I was talking in circles so that Travis wouldn't catch on to what was going down.

"Handle your business, Miss Thang. But you know that Daddy miss spankin' that big, beautiful ass of yours. I think I need a reminder of how goods it feels. Don't let that li'l nigga make you forget whose pussy that is," he said.

"Oh, don't even sweat that. I got you when I see you. I'ma make sure that the figures come out right," I said.

I tried to make the conversation appear to be strictly business. I could tell Samson was enjoying the fact that he had me tongue-tied. He let out a loud chuckle on the phone.

"Cool, get at me when you get a chance," Samson said.

"That's a bet. Peace," I said. When I hung up the phone, I turned over to find Travis' sexy behind glistening next to me in his birthday suit.

"Hey, beautiful. Who was that on the phone?" Travis inquired.

"Oh, that was Samson. He was calling to talk to me about business," I responded.

"Oh, I've been wanting to ask you about him. I read in one of them rap magazines a while back that there was a rumor that y'all messed around. Is that true? If you don't wanna answer the question, that's cool. I know I ain't ya man," he said.

He gave me the puppy dog eyes. He looked so cute with his deep dimples. This dude was seriously digging me. I could tell I had him in the palm of my hands. I wanted to tell him about my relationship with Samson because I didn't want to mislead him into thinking he was the only man my life. At the same time, I didn't want to tell, him because I didn't wanna fuck up what could be a good thing.

Not only that, Samson was the key to me having a long future in the music business. I would be damned if I let go of him before he made me into the megastar I wanted to be.

He had approached me recently with the idea of doing a solo album after the group's sophomore album was released next year. He said the public seemed to respond more to me than the rest of the group, and it was time for me to step out into the limelight on my own. I was a little hesitant at first because Latrell, Danita, and I always rolled as a team. However, after he mentioned that doing a solo album would bring me a million-dollar signing advance, my eyes became a little more open to the possibility. I guess fucking the boss did have its benefits.

"Nah, that was just a rumor. We're just friends outside of our business relationship. Samson is mad cool peeps. He ain't nothing for you to be sweating about. You're the one here with me now, ain't you? Do you need a reminder of how good this lovin' is that I put on you last night?" I asked.

"Hell no. I ain't forget about that," Travis said.

I started kissing on his chest lustfully as I massaged his dick in my right hand. With every up and down movement, his penis began to respond until it reached its full potential. Once I had him erect, I climbed on top of him to feel its full effect.

I sexed Travis crazy for about an hour before we both climaxed. I must admit that I had the best of both worlds with him and Samson. Samson was my rock that I could always depend on to have my back and to keep my bank account stacked. Travis was my distant lover who I could always call when I needed some stress relief from the hectic music bussiness. What more could a girl ask for?

28

Danita (D-Boogie)

We were the star attraction at the *Street Flavor* magazine awards show. We cleaned house, winning all of the awards we were nominated to receive. We got a chance to perform during the show and we tore the house down. We got a standing ovation from the packed audience.

Everybody in the crowd loved our performance, despite all the difficulties we had backstage. First of all, our wardrobe designer brought the wrong outfits for us to perform in. We had to improvise and wound up getting her to do an impromptu dash to the mall to find us all something to wear.

After that was taken care of, Latrell and Takeisha got into a big argument over some nonsense that really had no relevance. Takeisha was pissed that Latrell used up all of her makeup and deodorant, and complained that she was growing tired of her

mooching off of her stuff. Latrell shot back that
she was pissed that Takeisha tried to always hog the
spotlight. They almost came to blows before Samson came along and got them both to calm down.

The bickering between the two of them was starting to become more regular and more intense.
Their friendship was being put to the test. I, of
course, remained neutral and just watched from
the sidelines. Whereas they got caught up in the
flashing cameras and the spotlight, I remained re-
served and remembered that this whole rap thing
was a business, not just about who got the loudest
cheers from the crowd. I wasn't sure how much
longer I could put up with the demands of being a
member of the top female rap group in the industry. Something had to give.

After the awards show, we all decided to go to
the after-party at a club called Escapades, near the
beach. The party was being sponsored by Big
Pimpin' Records, and Kid Capri was gonna be DJ-
ing. The music was gonna be hot, and the place
would be filled to capacity.

We asked the limo driver to take us back to our
hotel so we could change into our party gear. After
we got dressed, it was off to the party to have a
good time. Silk was back at home in New York, so I
figured that I might as well have some fun with my
girls.

When we got to the party, the line to get into
the club was wrapped around the corner. Rolling
as a part of the Cash Rules family, we had VIP status. Our limo driver drove around to the back of
the club so we could get into the party from the
service entrance. That allowed us a chance to miss
the fanfare and all of the photographers trying to

snap our picture. We were out to just have a ball without the media frenzy. At least those were my plans.

Once inside the club, we were escorted to the VIP section on the third level. There were three different kinds of parties going on at the same time. On the first level of the club, they played Latino salsa music. That was where the sexy Latino mamis and papis got their swerve on, dancing in a seductive manner to the music. On the second level, there was the reggae room, where a whole lot of bodies were rubbing up against each other to the erotic melodies of the dancehall grooves. Finally, the room we were in was for the hardcore hip-hop heads. Kid Capri had the party hyped up. I planned to dance my ass off until I sweated my hair out.

Everybody that was anybody in the rap world was in attendance. I got a chance to meet all of the favorite rap artists I used to look up to in the game. I took pictures with the entire Wu Tang Clan. I met Nas for the first time, and he was even cuter in person. I got a chance to engage in an interesting conversation with Queen Latifah. She congratulated me on my success. After we conversed for a while, I was surprised to see that we had so much in common. We exchanged numbers and agreed to keep in touch.

As the evening wore on, the three of us were enjoying ourselves, being in the presence of so many of our role models. That was when the drama started. At around midnight, we were approached by the rap group, Gangsta Bitches 4 Life (GB4L). They were a rap group from the Miami area who hoped to get a record deal. They figured the best way for them to create a buzz was to challenge us to a battle at the party. Well, after performing at the awards, we were hardly in the mood to freestyle battle with anybody. We were just out to enjoy ourselves and bask in our success. However, these chicks had a different agenda.

GB4L was made up of four stern-mugged sistas that looked like they came from a hard life. These hookers were ugly as could be! The leader of the group, Sparkle, was about 5' 10" tall and looked like a cross between Tyra Banks and Rupaul, minus Tyra's good looks. Bubbles had to get her name from the bubble shape of her huge ass. La La had breath so bad it could melt your eyelids. Finally, Li'l Mama was the funniest member of this group of wanna-bes. She was a midget, standing about 4' 6" tall and tiny enough to fit into my pocket. This group of misfits had the nerve to step to us, wanting to see who had more lyrical skills. That was like somebody pulling out a knife in a gunfight. They were no competition for us.

When we refused their request to battle in the middle of the party, the trouble started. Sparkle made the mistake of getting up in Latrell's face, pointing her finger. She said that the KS Crew were a trio of prissy-ass paper gangsters from wack-ass Baltimore. Me and Takeisha were gonna just walk away and pay their BS no mind. We knew they were just trying to get some free publicity for their group. Some artists that can't get by on their natural talent and beauty will do anything to make it in this business. However, Latrell loved to be in the middle of some drama, so she fed into their nonsense.

Latrell nailed Sparkle smack dead in the mouth with a right cross that sent her flying to the floor, then pounded on her with both hands flying. The rest of the wack pack tried to jump in and help Sparkle out, but we weren't having that at all.

Takeisha looked at me and I looked at her, and we proceeded to handle our business to help out our homegirl. Right or wrong, the KS Crew always rode together in times like this. By the time the smoke cleared, we gave them an ass kickin' they would never forget, and we did it B'more style. Their hairpieces were all over the floor and blood was everywhere.

The club security team tried to break up the fight, but they were no match for us. When a group of sistahs get to scrappin', we're worse than a pack of dudes going at it. Besides, when Samson finally saw what was going on, him and his homeboys got in the way of them breaking up the fight. Knowing Samson, he got a thrill outta seeing us throw hands with these unruly bitches. He was probably glad to see that we weren't just some pretty faces that couldn't fight. He saw for himself that he had some real gangsta bitches in his stable.

The fight came to an end when the police arrived. The manager had called the law because the crowd got outta hand when everybody tried to get a view of the main event. We were carted off to the police station in the back of a paddy wagon. We were fingerprinted, processed, and placed in a large holding cell.

As for GB4L, they were also arrested and placed in a cell opposite ours. They were still talking shit from behind bars. Latrell responded to them—as if she really needed to do so. We had already proven that we were not to be fucked with, as bad as they all looked.

The fact that we wound up in jail on New Year's Eve still shocked me. The situation got totally outta hand. It was all Latrell's fault. If she had just kept her mouth closed, we could have smoothed over the confrontation without anybody getting hurt. Instead, she chose to fly off the handle and let her emotions guide her to act like a stone cold hoodrat. Me and Takeisha had to jump into the fight being that we were her friends. I knew she knew that we would have her back, and that was why she cold cocked that girl in her face the way she did.

Samson bailed us outta jail the next morning. We found out that those hookers pressed charges against us for assault because Latrell swung first. We were each released on $50,000 bail. Samson told us not to worry about it at all, that he would make it go away once he and his associates had a long talk with the GB4L crew. Just as sure as a clock was straight up and down when it read 6 o'clock, Samson was true to his word. In a few weeks, all of the charges were dismissed.

On a sour note, I began to reassess my friendship with Latrell. Her selfish ways had always been there, but for her to have involved us all in a public fiasco like that just brought them to the forefront. The more famous we became, it seemed, the more self-centered she became in her actions. Her parading around with so many different entertainers made us all look like sluts. I was getting tired of dealing with her uncouth ass. I started to feel as though I should distance myself from her and just keep my relationship with her strictly business.

The press had a field day with our arrest. We made the front page of every entertainment newspaper and magazine. We were the talk of the industry. Not only were we considered to be hardcore on the microphone, we now had a reputation for being hardcore out in the streets.

The fight only enhanced our street credibility. Samson said this incident would increase our record sales. That meant more money for us, but I wasn't happy with the negative image thing at all.

29

Scar

It had been almost two years since I got locked down and my life fell apart. My time in jail was a sobering experience. The everyday ordeal of seeing somebody getting shanked or some new, young inmate getting raped had me about to lose my sanity. I couldn't take it anymore. I had to find a way outta this hell. With all of the drama I saw either on the yard or on my tier, I knew I would either die in prison or eventually wind up killing somebody.

I didn't get any preferential treatment from the guards or the inmates at the various jails I had been transferred to throughout my incarceration. In fact, they made it their business to make my life as difficult as possible. The guards harassed me at every turn. Most of the other inmates were jealous of my fifteen minutes of fame and considered me to be a fool to have wasted it over the rape situation.

My street credibility carried no weight in the penitentiary. Without my crew to back me up, I was on my own to survive. I got into several altercations with other inmates. In fact, I wound up getting stabbed in the stomach by a cat named Eric over some bullshit about something he claimed was stolen from his cell. I recovered physically from the incident, but the mental effects of my injuries took their toll.

Another thing that weighed heavily on my mind was the success I saw the KS Crew had achieved while I was locked up. I was filled with jealousy over their climb to the top and my decline to the bottom of the barrel. I couldn't deny that.

I had constant memories of all the studio sessions I guided them through, how I helped them create their image and improved their lyrical flow. I thought about my relationship with Takeisha and how it ended so dramatically because of my egotistical ways. I could admit that I got caught up in my own hype. Nonetheless, with all of the support I gave them, I didn't even get as much as a sympathy card from any of them throughout my trial or my time in jail. I was seething with animosity. All of the platinum record sales and notoriety was supposed to be mine not theirs. *Fuck them bitches!* was what I told myself on a daily basis. Add that to the fact that I was convicted on the basis of a lie, and I was just one hateful motherfucker to be around.

While I had been locked down several times throughout my life, this bit broke my sprit. It showed in my physical appearance. I was no longer the poster boy image of a thug nigga, with my bulging muscles and rugged good looks. I had lost about twenty pounds since I first got my time, grown a full beard, and my hair that used to be a neat crop of waves was now a bushy forest in need of some serious trimming. The stress from my un-deserved reality had me on the verge of suicide, until I was presented with an opportunity to give some of my time back and get outta jail early.

It turned out that my drug supplier in New York, Miguel Salazar, was high up on the DEA's list of drug kingpins. The Feds were unable to gather any evidence from within his crew or from their surveillance of his operation to bring his organiza-tion down. Miguel kept his crew tight, and every-body knew that to cross him would mean certain death.

When the Feds found out from the Baltimore City police department that Miguel was my co-caine supplier, they contacted my lawyer and tried to offer me a deal in exchange for helping them convict Miguel. That was why two DEA agents came to the jail to see me. I wanted to hear what they had to offer.

I made my way down to the VI room and was greeted by Agents Horowitz and Drake. Horowitz was a tall, lean Jewish man with broad shoulders. He looked like a cross between Michael Rappaport and Ben Affleck. Agent Drake was a black man, about the same height as Horowitz, but he was thicker in build. He wore his hair in a medium Afro with sideburns. He had a cool demeanor, kinda like the '70s Blaxploitation hero, Shaft.

"So, Mr. Jones, how has prison life been treating you?" Horowitz asked rather sarcastically.

"Lousy. How the fuck do you think? Why you gonna ask me a dumb-ass question like that?"

"Tone it down, young man. You might wanna take that bass outta your voice. We're here to make you an offer that you can't refuse," Drake said, trying to ease the tension.

"State your business then. I ain't got all day to be fooling around with y'all clowns," I said.

"Don't let your mouth get you in more trouble. We can certainly find a way to add more time onto your sentence," Drake said.

"Hold on, partner. He didn't mean what he just said. He's just a little uptight. Let's see if we can't start this conversation from scratch," Horowitz interjected.

"You're right. I apologize, Mr. Jones, if we came off a little harsh. We need some information and we think that you can help us out. You scratch our backs and we'll scratch yours. Tell us about your relationship with Miguel Salazar," Drake said.

"Who, Micky? That's my man. What about him?" Scar asked.

"Well, we've been investigating your good friend for quite some time, but have come up empty. That's where you come into the picture. We need someone with inside information to help us bring his crew down," Drake said.

"Oh, you can forget about that. I ain't no motherfucking snitch. You barking up the wrong tree, homey." I had to play bard ball. I wanted to see how much they wanted to offer me for my information.

"We're not asking you to sell anybody out. We just need you to tell us a little bit about his organi-

zation and how it operates. Look, we already talked
to the Baltimore police department and we know
how you worked with them to get the drug charges
against you dropped. All we want is to offer you a
similar deal," Horowitz said.

"How the hell do y'all know about that?" I asked.

"We have our ways of finding out information.
We know everything," Drake said.

"I'ma say it again. I ain't no rat, dog," I reiter-
ated. In reality, if the deal they offered was right, I
was down to take it just to get the fuck outta this
joint.

"What would you say if we could guarantee that
you could walk outta here in six months if you
helped us out?" Drake asked.

"I would say that you were full of shit," I replied.

"Mr. Jones, Scar, we know you got railroaded at
your trial and that the girl was lying. I know you
wanna resume your rap career. You can't do that if
you're behind bars, now can you?" Horowitz asked.
Now he was talking a language I wanted to hear.

"Hell yeah, that bitch set me up. She fucked up
my life and took a chunk of my money. What y'all
want from me, man?" I asked. That street code of
honor of no snitchin' was about to go out the window. I was gonna get free by any means necessary.
That judge could take that time he gave me and
shove it up his ass.

"We just need you to break down Miguel's operation as plain as you can and we'll do the rest. Nobody will know it was you who gave us the
information. We may also need you to testify that
you purchased large quantities of cocaine from
him personally after we arrest him. That's just a
last resort. You do this for us, and we'll make sure

you get protection from any retaliation that may come your way," Drake said.

"I don't need no fucking protection. I'm Scar, nigga. Ain't nobody gonna fuck with me. What else you got to offer?" I asked.

"What do you want?" Drake asked.

"One hundred grand, a passport, and any information you can get me on that bitch that set me up, and whoever was involved in it with her," I replied.

"I think we could definitely arrange that. Have your lawyer contact us later in the week and set up an appointment. I knew we could work something out," Horowitz said.

The three of us shook hands to solidify our agreement then. I went back to my cell. I couldn't believe what I had just done. The old Scar would have never struck a deal with the law. However, I had a chance to get the hundred grand back that I spent to beat my other drug case, plus I would be a free man. At least these Feds were good for something. The tide was about to turn back in my favor.

30

Takeisha (T-Love)

I can't believe this shit!
That was all I could say after we left our meeting
with Samson's attorney, Richard Lewin. We had set
up a meeting to discuss the recent royalty statement we received, which stated that we were in
debt to Cash Rules Records for 500 grand. Consid-
ering the fact that our record sales were now over
the five million mark, that was totally absurd. There
was no way we owed money. In fact, according to
my calculations, we should have each received more
than a million dollars in royalty payments.

In the royalty statement, there were all kinds of
bullshit expenses charged against our account that
we were originally told would be covered by the
record company. I knew the cost of the elaborate
music videos we shot for our three hit singles
would be deducted from our royalties, but it was

the other charges that had me pissed. There were charges for things such as salaries for our personal assistants, wardrobes for shows, and travel expenses. All of these charges alone totaled up to almost 250 grand deducted from our account.

All of the other miscellaneous things we were being charged for were just too insane to mention. I saw things in there about child support payments for some of Samson's boys that were paid outta our account. I just couldn't fathom how he thought he was gonna get away with this kinda scam.

Not receiving any royalties at this time was gonna be a problem for me. My Lexus SC430 was paid for, but I still had a house note to pay every month. I only had about a seventy-five grand left in my bank account. That wouldn't last me for another six months. I had credit card debt up the ass to take care of as soon as possible. I was banking on my royalty money to bail me out. Without it, I was fucked. The repo man would come knocking real soon to take away all of this expensive shit I bought, like my fur coats and shoe collection.

I didn't wanna wind up being another one of those superstars you see on the E! channel, who went from riches to rags overnight. My pops had always told me not to go crazy spending money shopping for unnecessary things. Right now, I wished I had listened.

I was also surprised to see that Latrell had taken several sizable advances against her royalties, even after we got our initial advance. She received an additional 300 grand from Samson that Danita and I knew nothing about. What the fuck she needed the money for was beyond me. Besides, it was my understanding when we signed the record contract that whatever advances we took individually would be taken from our own third release, and not out of the royalties for the entire group. At least that was what the lawyer my father hired had told us. Obviously his ass didn't read the fine print.

The three of us met at Danita's house to discuss our situation.

"Yo, this is crazy! That motherfucking Samson better come up with our loot. He don't know who he fucking with. My niggas is gonna see his ass if he don't correct this with a quickness," Latrell said.

Her eyes were bloodshot with bags under them. She looked like she was up all night, but didn't seem to be lacking any energy. She seemed wired as hell. If I ain't know no better, I would swear she was on the pipe.

"Bitch, please. Why the fuck did you need all that other money that you took out? What the hell are you spending your money on? You need to be kicking me and D some money because we takin' an L because of your shit!" I said to her in response.

"What I do with my money is my business. The last time I checked, I was a grown-ass woman. You just tryin' to take up for that nigga because you fuckin' his ass," Latrell shot back.

"Fuck you, ho. All da dick you been sucking in the industry, you shouldn't be talking about anybody. You need to learn to keep your legs closed," I said.

"I got your ho, a'ight. You wasn't saying that shit when we was at Ricardo's house that night, was you?" she said.

My jaw almost dropped to the floor. I couldn't believe she put me on front street like that. That night we spent with Ricardo was supposed to be our li'l secret. Danita was never supposed to know about that incident. That was especially true after we witnessed Samson kill him. There was supposed to be no connection between him and us. The fact that Latrell mentioned anything about it in front of Danita, even though she was our girl, let me know that she was totally outta control.

Danita had no clue who Ricardo was and what Latrell was talking about. I wanted to make sure it stayed that way.

"Watch your mouth, bitch. Don't say something that might get your ass kicked," I said.

"Bring it, bitch. Bring it. I'm getting sick of your high and mighty ass always tryin' ta run shit anyway," Latrell said.

I prevented the situation from escalating to an all-out war by changing the subject. I tried to tell myself that Latrell was still my girl and we shouldn't be beefin' like this. We done been through too much shit together to become enemies. However, it seemed as though success had gone to her head and made her nearly impossible to deal with.

"I ain't even gonna go there with you. It's not worth my time. D, I'ma make time to go see Samson to see if I can straighten this whole thing out," I said.

"A'ight, girl. Let me know how it goes," Danita said. She gave me a hug as I walked toward the door.

"That's all you got to say to her ass for getting on me like that? You need to stop kissing her ass all the damn time. Oh, I forgot, she's your fuckin' role model," Latrell said to Danita, then laughed in a cynical manner.

"Whatever, Latrell. I ain't even got the time or patience for your foolishness. I want you to leave, please, so I can get some rest," Danita said.

"Fine, I'm gone. I had enough of y'all asses for one day anyway," Latrell said.

She swiftly walked toward the door and brushed up against me on purpose. She angrily walked out the door and slammed it with violent force.

I waited a few minutes until I was sure she was gone before I left. She was looking for a fight, but I refused to give her one. My mind was stuck on getting this money situation right with Samson.

Since we got our jacked-up royalty statement, Samson avoided me like the plague.

Every time I called the office for him, Malonda gave me some bullshit-ass excuse that he was in a meeting and couldn't talk to me. I called him on his cell phone and he never answered. Any other time, he answered when I called him, and now, all of a sudden, all I got was a chance to talk to his voice mail and leave countless messages. That made it clear that he knew he fucked us over with our money and didn't give a damn.

My next course of action was to contact the lawyer my father hired to look over our contract before we signed our deal. When I called his law firm, I was shocked to find out from the receptionist that he no longer worked there. He had been recently disbarred by the state of Maryland. It turned out that he was stealing money from his clients' accounts and using it to fund his lavish lifestyle. He bought a yacht, several luxury cars and a condo in the Bahamas, all paid for with the money he stole. He was facing several felony charges of embezzlement and theft that would land him in jail for a long time if he got convicted.

We paid that man ten grand for doing absolutely nothing. This news just added to my depression. I felt like strangling my father for finding this idiot to look over our contract. I decided to call Ace to see what solution he could come up with to help me.

When I spoke with Ace, we set up an appointment to meet for lunch in Baltimore, near BWI airport. I caught a flight outta Laguardia to meet him.

He told me about all the artists he was working with and how well things were going for him. He said he heard from Scar's lawyer that he was gonna be released from jail early, but didn't get any specific details. That sounded crazy to me. I was a little concerned about that situation, but I put that thought on the back burner. I had bigger fish to fry in my life.

I gave him a copy of our contract to look over with his attorney, to see if there were any loopholes we could use to get our money from Cash Rules Records. He got back to me later in the week and said that basically we were fucked, and there was not much we could do about our situation. Our contract was airtight. Samson had every right to charge our account for the excessive expenses listed in the fine print. Samson had it weaved in clever legal terminology that Latrell's personal advance could be cross-collateralized with the rest of the group's royalties, and we would be all held accountable for recouping that money.

The only thing Ace suggested was that we get to

work on our next album and not spend as much in production and video costs, to cut down on our expenses. That way, when we got our next statement, there was less money Samson could try to charge us. We would have to take this as a lesson about the shady side of the music business and learn from our mistake. I wasn't tryin' ta hear that shit. I wanted what was mine and I wouldn't rest until I got every penny that was due me.

After speaking with some of the other artists with the company, like The Assassins and Menage, I found out their money situations were jacked up too. They were also unable to reach Samson about their royalty statements not being accurate.

One of the members of the Assassins, Jimmy Black, went up to the Cash Rules office with a baseball bat and demanded to see Samson. Samson's boys gave him a severe beat-down. He suffered several broken ribs and a broken wrist. He planned to sue Samson and his crew for his personal injuries.

I also got a hold of Joe, from the Smith Brothers, and what he told me shocked me even more. When they confronted Samson about the discrepancies with their royalty check, he brought them a funky move even worse than the one he did on us. He strong-armed them into signing over their rights to us for $200,000 in hush money. In exchange, they were to keep their mouths shut about Samson's shady business dealings, and they would be allowed to continue their musical career as producers.

Although he dissolved their label agreement with Cash Rules Records, Samson agreed to let them do some production for him on a project to project basis. That was his way of making it appear to the public that there was an amicable separation between them and the label.

At first, I was pissed at them for selling us out. However, after I thought about it, I realized their backs were against the wall just like ours. They had no choice in the matter. Samson was a powerful and unscrupulous man, and to go up against him would mean the possibility of death. I just wished them well and hoped we got a chance to work together in the future.

It appeared as though Samson was getting rich off of us while we starved. After all of our hard work to put out hit albums, Samson had stabbed all of his artists in the back. All of that talk about the Cash Rules family and how he would go the extra length for us was garbage. With family like Samson and his crew, you didn't need enemies. He certainly wasn't gonna get another piece of this pussy after the way he screwed me over.

Throughout all of this bullshit in my life, the only source of relief I had was the time I spent with Travis. All the fake smiling for the cameras and acting like everything was all good between the KS Crew and the record label was making my nerves bad. Travis always seemed to know the right thing to say and to do to make me feel better. His massages soothed my tension. He knew how to make me laugh when I felt like crying. He was my bright light in this dark time in my life. I had to admit that he had become someone very special in my life.

I think my relationship with Travis was also part of the reason Samson wasn't returning my calls. It had been a good minute since we had sex. He had tried to get with me several times, but when he called, I always made up some excuse why I couldn't see him. The last time I turned him down, he was pissed. I think his ego was bruised because he always liked to be in control. Since I didn't give him what he wanted, he was probably happy to pay me back in a way he knew would hurt me—in my pockets.

Travis and I were relaxing in the living room after we returned from dinner in Manhattan. He massaged my feet while I sipped on a glass of Cristal. It felt so good to be in his company. We playfully kissed and cuddled as we watched the movie *Love and Basketball* for the umpteenth time. Our moment of peace and tranquility was broken when the telephone rang

"Hello."

"What's up, sexy? Are you alone?"

"Samson, is that you? Why the hell you ain't returned none of my calls?"

"I been busy, baby. Plus, you wanna act all stingy with the pussy. Why the fuck should I rush to call you back?"

"Never mind all that. We need to talk. You and your accountants need to get our money right. Ain't no way in the world the KS Crew should be in the red to the record label."

"Calm your ass down. We can straighten this shit out easily. When do you wanna get together to discuss the matter? Oh, and it's just you by yourself that I wanna meet with at my office. Wear that sexy red dress I bought you. You know the one that hugs that pretty li'l ass of yours."

"Whatever, Samson. We can get together tomorrow at eight. This some fucked up shit you done did, and I just want you to know that."

"Yeah, yeah. I'ma see you then. Oh, tell your li'l boyfriend that I said hello."

I didn't even respond to his last comment before I hung up the phone. When I turned around, Travis was up in my face. He wanted some answers to obvious questions. I couldn't just brush him off like I used to when we first started messing around. Our relationship had changed drastically, in a good way. I had to explain to him what was going on with me.

"So, are you ready to tell me everything yet?" Travis asked.

"Yeah, I guess I might as well now," I replied.

I proceeded to tell him everything about my relationship with Samson. I apologized for lying to him. He accepted my apology. The only information I didn't tell him was about the videotape of me, Latrell, and Ricardo and how Samson had murdered him. I was feeling Travis a lot, but I wasn't that crazy to say something about that situation.

"Takeisha, I care about you a lot. I wanna take our relationship to the next level, but, this thing between you and Samson has gotta be over. You have to promise me that. You also have to promise me that you won't ever lie to me again," he said.

"You mean you don't wanna leave me alone now?" I asked.

"Nah, I don't go away that easy. He might got more money than me, but he can't do the things that I can for you. He can't make you happy, but that's all I wanna do for you," he said.

"I promise you I won't lie to you anymore. Me and Samson are done as far as us messing around, but I still have to deal with him on a business tip because he's the president of our record label," I said.

"I understand. I can't argue with that as long as it's just business," he said. We got back to enjoying the rest of our evening because he had to leave in the morning to return to Baltimore.

The next evening, Samson came to pick me up in his limo. I was dressed in the sexy red mini-dress he bought me. The dress made my ass stand out from the rest of my body, and Samson was almost drooling when he saw me in it. He was dressed in a black, tailor-made leather set and a pair of Steve Madden shoes. If I wasn't so pissed at his ass, I would've admitted that he looked fly as hell.

The driver opened the door and I got in the limo before Samson. His hands found their way onto my ass before I had a chance to sit down.

"Don't touch the merchandise, please. This meeting is strictly business, not personal," I said. I had my game face on and I was ready to handle mine.

"Why it gotta be like that, baby? You used to like it when I felt on that big ass of yours. That was before you had that little boyfriend and what not," he said.

"Times have changed. We don't get down like that. Remember when we said that our relationship was casual?" I asked.

"True dat. Now, what problem do you have with me?" he asked.

I couldn't believe this nigga had the nerve to ask me such a stupid-ass question. He was gonna sit here and act like he did nothing wrong by stealing our money with his shady-ass contract. This bastard was arrogant times ten. He was definitely feeling himself, so much so that if he could suck his own dick, he probably would.

"Let's cut the bullshit, Samson. You know you fucked us on the royalty tip. All the records we done sold for you, how the hell are you gonna do us like that?" I asked.

"Hold up, baby girl. I gave you a chance to have the contract looked over before you signed it. It ain't my fault that your lawyer didn't beef about the small print. All the money I kept is mine legally. The same goes for all of my acts. If y'all try to challenge the contracts, you will lose," he said boldly.

I had to admit that he was right. We did sign the deal. We did have a lawyer look it over first. However, I refused to back down before I got something outta this deal. I had to show Samson a thing or two about how us East Baltimore bitches negotiate.

"Fuck that. You know you owe us for all we did in helping you take Cash Rules Records to the next level. Your company was just another rap label before we signed onto the team. Now everybody is trying to get down with the label because of our success. You need to treat us right on the strength of that," I said defiantly.

"I don't need to do shit except stay black and die, shorty. You better watch that tone and remember who the fuck you talking to here," he said.

I knew that he was dangerous, but the way I was feeling, I didn't give a fuck. I was on a mission, and taking no for an answer was not an option.

"You need to remember who I am and what the fuck I know about you," I said.

I was talking about Ricardo's murder. I knew Samson was not the type to be blackmailed, but I had to at least try my hand. That was the wrong move. Before I could blink, Samson grabbed me around the neck with his enormous hands. I was terrified, even though I tried to show no fear.

"You li'l bitch, don't you ever threaten me or I'll have your ass floating in the bottom of the Chesapeake Bay with some cement shoes on," he said. He removed his hands from my neck and reclined back in his seat. Out of nowhere, he let out a loud laugh.

"That was a good try, Miss. I gotta respect ya gangsta. You got some balls on you. I ain't hardly worried about you going to the police. All you would be doing is indicting yourself as well. Besides, I have my own little security blanket that I decided to hold onto, just for this occasion. We wouldn't want your daddy to see this tape, now would we?"

He held the videotape in his hand. It was no doubt a copy of the one he took from Ricardo. He said he had destroyed it, but obviously he lied. I should have known not to trust him. A snake never told the truth in any situation, and that was exactly what Samson was, a low-down, slimy snake.

"I thought you said you destroyed that tape. That's fucked up. I thought we were cooler than that Samson, but now I see how you get down," I responded. He just laughed, but I didn't find a damn thing funny.

"Yeah, I did have a good time watching that tape. It served as a reminder of how freaky your ass was before you started holding out on me with the pussy. Your girl, Latrell and I watched it together a couple of times when she came by and broke me off. Her pussy ain't as good as yours is, though. Nonetheless, you supposed to be from the streets. You should know that you should cover your own ass and not trust nobody," he replied.

Samson threw me for a loop when he told me he was fucking Latrell and me at the same time. She was a snake typa bitch, and her ass was getting kicked when I got a chance to get at her. I couldn't believe she wouldn't tell me that he still had a copy of the tape. Our friendship was through at this point, and that shit was official.

"This is so fucked up! This is so fucked up! I just can't believe this is happening to me!" I said repeatedly.

A few minutes later, we arrived at the Cash Rules office. I was numb all over at this point. Samson grabbed my arm and helped me out of the limo.

As we walked toward his office, I began to come outta my trance. In the office, I took a seat. Samson poured himself a glass of Hennessy on ice and began to speak.

"Calm down, shorty. I'ma tell you what I'ma do for you because I like you. I said that I always wanted you to do a solo album because I think you're the star of the group. Them other two bitches ain't shit without you. Latrell, she's a ho, and she ain't gonna last long in this business. Danita, she's a good girl and all, and she's gonna always get her money writing songs. However, one or two more albums and the group is will have run its course. I'ma give you five hundred grand as an advance for your solo project. Here's half now as an act of good faith. How does that sound to you?" he asked.

Samson pulled out a briefcase filled with neatly

stacked rows of $100 bills. Seeing all that cash at one time seemed to make my anger disappear.

"I thought you said you was gonna give me a million."

"Look, beggars can't be choosers. You better take what I'm offering because in a minute that amount goes down by half again," he shot back.

I came to my senses real quick. I needed that money in my life like yesterday. I would be damned if I turned it down like I was a fool or something.

"What I gotta do in return?" I asked.

"Nothing major. I just want you to convince your girls that trying to recoup any money from that first album is a dead issue. All artists get fucked on their first album. I need you to put your anger with Latrell aside, and for the three of y'all to put together a banging second album for me in the next three months. I'll give you all two hundred grand a piece as an advance for the project under a new contract. It'll be fairer than the first contract that y'all signed.

"If you play ball with me, I'll play ball with you. We need to resume our little personal arrangement. Fuck that li'l soft-ass, model-looking boyfriend of yours. That pussy belongs to me. If you can't make this happen, then I'ma have to go public with the tape," he said.

I had to admit that the offer was tempting the hell outta me, even if it was blackmail. All this cash in my face was very persuasive. Shit, it was time for me to think about my future. Latrell wasn't my friend any longer, and Danita would be a'ight financially, with or without the group, due to her songwriting. I couldn't risk letting that tape go public, so I had no choice. Even though I wasn't sure if I could trust Samson to keep up his end of the bargain, I had to take the chance. At worst, I would at least have the 250 grand on hand right now. Giving him a little pussy as a bonus might actually work in my favor. It might make him less of a threat to me if I gave him what he wanted.

"You got yourself a deal," I said.

Samson and I shook hands and made our agreement official. We were off to his place to conduct another one of our private, freaky sessions. I had made a deal with the devil to find my way outta hell. I hoped I didn't also sell my soul in the process.

31

Danita (D-Boogie)

Takeisha called me and Latrell and asked us to meet at her house. She wanted to talk to us about our situation with Cash Rules Records. I hoped she had some good news because it just wasn't right what Samson tried to get away with. I knew that if anybody could persuade him to do the right thing and give us the money we deserved, it was her. T could convince a crazy man that he was sane if she wanted to. She just had the gift of gab when it came to most men. She'd been that way for as long as I could remember.

Even though I remained optimistic that things would work out for us, I also prepared myself for the worst case scenario. If Samson didn't agree to pay us our royalties, then I refused to record another album with him. While it was true I wanted the money I was owed, I didn't need it that bad.

Unlike T and Danita, I was conservative when it came to how I spent my advance. I didn't have to buy a house because I lived with Silk at his crib. That alone saved me a lot of money. He paid all of the bills. I wanted to help him with some of our living expenses, but he insisted that since he was the man of house, he wanted to be the one that took care of everything. He felt it was his duty as a man to financially provide for his household. Who was I to argue with him if that was how he felt? I was happy I had such a good man.

I did buy myself a cute Benz as a gift to myself for all of my hard work. While my girls went crazy shopping for new clothes almost every chance they got, I budgeted out my shopping sprees. I didn't need all of the expensive jewelry they wasted money on.

The one thing I admit that I inherited from my mother is my ability to make a dollar stretch as far as it can. I still had almost half of my advance left over. Not only that, I knew I was gonna get paid soon for all of the songs I co-wrote with Silk for other artists.

It was good fortune that Samson had no control over my publishing rights when it came to that part of my income. Otherwise, I would be as stressed as my girls were over our royalty money.

Silk's album, *Thug Luvin'*, went double platinum and spawned three number one singles that we co-wrote together. We would clear almost $2 million in publishing royalties to split for the next royalty cycle in six months thanks to the hit songs we wrote for his album and for artists like Mary J. Blige, Faith Evans, and Gerald Levert.

When I arrived at T's house, I noticed Latrell

sitting in her car. Since her and T weren't as cool as they used to be, I figured she had to be waiting for me to arrive before she went in the house. That way she wouldn't be alone with T, forced to have a phony conversation with her.

I parked my car and walked over to her vehicle. As I got closer, she got out of the car and walked toward me. Her hair was all over the place and her clothes were wrinkled. She looked a mess, like she had been out partying all night.

I wished she would slow down and not party so much. Silk told me he heard rumors around the industry that she started using harder drugs, like coke and dope. I hoped that wasn't true. However, with the wild crowd she hung with, that was a possibility. I planned to talk to her about that in the near future.

"What's up, girl? Whew, I'm tired. I was out hanging at this crazy party last night that P. Diddy had in the Hamptons. It was off the hook," she said.

"Latrell, you need to slow ya behind down. You party too much," I said.

"D, I'm straight. You ain't my mother. I'm a big girl. I can handle my own. Never mind that. I wanna see what this bitch got to say about our loot. She better have some good news for me. I need my money," she said.

"I feel you, but y'all two need to stop arguing so much. We're supposed to be family. What happened to our old saying, KS Crew for life?" I asked.

"D, please. You always was the one that lived in a fantasy world. Things change. People change. Me and you are gonna always be cool. As for Takeisha, that's a whole other story. We can talk about that later. Let's get up in here so we can see what's up with this money," she said.

Takeisha greeted us at the front door. She gave me a hug and shot Latrell an evil stare. I wished they would stop this foolishness and just make up like they used to do all the time.

"I think we all know why we are here. I talked to Ace, and he said that we're basically locked into this deal with Cash Rules Records. All of the excess expenses the label charged to our accounts are legal, according to our contract. The lawyer that my father hired fucked us," Takeisha said.

"Tell us something we don't know," Latrell said.

"I'm not even gonna respond to that comment. Anyway, I also talked to Samson. I wanted to try and make the best outta this situation. He agreed to work out a new deal with us for our next album. We're gonna be signed directly to Cash Rules records this time. He said he's gonna give us two hundred grand apiece as an advance. Shit, the way I figure it, any money is better than no money at this point. Wouldn't you agree?" she asked.

"T, that is crazy. How you gonna come up in here and try to make us think that what Samson said makes any sense? How is he gonna offer us that li'l bit of money after what he gave us up front for the first album? There has gotta be some kinda way that we can get our money back," I said.

"D, if it was, don't you think I would have made it happen? This whole thing is what it is. This is the game we're in. We're fucked. Either we play ball or we lose. Me, I'm trying to get whatever I can outta this mess. My funds are getting low, and I need the money," Takeisha said.

"Always looking out for yaself. I wonder what

else Samson offered you to bring us this bullshit offer," Latrell said.

"Look, bitch, I'm trying to be civil with you for business only. If you only knew what I had to go through to get him to agree to what he offered us, your ass would be grateful," T said.

"Yeah, whatever. So, what's it gonna be? Are we doing the album or what? I need the money," Latrell said.

"Well, I agree that we have to make the best of a bad situation. After this album, I'm done with Cash Rules Records, period," I said.

"Agreed. He said that he would have the contract drawn up and in our hands next week. This time we're gonna hire our own lawyer. I contacted Barry Michaels to represent us. He's the best entertainment lawyer in the business. Samson said we have three months to record the album. That means we gotta get to work real soon," T said.

"Is that all? Are we done yet?" Latrell asked.

"Yeah, we're done. Please get ya ass outta here. I don't wanna be around you any more than I have to. D, I'ma holla at you later. I need to get some rest," Takeisha said.

With that taken care of, Latrell and I bounced. I wondered how the friendship between my two best friends got so far off track. Was the fame and fortune worth what it had cost us? It seemed like this business just made a person become selfish, doing whatever was necessary to keep the fame and fortune.

I thought about the relationship between T and Samson. Her comment about what she had to go through to get Samson to give us a new contract planted a seed in my mind. I wondered if she got something else outta this deal that she didn't tell us about. She seemed too willing to convince us to go along with his offer. It wasn't like her to concede so easy. For now, I kept my suspicions to myself because what's done in the dark always had a way of coming into the light.

32

Latrell (Luscious) and Miguel

Latrell ran into Miguel Salazar at the Shark Bar. She was hanging out with her hairstylist, Shannon, and her girlfriends. Miguel sent her a bottle of champagne from across the room, and she eagerly accepted his generous offer.

At first, Miguel couldn't recall where he knew this fine caramel honey from, but then it clicked. He recognized her as the girl Tank sent to cop some coke from him on several occasions. He also realized that she was the same girl he saw on BET in the videos. After Latrell accepted his bottle of champagne and sipped on it generously with her crew, she made her way over to Miguel's table to thank him.

Miguel was seated at a table with his entourage surrounding him. He had Manuel and Sosa, his two burly bodyguards, posted up at the table for protection. He also had his little brother, Pedro, as well as his right hand, Martinez, with him. He was teaching Pedro the family business because he hoped to turn it over to him one day. Pedro was the heir apparent to his powerful empire, controlling approximately seventy percent of all the cocaine trade on the East Coast. Miguel had the drug game on lock down and ran his crew with a tenacity and brutality not seen since the death of Pablo Escobar.

"So, I see that you've come up in the world, huh? Who woulda thought that my man Tank's sexy li'l mule would be a rap superstar. You've come a long way from making them trips to see me on Greyhound," Miguel said.

"Yeah, I made a coupla moves. A sistah had to do her thing. You can't be in the game forever, ya know what I'm sayin'? Everybody ain't on ya level," Latrell said.

"True, true. I see you're working with Samson Miles. He's a good friend of mine. We go way back. Tell him I said hello," Miguel said.

"I don't fuck with him like that. He's a snake," Latrell said.

"Samson is a stand-up guy. Why would you say a thing like that?" Miguel asked.

Latrell proceeded to tell Miguel about her troubles in the music business dealing with Samson and Cash Rules Records. She detailed how he beat them for their royalties for their first album. She told him about the deal Samson offered to make up for screwing them over. She never stopped to think that she was giving up all of her personal info in front of a group of total strangers. After he heard her tell her story, Miguel shook his head and took a sip of his drink.

"That doesn't sound like my good friend Samson. Would you like me to talk to him for you? He respects me. I may be able to reason with him," Miguel said.

"Hell yeah. If you could do that for me, I would be eternally grateful," Latrell said.

"I'll do what I can for you. Also remember, I like to collect on my debts. You seem equipped to handle whatever arrangement I set up as repayment," Miguel said as he eyed her up and down.

"Fa sho. I know we can work something out," Latrell said.

In exchange for his assistance, Latrell agreed to do some work for him, transporting cocaine outta state to Baltimore, DC and Richmond. He agreed to pay her three grand per trip.

He told her that she could use her celebrity status to get through the airport checkpoints easier. She could hide the drugs in the secret compartments of her suitcases. Airport security would be less likely to search her belongings as thoroughly as they would an average citizen. He could tell from her physical appearance that she was using coke heavily, and he planned to capitalize on her habit. He knew that the offer of money would be enough to entice her to do anything he wanted.

Latrell needed the money to fund her lavish lifestyle and growing cocaine habit. She had developed a thousand-dollar a day crack habit that grew with each pull she took off of that glass dick. All the partying and living in the fast lane started to catch up with her. As a kid, she swore she would never be strung out on drugs like her brothers. However, here she was, a full-fledged addict, living in denial of her self-destructive reality. She was becoming a victim of her own greed and undisciplined behavior.

Despite her personal struggles, she pulled herself together enough to create magic in the studio once again with her crew. For the next few months, the KS Crew worked at a feverish pace in the studio to get the project completed. Latrell and Takeisha agreed to put their personal differences aside for the sake of the group's success. Danita did her part, coming up with most of the hooks for their songs. Despite all the personal issues in the group, their chemistry in the studio was as crisp as ever. The second album was finally completed after countless hours of hard work. It was called *Bringin' the Heat*, and it was scheduled for release in September 2002.

Since the night they hooked up at the Shark Bar, Miguel and Latrell had become better acquainted, both professionally and personally. She had made several successful runs for him with no glitches. In addition to getting paid for her trips, Miguel gave her a never-ending supply of coke for her personal use.

Latrell had lost about ten pounds from her frame, but she was still fine. Miguel also started indulging in cocaine use with her, and the two spent many nights together having steamy sex and taking turns hitting the pipe. Latrell used her charm and skills in the bedroom to entice him into her world of bangin' sex and getting high. He had dibbled and dabbled with sniffin' blow, but it never became a problem for him until he met Latrell.

Miguel had violated the number one rule in the game: never get high on ya own supply. Their relationship was a powder keg of disaster, ready to explode

As his drug habit increased, Miguel's once sound business mind began to dull from all those late nights partying with Latrell. His crew recognized this fact, but they were afraid to approach him about his erratic behavior. He became increasingly paranoid, thinking everyone in his crew was out to get him. He had several of his top soldiers executed on this premise. He became more brutal and hard to deal with in his immediate circle of associates.

Miguel didn't know that thanks to Scar, the DEA was able to infiltrate his organization like never before. They now had informants in his camp who were able to gather useful surveillance to build a case that would stick. Some of his lower level soldiers were singing like canaries in exchange for lighter sentences. They had Latrell on videotape receiving cash and delivering drugs for him. They were all caught dead to right. All that was left was for them to get the arrest warrants typed up and signed by the judge to bring Miguel and Latrell into custody.

An explosion was exactly what happened one dreadful night. On the day the Feds came to arrest Miguel, they burst into his Long Island estate to find him in bed with Latrell. The two of them were ass naked between the sheets and high outta their minds. The agents found half a brick of raw coke and about an ounce of rock cocaine, along with crack pipes and other drug paraphernalia scattered about Miguel's house.

Latrell was so hysterical it took several agents to

restrain her. Miguel stayed cool, calm, and collected throughout the entire process. He figured that since he had money, his lawyers would be able to make this whole mess go away. His arrogance didn't allow him to see the reality that his reign as the king of the streets of New York was over.

Of course, Latrell's involvement in the situation made the case front page news all across the country, in every newspaper and every music magazine. Her desire to live life on the edge had finally caught up with her. How this would affect the rest of the KS Crew remained to be seen.

33

Samson

Sometimes being the CEO of my own company could be a headache. Dealing with these artists and all the drama that came along with their fucked up lives was more than it was worth. The money didn't equal the problems in some situations. It's like these bastards were my kids and I had to bail them outta more than enough jams just to get my money's worth outta them. With all the money I put out to make these artists into stars with hit records, I had to come out on top with a lion's share of the profits. That's why I didn't feel any guilt if they complained when their royalty checks came up short.

All the time in the news, music artists claimed their record company had robbed them blind of their royalties. They acted as though the money that record companies spent to produce, promote, and distribute their music was nothing, and they were entitled to a larger share of the money pot. That was just pure bullshit! These motherfuckers didn't have to come outta their pockets with no loot to get their music out into the mainstream, but they were the first ones to complain about how the money was divided up between them and the record company.

Shit, the way I saw it, us record companies took all the risk that their records were gonna sell. Of course, if their record bombed, we took the loss and they were free to walk away from the situation with a hefty advance, while we had to figure out a way to recoup our financial losses. That's why I said "fuck 'em all," and I gave my artists the bare minimum.

Add up all of the money that was spent on producing an album and selling it to the public, and we would be talking about a whole lotta bread. That's in addition to how much money I had to spend on these immature assholes to get them outta so many legal jams. When any of my artists got arrested or had a problem with the law, they called me and I had to bail them out. I couldn't make my money back if they were locked up. On top of that, I paid my PR people and attorneys crazy money to fix up any of the messes they created. I felt like a father with a set of bastard kids that was taxed by the State for child support. I'd be damned if I paid them more money than I paid them now. All the headaches they put me through, I deserved to be a filthy rich tycoon.

For example, a few weeks ago, The Assassins got pulled over in North Carolina after a show. They were riding three cars deep in the South and smoking weed with the windows rolled down and the music blasting. That was just asking for trouble, riding dirty in the South, with these racist hillbilly cops just looking for a reason to stop a brother. Common sense always seemed to escape these silly-thinking rappers.

When the cops searched all three cars, they uncovered about a half-pound of weed, two grams of coke, and a couple of pills of Ecstasy. That's not even mentioning the loaded .45 and 9mm they found under the seats of one car.

The police arrested these idiots, along with their entourage, and impounded their vehicles. They happened to be riding in a Lexus GS 400, an Acura RL, and a 7 series Beamer. My company leased all of the cars for them. I had to get my legal team on the job to bail these fools outta jail and it cost me plenty. Make no mistake, I was gonna recoup these costs outta their future royalties.

Just to think, one of them dicks wanted to sue me because my security team had to whip his ass for coming to my office in an unruly manner, demanding more money from me. That was insane because if it wasn't for me, their broke asses would stay in jail until their cases went to court. They owed *me* for their freedom. If it were up to them to make bail for themselves, they would be shit outta luck.

These ignorant-ass entertainers only lived for the here and now, and didn't believe in saving money for a rainy day. Instead of investing their royalty money wisely, they would waste it on jewelry, flashy cars, and paying their crew for doing absolutely nothing. Most of these other companies would have left them for dead when their legal troubles began to cost too much. However, coming from the streets, I understood the madness that made many of them do the stupid-ass things they did. I used to be the same way when I was younger, running wild in the streets of Baltimore. I tried to guide them the best that I could, but most of them had to learn from their mistakes.

This wasn't the first time I had to get The Assassins outta a jam, and I knew it wouldn't be the last. Just last week, I had to deal with paying out large sums of money for my young rapper from Detroit, Chaos, who had yet to release an album. He owed money for the paternity suits he had in Michigan with several different broads.

I could go on and on giving examples of the BS I had to put up with to be a successful CEO, but it would be senseless and too damn time consuming. Smoking on a nice fat Cuban cigar was my way to unwind from the stress of my long days at the office.

Ever since me and Takeisha had reached our little understanding about resuming our relationship, I had her right where I wanted her. That fine bitch was gonna make me richer than I already was, plus keep me sexually satisfied. Her little boyfriend, Travis, would just have to accept our arrangement because there was nothing he could do about it. Takeisha might've liked him, but she loved money. I had more than enough of it to dangle in her face to keep her interest. He was made to realize this fact when he caught us together at her place.

We were there one night, mellowing out to the smooth sounds of Gerald Levert, when he decided to pop into town unannounced. She had given him a key to her house to let himself in whenever he was in New York and she was out in the city, handling her music business.

When he put his key in the door on this particular night, he walked in and saw her giving me some straight neck on the living room floor. His eyes almost popped outta his head. The little pussy's heart was broken to see his girl sucking me off and enjoying it. That was when the drama jumped off.

"T, what the fuck is going on? How the hell could you do this to me?" he said.

He sounded like a cold bitch. While he awaited her response, I got up off of the floor and pulled up my pants. I took a seat on the couch and just sat back to watch these two fools go at it. This was better than watching a comedy show.

"Travis, it's not what you think. Please just give me a chance to explain, " Takeisha said.

"What do you need to explain? I walk in and find you sucking another man's dick. I think that says enough right there," he shot back.

I was just laughing my ass off. I loved this shit. I had to throw my two cents into the mix.

"That's a good point, homes. He got you there, T," I interjected.

"Who the fuck asked you anything, nigga? This is between me and my girl," Travis said.

"Slow your roll, college boy. Don't bite off more than you can chew. You don't want no parts of me," I said.

"Samson, please, I got this. Travis, let's go into my room so we can talk," Takeisha said.

"Fuck you and fuck him. Ain't nothing we need to talk about. I should've known you was just another no-good ho. Latrell was right about you," he said. Takeisha was caught off guard.

"What did you just say? When the fuck did you talk to her? What she got to do with this?" Takeisha asked.

"She told me a while ago that you was still seeing this dude. I didn't wanna believe her, but now I see it's true," he responded.

"What the fuck were you doing with that skank? Did you fuck her? Did you?" Takeisha asked.

"Don't try to change the subject from what I just walked in on. You lied to me. You said it was over between you and this nigga. I see the joke's on me. I loved your no-good ass. To answer your question, yes, we did fuck. Her pussy was gooder than a motherfucker," he said.

That was the wrong move. She already knew I had fucked Latrell, and now to find out that her golden boy had done the same, she was steaming. Before he could blink, Takeisha slapped him across the face. She followed that up with a few sharp blows to the gut.

He didn't make an effort to hit her back. He just tried to grab her and hold her down. This was getting better by the minute. I jumped up in an attempt to break them apart.

"A'ight, kids, that's enough," I said. I pulled them apart because Travis had Takeisha in a bear hug in an effort to stop her from hitting him.

"Fuck you, nigga. This is all your fault. Your greedy ass don't care nothing about her. You fucked up our relationship," he said to me.

"College boy, I done told you once that I ain't the one. If I gotta tell you again, it's on. Now, I ain't break up shit between y'all. T and I just have an understanding. We hook up every now and then when you ain't around to have a good time. I know she's ya girl, but she's my plaything. She'll tell you how daddy keeps her bank account fat as long as she gives me what I want," I said. Takeisha said nothing because she knew I held all the cards here.

Travis was pissed off about my last statement. He balled his fist and made an attempt to hit me in the jaw. However, with my reflexes and strength, I caught his punch and deflected it with the palm of my hand. His fist was swallowed in mine like a hand in a catcher's glove. He was no match for me. I twisted his arm around until he went down on one knee. I continued to bend it until I heard a snapping sound. He yelled out in pain. I knew I had broken his arm.

"Samson, don't hurt him anymore, please. I'll do anything you want. Just let him go," Takeisha pleaded.

"Nah, college boy wanna try to be a gangsta then he gotta learn how gangstas get down. I tried to warn him, but he wouldn't listen. He gotta learn the hard way," I said.

He was balled up on the floor, gripping his arm. I kicked him several times in his face and groin. I turned him over to face me and began to pound on his grill piece with both hands. That pretty boy mug was gonna be battered and bruised when I was done.

"Stop, man. I didn't mean what I said. I'm sorry," Travis yelled. Feeling sorry for the kid, I let him up after I noticed all of the blood that had stained the carpet. He had learned a lesson for disrespecting a nigga of my status.

"Take this as a lesson, young blood. When a grown man is talking, show him his proper respect and play ya position," I advised him.

Takeisha stood off to the side in tears. I gathered up my things and made my way to the door. After tonight, that fool and Takeisha knew that her pussy belonged to me. He was just allowed to play with it while I was doing other things. I knew she wouldn't call the police because of the tape I held over her head like a dark cloud.

Takeisha went over to comfort Travis and help him with his injuries. I threw my jacket over my shoulder and lit up a cigar as I walked out the door. I left them behind to sort out their li'l love affair.

34

Takeisha (T-Love)

Since the night of our big blowout, Travis wouldn't return my calls. It had been almost a month. The one time I did talk to him since the incident with Samson, he was mean and nasty to me. He told me it would take about six weeks for his broken arm to heal. He told me it was my fault; he hated me, and never wanted to see me again.

He went on and on, telling me about the night that he slept with Latrell, just to get under my skin. It happened one night at my house when she had called looking for me and he was there alone. I was at a photo shoot with Samson, taking photos for my album cover. When she found out I wasn't there, she made it her business to stop by. She told him I was sleeping with Samson and gave him specific details. The details he knew about my encounters with Samson had to come from only one source. Samson must have run his mouth like a bitch to Latrell about us.

Travis told me how they had a few drinks, one thing led to another and they had sex on my living room floor. He cleaned up any evidence of their encounter before I got home.

I wanted to be mad at him, but I couldn't because I was cheating on him with Samson. We were both guilty as hell. I just hoped in time he would forgive me. He was a good man and I needed him in my life. He always treated me like a lady and he gave me the utmost respect. The more I thought about him, the more depressed I became. Damn, I missed his ass. He had to come back to me.

As for Samson, I hadn't slept with him since that night, but I spoke to him several times over the phone and at his office. He acted as though nothing was wrong between us, and only wanted to talk about my solo album. That let me know he was a cold-hearted motherfucker who only saw me as a sex object—and a cash cow he could make a fortune off of in the near future. I had put myself in a bad situation and had to make the best of it that I could.

Latrell's arrest was all over the news. MTV ran a half-hour long special on her, detailing the charges she faced. BET highlighted the story as well. My phone rang off the hook because every major entertainment news reporter wanted my view on her arrest. Danita got just as many calls as I did.

We were instructed by Samson to make no comments to the press and to keep a low profile. Samson had his PR people on the job, trying to do all they could to make the best of a bad situation, but the damage was already done. Add Latrell's legal problems on top of the recent situation involving The Assassins, and Cash Rules Records was sure to be the next rap label to be under investigation by the Feds for being an alleged criminal enterprise. I knew Samson wouldn't be happy about the heat this situation brought him, and I was sure that all of us, as his artists, would feel his wrath.

This bitch had seriously lost her mind this time. Danita told me about the rumors she heard from Silk about Latrell's drug habit. Now I saw the rumors were true. With her arrest on major drug charges, I had no choice but to accept the obvious—Latrell was a bonafide drug addict.

I wanted to feel sorry for her because we were friends for so long, but I just couldn't muster up any sympathy. This ho had fucked both of my men. She got what she deserved.

She had the nerve to call me from jail. I let her have it with full force.

"T, I need ya help. Samson said he won't bail me out. Do you believe that shit after all the money we made him? My bail is $250,000. Please get me outta here as soon as you can," Latrell said.

"Bitch, please. I'm glad he didn't get your triflin' ass outta jail. If it were up to me, I would leave your ass in there until your stank ass rots to death. I talked to Travis and he told me you fucked him. I also know about you and Samson. Dumb bitch, I guess you must have always wanted to follow in my footsteps. I guess fucking every nigga that I did was your way of trying to be me, huh?" I asked.

There was silence for a moment. I could tell she

was caught off guard, not expecting my onslaught. Finally, she gathered up the nerve to respond.

"T, I'm sorry for everything I did. I know I done did some fucked up things. I can't make them up to you now, but I promise I'ma make things right between us if you get me outta here," she said.

She wanted some sympathy. However, from me, she had no love coming. She didn't even try to deny that she slept with my men. Her fake-ass apology was just her way to trick me into bailing her ass outta jail. Not a chance.

"You got a better chance of getting the Pope to get you outta jail because I can't do nothing for you," I said coldly.

"Come on, T. Don't be this way over no niggas. We supposed to be tighter than that. It's supposed to be KS Crew for life, remember? I know these drugs got me all crossed up. I'ma get some help if you get me outta here. I promise," she said.

"I done told you that I can't do nothing for ya. Before I hang up, do you have anything else to say? You're running up my phone bill," I said.

"If that's how you wanna carry it, then fine. I see how you are. One day, you're gonna need me, and I won't be there. Fuck you, bitch. Yeah, I fucked your men and loved every minute of it. If Scar hadn't went to jail, I would have fucked him too. I'ma get outta here some way and when I do, I'm coming for ya ass. You better watch ya back!" she shouted at me.

"Whatever, trick. Bring it, ho. Bring it!" I replied.

Before she could respond, I hung up the phone. My heart wanted to feel bad for her, but her actions made me pay that no mind. If she wanted some drama with me, then drama it would be. Just like I waxed that ass in elementary school, I would do the same now, but much worse.

Fuck the KS Crew. This group is history after this next album.

D and I were always gonna be cool. As for Latrell, it was on when I saw her ass again. At least I had my solo career to look forward to when my album dropped sometime next year.

35

Danita (D-Boogie)

I had to be a fool to bail Latrell outta jail. After T told me about her sleeping with Travis and Samson and all of the crazy things she had done since we got our record deal, I should've let her ass sit in jail and rot. However, my conscience wouldn't let me do it. Right or wrong, she was my girl and I had to be there for her when she needed me. With all of her faults, she had been there for me more than enough times in the past, and this was just my way of returning the favor.

T, however, wasn't trying to hear it. She was through with Latrell. Nothing I said could convince her of anything different. When I talked to her on the phone, she made her point loud and clear.

"Come on, T. How long have the three of us been friends? You remember how back in elemen-

tary school y'all took me under your wing and
looked out for me when everybody else used to
tease me? Y'all to go back too far for your friendship to be over because of this nonsense," I said.

"I don't even wanna hear that, D. She done
crossed me too many times. Fucking with Samson
was one thing, but to sleep with Travis was a whole
other story. And she did it at my house. She knew
how much I was feeling him. Homegirls don't
cross that line," she said.

"Everything you're saying is right, but you ain't
no better. Look at how you did Travis to mess with
Samson. You carried him greasy, and he worships
the ground you walk on." I said.

"Fuck you, D. You ain't got no right to judge
me. If you wanna be that bitch's friend, then so be
it. I'm done with this conversation," she said and
hung up on me.

Takeisha thought she was perfect and never
made mistakes. She must've forgot how the two of
them ran game on the same guys countless times
in the past.

She should not have let a man come between
the crew. In this situation, I kinda agreed with Latrell about how Takeisha acted like her shit didn't
stink sometimes. She never accepted any blame
when she did something wrong. She had always
been this way. I just chose to ignore it most of the
time.

For her to curse at me like that, it seemed like I
was the only one of the three of us that was sane.
She had no right to talk to me like that. I wasn't
gonna speak to her until she apologized.

Latrell's bail was set at $250,000. Luckily, my
royalty checks from my songwriting had left me

well enough off that it wouldn't put a huge dent in my finances. However, make no mistake about, she was gonna pay me back every penny of my money. I had my attorney draw up an agreement so the money I put up for her bail would be paid back to me outta her future royalties from Cash Rules Records. She had no choice but to sign the agreement if she wanted to get outta jail. Being friends was one thing, but I didn't fuck around when it came to my money. I worked too hard to get it, and I would be damned if I threw it all away for nothing.

When I saw Latrell after she got released, I couldn't believe my eyes. She looked nothing like the girl I had known for so many years. Her clothes looked rough, her hair was a mess, and she had bags under her eyes that were big enough to carry groceries. She looked a lot lighter than the last time I saw her. I couldn't believe how she had fallen off so quickly.

I tried to talk to her about going into a drug rehabilitation center, but she gave me the brush-off. As soon as she hit the streets, she was off to the races. The crack pipe had a hold of her soul, and she was on a mission to get as high as she could. The seriousness of her legal situation instantly left her mind. I knew it was the drugs and not her that drove her to do the things that she did. I just prayed she would get her life together.

Sometimes when I was alone, I thought about how close we used to be before we got into the music business. It hurt me inside to see Latrell and Takeisha as enemies when I knew how much we had been through together. Memories of all the years we spent as a crew, kicking up dust in B'more, pervaded my thoughts. It seemed as though all those years weren't real, but just one big fantasy.

Since we finished recording our album, we didn't see each other much. Latrell was busy doing her, partying all the time, and I was busy with Silk, enjoying our relationship. Takeisha and I spoke at least two times a week, but not even our friendship was the same. We all seemed to be drifting in different directions. I knew it wouldn't be long before the group fell apart as well. It was a depressing thought but a growing reality about to manifest itself.

My thoughts were interrupted by Silk's strong hands massaging my shoulders. He had been so supportive of me and my dilemma with the group that I sometimes felt as though I didn't deserve him. He never criticized my friends in front of me, no matter what they did wrong or right. He just let me know that whatever I chose to do, he had my back. I had fallen head over heels in love with this man. I knew he felt the same way about me.

"How does that feel, baby?" Silk asked.

"That feels so good," I replied.

"Don't let Latrell and Takeisha's beef get you all stressed out. They have to work that out on their own. You can't be the peacemaker all the time," he said.

"I know, baby. I just want things to go back to the way they used to be," I said.

"Maybe they will or maybe they won't. Nonetheless, you have more important things to worry about, like yourself—and making me smile," he said jokingly. He began to tickle me and I started to laugh.

Silk gave me the sense of security I had always

wanted since my father walked outta my life. He took away the pain and the void that Larry's untimely death had left me feeling. Silk was making my life complete, and now we were going to be parents. I found out recently from my doctor that I was almost four months pregnant with his child. He was as happy as I was about the news. Now, if I could only get my child's two aunts to act like they had some sense then everything would be fine. I needed my girls in my life to help me raise this child.

36

Scar

I washed the sleep outta my eyes as I arose to go about my business for the day. I was happy to be back out in society. For the past two weeks, I felt like a new man with a new mission and purpose for life.

I was released from prison to relatively no fanfare or media attention. In the music business, you can be a star today, then tomorrow somebody else comes along who's hot, and you're forgotten. It was as though all those millions of people that bought my album didn't know I existed anymore. I guess that was the downside of fame.

There was a small blurb on MTV about my getting outta prison, but that was it. The story reported that I was released because the police didn't follow proper procedure when they bagged me. It was stated that they failed to read me my Miranda rights before they questioned me. As a result, my conviction was overturned on an appeal and I was set free.

Of course, that story was all bullshit that the DEA manufactured to keep their agreement with me. My information led to the arrest of Miguel Salazar in their drug sting. Luckily, they wouldn't need me to come to court and testify against Miguel. The information I gave them was enough to build a case. Therefore, my status as an informant was a secret known only to the DEA and me.

These government assholes were some clever, conniving, lying predators when they wanted to be. They could feed any kind of lie they wanted to the media and people believed it was true. Just to think, when I was hustlin' out in these streets, they called me a criminal, as crooked as they were. Ain't that some hypocrisy for ya ass!

Since I was locked up, I had lost my passion to write rhymes. Most of my time behind bars was spent trying to survive and deal with the madness of prison life. However, I knew that writing rhymes for a poet was like riding a bike—once you perfect the craft, you never lose that ability. I was kinda rusty, but I still felt I could hold my own with the best MCs in the game. That was why I had a meeting scheduled with Ace at Fisherman's Wharf.

Since Marquee dropped me from the label after I was convicted, we planned to discuss getting me a deal with another record company. Looking at my sales figures from my first album, I saw no reason why I wouldn't get picked up by another label. The one thing all the record executives had in common was that if they felt you could make them some money, they would take a risk on signing you to a deal.

As I sipped on a glass of Hennessy and Coke, Ace walked in and greeted me.

"What's going on, bro? I'm glad to see you got out," Ace said.

He gave me one of them Hollywood typa phony-ass hugs. I could see that his success since I was locked up had changed him. He had fifteen acts, some R&B and some rap, that he now managed, bringing major money. He was now a brother that had infiltrated the Establishment. He had *arrived*, as they said in those uppity circles.

"Just trying to hold on, ya know. I'm glad to be out. I see you done blew up and you da man, now, huh?" I asked.

"Yeah, I'm doing my thing. I always told you that hard work paid off in the end. I got a check here for you from Marquee Records for your last royalty period," he said. He handed me a check in the amount of 100 grand.

"Now, that's what I'm talking about. There ain't nothing like coming home to a shit load of cash. Old money spends as good as new money, ya smell me? I'm ready to get back in the game, Ace. I was hoping you could work ya magic and get a brotha a deal," I said. I sensed some hesitancy on his part.

"I would love to, dog, but right now, my plate is full. All these acts I have keep me so busy I hardly have time for my family," he said. He sent me a letter while I was locked up to tell me he got married. He and his wife now had one child and another one on the way.

"So, you saying you ain't got time to do this for

me? You forgot who took a chance on you when you were a nobody in this game? Stop bullshittin' with me, Ace," I shot back.

"Nah, I ain't forget that, Scar. You know we cool. To be blunt with you, you're damaged goods in this business, with ya legal problems and the fact that Marquee dropped you from ya deal. It's been over two years since you had a record out. So much has changed in the rap game since then. Two years is like a lifetime in this business. A lotta companies ain't gonna take a chance on you. They think you're shot as an artist, and it would be too costly to try to revive the buzz you had back then. That's just the facts, man," he said bluntly.

I wanted to argue with him about what he said, but I couldn't. Everything he said had to be true. Ace was always on point when it came to his business. When you're hot, ya hot, but once you cool off, it's hard to get ya fans back. That's just how it goes in this business. My music career was over. As bitter a pill as it was to swallow, I had to accept it and move on.

"I feel you, man. At least I had my fifteen minutes of fame, right? Let's get something to eat. You can tell me about some of these new acts you got signed," I said calmly.

We ordered our food and ate it as we reminisced about the crazy times we had getting into this rap game. I couldn't hate on Ace. I was glad to see him do his thing. He deserved his chance to shine. I had no time to dwell on something I couldn't change because I had other business to tend to. Somebody had to pay for fucking up my career, and I knew just who it would be.

37

Takeisha (T-Love)

Our second album dropped on schedule and it did pretty good numbers. We didn't move as many units as our first album did in its first week, but we still managed to make number one on the Billboard charts, with 390,000 CDs sold.

The music critics were harsh on our album, and gave us disappointing reviews. The *Source* only gave us two mics, saying that our lyrics were not as fierce as they were on our debut album and our music production left a lot to be desired. The critic for *Vibe* magazine said the album appeared to be rushed, probably in hopes that we could capitalize on the press from Latrell's legal situation. All of the other reviews pretty much echoed the same sentiments, calling us everything from has-beens to one hit wonders. Nonetheless, Samson said that at least we were guaranteed another platinum album when it was all said and done. As long as we kept our expenses low, we would be in good shape to receive royalties. I just hoped he paid up this time.

Danita was coming along in her pregnancy and appeared to be happy in her relationship with Silk. They made a cute couple. After I cursed at her for taking up for Latrell, I called her to apologize. I was dead wrong to take out my frustration on her. She forgave me, as she usually did. D had such a good heart. I wished some of her ways would rub off on me. Then maybe I wouldn't get myself into some of the situations I had to face.

For health reasons, D couldn't do too much touring and traveling if she wanted to have a healthy baby. Also, me and Latrell still weren't on speaking terms. Without the three of us out in public to push this album like we did the first one, our sales suffered. Samson did the best he could to promote the album without us all in the same place at the same time. His PR people made up excuses for our low profile.

Samson also kept his word and paid us the money we agreed upon as an advance. The money came in handy and bailed me outta my financial jam.

Latrell was more off the hook than before. Her drug use was outta control, and it could be seen in her appearance. She had lost a lotta weight and looked like a full-time crackhead. That was another reason Samson kept her outta the public eye as much as possible. She had become an embarrassment to the group, as well as Cash Rules Records. I knew it wouldn't be long before Samson dealt with her in his own way. I felt no sympathy for her, especially after our last altercation.

After D mentioned to me that Latrell told her everything about our night with Ricardo, the videotape, and about Samson killing him, that bitch rose to the top of my shit list. I went to her house to confront her about her loose lips and give her the ass whipping she deserved. When she came to the door, I rained down on her ass before she could get it all the way open. I burst through the door, and I was on her like stink on shit.

"Bitch, why the fuck you had to tell D about Ricardo? Didn't I tell you to keep your fucking mouth shut?"

I was on top of her, pounding on her face like nobody's business. In the past, she might've given me a run for my money, but her getting high made her no match for me today. She didn't have the strength to mount a defense. Nonetheless, she still managed to talk shit to me.

"Get off of me, T! I ain't tell her shit. She already knew everything. Samson told her, not me," she said.

I knew that was a lie. Samson was too smart to tell anyone about the murder. She wanted to get me to let up off this can of whip-ass I was administering. Because she lied to me, I continued to beat her ass until her face was a bloody mess. Her hair was everywhere as she tried to turn her face away from my onslaught of blows. I connected with more than enough shots. After a while, I got up off of her and began to kick her midsection. I relentlessly released every bit of my rage toward her before I figured she had enough.

"If I found out you told anybody else about that shit and it come back on me, that's your ass. You can take that to the bank, you stank ho!"

I left her on the living room floor, wincing in pain. She grumbled under her breath about getting revenge on me. She said some shit about this not being over between us, that she would have the last laugh. However, I think she knew better than to test my hand again. Besides, once the Feds got finished with her ass, prison was gonna be her home for a good minute.

After I whipped Latrell's ass, I received an unexpected surprise visit from Travis. It had been a few moths since I last saw him. I thought for sure that he was through with me. However, since he was at my front door, maybe there was still hope. At least, that's what I hoped for my sake. I felt weak in the knees when I looked into his eyes. He still had a hold on me. I missed him like crazy.

"So, are you gonna let me in or are we gonna stand here at the door all day?" he asked.

"Oh, I'm sorry. You just caught me off guard," I said as he walked past me into the house.

"I know I probably did. I caught myself off guard too. I've been trying to get you outta my system, but for some reason I can't seem to shake my feelings for you," he said.

"Really? I've missed you too, Travis. I know I messed up big time, but so did you. How did we get so off track?" I asked.

"I don't know, T. I was mad at you for messing with Samson, and I acted out off of my feelings. I was wrong for sleeping with Latrell. I'm not too proud to admit that," he said.

"So, do we still have a chance? Travis, I want you

back in my life. Everything is just so crazy in my world right now. Being a star ain't all it's cracked up to be. I almost feel like the money ain't worth it. The only time I've been truly happy was when I spent time with you.

"Let's give this thing another chance. I know I said this before, but I mean it this time. I promise not to lie to you anymore. My defenses are down. I need you in my life," I said.

"I need you in my life, too, baby. I'm willing to try to make things work with you," he said.

I jumped up off the couch and into his arms. We kissed for what seemed like forever. I was glad he was back in my life.

I swore to myself I wouldn't mess things up between us this time. At that moment, he made all the drama in my life seem nonexistent. My problems with my girls didn't matter. I didn't think about dealing with the drama with Cash Rules Records or my career. I just hoped that nothing came along to mess this up. However, with my luck, who knew what could happen at any moment.

38

Latrell (Luscious)

With my trial coming up in the near future, I didn't give a fuck about much of anything. Making music was the last thing on my mind. According to my lawyers, with the case the government had against me, I was sure to be going to jail for a good minute. Consequently, I tried to live life to the fullest while I was free. I just wanted to get high and not think about how fucked up my life was.

The way I felt, I had nothing to lose at this point. I had lived my dream to become a superstar in this rap thing. I got to mingle with all the celebrities I grew up admiring on TV. I got a chance to fuck some of the biggest niggas in the business. I knew what it felt like to be rich, to be able to buy whatever the fuck I wanted. I got a chance to be in the spotlight that I never got growing up in my fucked up household. That alone made me feel like I was worth something as a person.

As twisted up as I was from my drama-filled life, I didn't appreciate my success when it came my way. I knew I had messed up big time, but I wasn't the typa person to beat myself up about my mistakes. I just said "fuck it" and rolled with the punches. What was gonna be was gonna be for me in this world. I lived for today because my tomorrow was surely not promised. I planned to go out with my guns slinging.

That bitch Takeisha was gonna pay for what she did to me. That siditty-acting ho musta thought she was better than me. Ever since we became friends Danita and I always had to do things her way or on her terms. Danita might continue to lie down and let her walk all over her, but not me. She was gonna regret bringing me a move like she did. I would see to it that I got some get-back on her, thanks to my man Scar.

I ran into Scar when I was in B'more visiting my family. He stopped by my old house, where my brothers still lived, and left a message for me to contact him. When I got his message, I got in touch with him right away. I always wanted to get with his fine ass. I always knew he was attracted to me, because what nigga didn't want me back then? I never made a move on him because Takeisha was my girl and all. I left his ass alone, trying to be a loyal friend. However, today was a different day. Fuck that bitch and everything she stood for.

Scar was eager to help me release my sexual tension. I booked a room at the Radisson in downtown Baltimore. I got the penthouse suite because I wanted to enjoy the night in each and every way.

Scar didn't get high, so I made sure that I smoked enough coke beforehand to last me through the night. The main thing I liked about smoking crack was that it increased my sexual pleasure. I got turned on to it one night by the R&B superstar, Raven. He convinced me to try it and after I did, we had the kinkiest sexual odyssey between him, his girlfriend, Tahira, and myself. I was hooked from that point on.

The things Scar did to my body had me reaching for the ceiling to get away from his nasty ass. It's true what they said about a dude that just came home from jail—he would fuck the life outta the first piece of pussy he got his hands on. Scar made me cum so many times I lost count. His love stick had me moaning and groaning each time he went in and outta me. Takeisha was a fool to let go of this dick. Scar had the kinda dick that drove a bitch crazy. It would have you ready to kill another ho if she tried to get a dose of it.

Scar licked me in every hole his tongue would fit into with ease. He made my thighs shiver when he tossed my salad as I leaned over the edge of the jacuzzi. His backstroke was just as wicked when he fucked me doggy style. We did it in the shower, on the floor, on the dresser and even in the closet. He gave me that thug lovin' like a nigga was supposed to, and it was just the way a bitch like me liked it.

I gave him just as much pleasure with my mouth, bringing him to climax several times throughout the night. The way I moved my hips had him slippin' 'n slidin' outta my pussy with ease and feeling the ultimate sense of sexual delight.

I had never felt such a high from having sex. I knew I was that bitch he needed in his life.

Feeling no sense of loyalty to Takeisha, I told Scar all of her business. I told him about her fucking with Samson and Travis at the same time. I told him about our threesome with Ricardo. I even told him about niggas she had got with while they were together.

He told me he found out from the Feds that Rachel and Rock had set him up to take a fall. He also told me that he was pissed at Takeisha, although he never explained why. I really didn't care, because I could use his help in getting back at that bitch.

"So, what's up? You tryin' to help me set that bitch up or what?" he asked.

"Hell yeah, nigga. What you got in mind?" I asked.

"I got something set up that's so sweet. I'ma get rid of her ass and that bitch-ass nigga Samson. I can't stand his ass," Scar said.

"What did Samson do to you? How do y'all know each other?" I asked.

It turned out that Scar's father and Samson had beef years ago in the streets of Baltimore. Scar's father was the man in B'more at the time that Samson was a young star on the rise in the game. Samson was determined to be the top dog out in the streets, and down to take out whomever stood in his way.

One of Scar's father's top associates, Lonnie, wound up getting killed in a confrontation between the two crews. Lonnie was like an uncle to Scar. As a result of his murder, bad blood existed between Samson and Scar, on behalf of his pops.

"Damn, that's fucked up. That nigga Samson is a cruddy motherfucker. Whatever you tryin' to do,

I'm down for it, 'cause at this point, I ain't got shit to lose," I said.

He ran down his plan to me, and it sounded on point. With a common enemy, we could definitely do some business that was mutually beneficial. He would make the perfect ally for me to carry out my plan of revenge. Shit, if I went down, I planned to take her and Samson along with me.

39

Samson

I sent Lem home early. I wouldn't be in need of his security services, so I let him leave early to spend time with his family. Lem was married and had three kids, a boy and two girls. His wife, Cassandra, had been with him throughout all of our slangin' and bangin' days in the streets of Baltimore. He figured that since she held him down while he was serving a seven-year stretch for aggravated assault, she was the perfect wifey material.

I really didn't need security because my street rep pretty much carried enough weight. However, I still hired him as my personal bodyguard so he had a legit way to make a living after he came home from prison. A dude from the streets who came home from jail didn't have a chance in hell to make it in this society unless one of his own looked out for him. Fortunately for him and many others, I was that olive branch to getting legit paper.

I was alone in my office, looking over the promotional campaign I had planned for T-Love's solo album. My graphic design department had done a good job coming up with a hot cover for the album. T and I had put our personal differences aside to create a bangin' collection of material. The album was entitled *Holdin' My Own*, and it was gonna be one helluva coming out party for my top artist. All of my other acts did pretty good sales figures, but Takeisha was about to take Cash Rules into the stratosphere. As a solo artist, I saw her being larger than Missy Elliott in terms of crossover success.

I had to admit that I had caught feelings for Takeisha. As twisted as our relationship was, she held a special place in my heart. It wasn't my practice to show affection to a woman, given my hardcore upbringing in the streets. That was why I never let it be known how much I really was feeling her. That woulda made me seem weak or vulnerable. However, I planned to change all of that soon. Once I made her into the star I wanted her to be, our relationship was gonna change. I let her have her fun with that busta, Travis, for now. When the time was right, he was gonna be history, one way or another, and it would just be me and Takeisha, on top of the entertainment world.

Because I was a don in this business, even a has-been like Scar reached out to me. I received a call from him the other day. I remembered that little punk motherfucker from my beef with his pops back in the days. His father was a sheisty-ass nigga that tried to stop me from taking over the streets of Baltimore when I was on my grind. He couldn't accept the fact that his time came and went in the drug game. I was the new kid on the block and I had to make him feel me. I personally killed his ace boon coon, Lonnie, to let him know I wasn't scared to put my murder game down. It was too bad Nate got knocked off before I had a chance to lay him and the rest of his team down.

When Nate went to jail, the streets were all mine to rule. Years later, Scar came up in the game. He had that natural knack for the street life, just like his father. Hustlin' was in his genes. We crossed paths a few times in the streets. He was a youngsta on the come-up, just like I once was. At that time, I was on my way outta the game. He never mentioned my beef with his father because he knew that would mean sure death for him. He just played it cool when he saw me, and gave me my proper respect.

I heard about him getting outta jail on a technicality, and it sounded like BS to me. With all the years I had been out in the streets, I knew how the system worked. He had to rat on somebody to get an early release, but the Feds just made it appear otherwise.

I sensed something shady was up with his case when it was written in the news during his trial that the drug charges he faced were mysteriously dropped. Drug charges don't just disappear. You either copped a plea, got convicted, or turned informant. The game was what it was.

Nonetheless, Scar had reached out to me about signing him to a record deal. I knew he had a buzz on the streets with his debut album, so I was open to seeing if I could rekindle his career. Even if he had lost most of his fan base, I could still turn a profit off of him with a mediocre album.

Old rivalries from the streets never stood in the way of me making legit money today. Cash ruled everything around me in my world, and I was in love with it. Besides, if he did wanna try and take on his old man's beef, I had no problem merking his punk ass like I did Lonnie.

Scar arrived at my office at about 9:30 in the evening. When I saw him, he looked like the spitting image of his pops, with his height and physical build. He was dressed in a Sean John sweatsuit with white-on-white Nike Airs. He wasn't wearing the platinum jewelry I remembered seeing when he hustled. I guess times were hard since he fell off. Instead, he appeared to be rather calm and humble when he approached me to shake my hand.

"What's going on, young man? You look just like ya pops. I used to look up to him coming up, ya know? How is he anyway? I know he's doing his time like a soldier. He always was a stand-up guy," I said.

"Yeah, I know. He told me all about you and y'all *relationship*. He's doing as good as could be expected under the circumstances. He's doing his time and not letting his time do him," Scar replied.

I detected a hint of sarcasm and subtle anger in his voice. My beef was with his pops, not him. However, if he wanted to start some shit, then so be it. Whatever thoughts he had of testing me, I would have to diffuse that real quick.

"Slow ya roll, young blood. Before we get down to talking business, we need to get one thing straight.

Whatever happened in the past between your father and me was just that, *the past.* If you can accept
that, then we can be cool and proceed. If not, then
it's best that you walk back out that door and never
let me see you again. Is that clear?"

He was from the streets, and he knew my words
were a gentlemanly warning, not to be taken lightly.
Anything I said, I could back up with action. My
reputation spoke for itself. Samson Miles was as
gangsta as gangsta could get.

"I hear you. You right. I ain't got no beef. Besides, this is the music business. This ain't the drug
game. I'm an artist now. I'm tryin' ta get a deal.
You got the hottest label around and I'm tryin' ta
get on," Scar said.

He seemed to take my warning to heart. I relaxed in my leather executive chair as I tried to
feel him out some more. I couldn't front because
he had skills as a rapper, and his street credentials
would make him a perfect fit for the most notorious record label in the game. I just had one more
thing I had to be sure about before I made him an
offer.

"I'm glad you see things my way. It's just one
more thing that concerns me that I need to address. I know you done heard about ya old girl,
Takeisha, and me, and how we get down. I need to
know if that's gonna be a problem for you," I said.

"Nah, that ain't even an issue to me, man. She's
old news. I had that back in the day. You can do
what you want with her. Besides, she'll tell you that
I broke it off with her and not the other way
around," he responded.

I could see his ass was trying to throw me a slur

on the low, as though I got his leftovers. Fuck that! Samson Miles never took sloppy seconds from no nigga. He had to pay for that comment, and I knew just how to make that happen.

"A'ight. This is what I'm willing to do for you. I'll give you fifty grand to sign and start you off at the new artist rate of twelve points," I said.

I knew he would take my offer as an insult, given that his first album did such awesome numbers. To offer him a new artist deal was a major slap in the face, but fuck it. I was the boss of this game, and I set the rules. I expected him to explode, but he didn't.

"I'm with it. When do I sign the contract?" he asked eagerly.

"See me next week and we can go over the paperwork," I replied.

"You got that. I appreciate it, man. Since Marquee dropped me and I got locked down, I thought I would never get another chance to do my thing. My old manager said that I was damaged goods. Thanks to you, I get a chance to prove him and everybody else wrong," he said.

We shook hands and he walked toward the door to make his exit then turned back to me with a sinister look on his face.

"Oh, Samson, I forgot one more thing. I want a copy of the tape that you got of Latrell and T fucking that dude that you killed. And after I get that, your ass is dead," he said.

His statement stunned me. By the time I gathered my faculties, he had reached into his dip and pulled out a loaded .45. This motherfucker had lost his mind.

"What the fuck is this, a stick-up? You trying to rob me? How the fuck you know about that tape?" I asked.

Before he could respond, I saw Latrell and his boy Trevor walk into my office now. I had the answer to my question. This stupid bitch had helped him set me up. She told him about the tape. Some way, some how, they were gonna try to extort money from me. I had to play it cool because they had the drop on me.

"That's right, Samson. Hand the fucking tape over. You ain't so big and bad no more, is you, motherfucker?" Latrell said. She looked like death warmed over. The crack pipe had her by the balls for sure.

"A'ight, people. Let's think about this here. This is some serious shit y'all about to get into. You know who I am and how I get down. Are you sure you wanna go this route?" I said.

"Fuck that shit you talking. Nobody knows you're here. We saw ya boy, Lem, leave out hours ago. Ain't nobody here but you and us. Now, hand the tape over before we have to smoke your big ass!" Trevor said. He was holding a .38, with his hand around the trigger, and he appeared eager to squeeze it.

"Oh, yeah. We want all the money you got in that safe next to ya desk, too. Hurry the fuck up so we can get outta here," Scar said.

Damn that bitch! Latrell told him about my secret safe where I kept the tape. She had seen me go in there on numerous occasions when she was in my office giving me a blowjob. I also kept over 150 grand in there in case of an emergency. It was one of my old habits from my days of hustlin'—always keeping a secret stash of money on hand.

She didn't know what else I had in there. That was my surprise.

"You got me, dog. Give me one minute to unlock the safe. Why don't y'all stop pointing them guns at me, though? They're making me nervous. Relax, y'all about to get paid," I said.

Scar and Trevor looked at each other. At the same time, they lowered their weapons and waited as I bent down to punch in the numeric code. After I put in the four-digit code, the safe opened. Inside was a copy of the tape, the money, and my handy 9mm. I placed the tape on my desk and began to pull out the stacks of hundred dollar bills. They were so excited to see all money that they took their attention off of me for a second. That was the wrong move!

Before they could think, I had the nine in my hand. Their weapons were still lowered. I pushed myself up against the wall as I prepared to empty my clip into these motherfuckers.

When Scar recognized that I was armed, his reflexes kicked in. He fired his weapon. Trevor followed suit right behind him, letting off several shots.

I squeezed the trigger on my gun. As I fired, I felt a burning sensation in several different parts of my body. I fell to the ground.

40

Scar

We interrupt this broadcast to bring you this piece of groundbreaking news. Samson Miles, CEO of the notorious rap label, Cash Rules Records, has just died from multiple gunshot wounds sustained in an apparent armed robbery at his Manhattan office.

He was on life support for the past week, until the hospital was given permission by his family to take him off when his chances of survival diminished. The police have no clues pointing to any suspects or any witnesses at this time.

This is just another tragic moment in the world of rap music, where its artists live a lifestyle plagued by guns, drugs, and violence . . .

The reporter went on to document Samson's rise to the top of the rap world. He spoke about his violent past as an alleged drug kingpin in Baltimore, and how he carried many of his same violent tactics into the music business. Other record company CEOs described him as an intelligent but misunderstood man, and said that his death was a tragic loss to the industry. Many of the Cash Rules artists who complained about him raping them of their royalties appeared to be sad about his death when confronted by the press for a statement.

I was content with the fact that they said they had no suspects in his murder. That meant we were in the clear. I didn't feel guilty that I killed that greedy bastard. He had it coming for the dirt he did in the past. He earned them shells he caught for killing my uncle Lonnie. My pops would be proud of me for avenging his best friend's death. Now all I had to do was take care of this silly bitch, Latrell, and I would be in the clear.

I really didn't want to fuck that grimy bitch, but sometimes you had to make sacrifices for the cause. She used to be fine back in the day, but her best days were behind her, thanks to the crack rock. When I met her she was a ten, but since the pipe had a hold of her, she was lucky to be considered a five.

To give a dumb bitch some good dick sometimes was the best truth serum. She gave me some good info about her girl Takeisha. She also helped me set Samson up lovely.

I told her she would get a equal cut of whatever money Trevor and I got outta the deal, but I never planned to cut her in on it.

At this point, I had to get rid of her because there was a chance she would talk. That bitch had a lot to gain if she were to turn on me with her trial coming up soon. Information on a high-profile murder would go a long way in getting her outta serving time.

That's why I had Trevor take her ass somewhere to dispose of her as soon as possible. By next week, she would be history. I told him to make her death look like a crack overdose so no one would be suspicious.

Now Latrell would be gone, and I had already taken care of another one of my problems. I used the information from agents Horowitz and Drake to track down Rock and Rachel. Them two dumb asses had relocated to Miami after my arrest and conviction. It turned out that they had used the money Rock stole from me, and the money Rachel got in her civil suit, to open up a day spa on the beach.

Once I caught up with their asses, they were surprised as hell to see me. They must have thought I would be in jail for a long time and they were in the clear. Trevor and I made quick work of them, disposing of their dead bodies out in some deserted swamp area.

Before we killed them, Rock, being the rat that he was, spilled the beans that Takeisha was involved in their scheme to set me up. That totally threw me for a loop. She had to answer for that shit. I planned to pay her a visit for old time's sake.

41

Takeisha (T-Love)

The studio audience was packed to capacity. All eyes in the rap world were on me. I was the featured guest on *106th and Park*. My solo album dropped that day and I had to make an appearance to promote it.

The album was released two months later than expected, due to Samson's death, but the expectations for me to do well were high. My future appeared to be so bright, but I felt like dying inside. My world had been turned upside down with all of the insanity that went on around me.

Since Samson died, his right hand man, Greg, took over running the company. Greg was the vice president of Cash Rules Records, and the obvious choice to be the heir to Samson's seat on the throne. A tall, dark, and handsome brother, he had an approach to business similar to Samson's. That was why Samson had always trusted him to handle a lot of responsibility in the company.

After the shock of Samson's death wore off, Greg got back to business and saw to it that my album was released. He knew Samson would've wanted him to carry on the legacy of Cash Rules Records. My album was to be the bridge for the company to go to the next level.

While it was true that Samson put me through a lotta shit, he also did some positive things for me. He gave the KS Crew a chance when no one else would. For that, I was eternally grateful. Despite his shady business dealings, he made us into a household name. We owed our success to him. Without his vision and hard work, we would've been another group of female wanna-be rappers.

Our personal relationship was a whole other ball game. We went through more ups and downs than a roller coaster. There were times he could be so compassionate and cool to kick it with, then there were times when he was a nasty, hateful motherfucker I didn't want to be around. In his own crazy way, I believed he cared about me, but was afraid to show it.

A man like Samson was larger than life, one that only came along once in a lifetime. Love him or hate him, you had to respect his gangsta. The man got results by any means necessary.

The police still had no leads about who killed Samson. Given their dislike for him, I don't believe they put much effort into finding his killer. However, I knew that if the police didn't catch the killer, Samson's crew would. They would definitely administer some street justice for their boss.

I was surprised to hear that he was alone when the altercation took place. He almost always had Lem with him. I began to believe that his death was an inside job from amongst his crew, but I had no proof and no intentions of trying to find any. I guess his death just went to show that no matter how gangsta you carried things, somebody always came along who was bold enough to come for your spot on the top.

To deal with Samson's death was more than enough, but to find out about Latrell's death from a drug overdose not long afterwards just added insult to injury. When I found out that Latrell was dead, I almost had a nervous breakdown. I thought back to the last time I saw her and how I had whipped her ass for sleeping with Samson and Travis. Inside, I felt numb because our fight was the last memory I would have of someone who at one time was my best friend.

In spite of our differences, she was my sister and I loved her. It was just the things that she did that made me angry. The lesson I learned from losing her was that one should never take friendship for granted and let other things, such as money, fame, or a man, get in the way of that bond. Unfortunately, now it was too late for us to make things right with each other. All I had to hold on to were the memories of the past.

When I went to her funeral, the person I saw in her coffin wasn't the Latrell I grew to love as a friend, but a whole other person. She went from a classy, fly-dressing diva to a broken down drug addict. Her wild and crazy ways that made her the person she was, caught up with her and wound up

being her downfall. For all of her faults, I was
gonna miss that off-the-hook bitch. She was my
dog for life.

On top off that, Danita wasn't speaking to me
right now. She was pissed that she had to find out
about my solo album coming out from the media
and not from me. She felt I was being selfish and
conniving to have cut a side deal with Samson, outside of the group. I tried my best to explain to her
why I did things the way I did, but she didn't buy
my explanation. She said our friendship was over
and she never wanted to see me again. That hurt
me more than she could ever know. Now that
Danita was mad at me, I felt alone. I had to find a
way to get her to forgive me if it was the last thing I
did.

When Free and AJ called me out to do my inter-
view on the show, I was a mess inside. I answered
their questions in a monotone, nonchalant voice.
They could sense that I wasn't my usual vibrant
self. With all that had gone on in my life recently,
they understood and didn't ask a lot of probing
questions about Latrell's and Samson's deaths or
the rumors about my strained relationship with
D-Boogie.

I appreciated that and went about the business
of talking about the album. The lead single and
video was a remix of the Wu Tang Clan classic,
"C.R.E.A.M." featuring Method Man and Ghost-
face Killa. The Smith Brothers produced the track.
When the video played on the projection screen
TV in the studio, the crowd went crazy. I knew I
had a hit on my hands.

After the taping of the show was over, I mingled
with the crowd for a while. The love I got from my

fans was what I needed at this time in my life to fill the loneliness without either of my girls around. The KS Crew was officially history, and T-Love, the rap superstar, was about to blow up in a major way. The chance to shine in the spotlight on my own was now at my fingertips and within my power to control. However, I began to ask myself if the price I had to pay was worth it in the long run. Only time would answer that question for me.

As I was guided outta the studio by my security team, I saw a face in the crowd that almost made me faint. It was like I had seen a ghost. I hadn't seen Scar since our breakup four years ago. He sent a chill down my spine. I knew he had been released from jail, but I didn't expect to run across him here, of all places. What the hell was he doing backstage on the BET set? I had to find out.

Old feelings I thought were gone were rekindled inside of me, and I had no clue why. He looked fine and all, with his sexy body, but Travis was my man now. I couldn't lie, though, because I felt guilt over what I had done to his career.

Our eyes locked in on each other in a tense moment as I walked toward him. My security guards were thrown off guard by my sudden change in direction. When Scar and I were face to face, he whispered in my ear that we needed to talk. We exited the studio with my entourage, headed to my place to have a long overdue discussion.

42

Scar

The ride in the limo was intense. Her two body-guards sat up in the front so we could have some privacy. We both tried to feel each other out, since this was the first time we were face to face in a good minute. I had changed, and it was obvious she had changed as well.

Back in the day, I was the man with the fanfare and notoriety and she was my understudy. Now the tides had turned, and she was this mega star while my career had dwindled away, thanks to *her*. It was an awkward moment as she tried to read my thoughts. I knew I had her off balance, and I planned to use that to my advantage.

"So, I see you done came up out here and all. I always knew you were born to be a star. I'm proud of you, T," I said.

"Thanks, Scar. It took a lot of hard work to get

here. You helped us a lot in the beginning. I could never forget that despite what happened between us," she said.

"I *hear* you. Is that why you wrote me all those letters while I was locked up to show me love and support?" I asked.

"Come on, Scar. Ain't no need for you to be sarcastic. Let's keep it real. We weren't on the best of terms. Let's not dredge up those bad old memories, *please.*"

"You right, T. The past is the past. Let's forgive and forget. I was wrong and you were wrong as well. Let's let bygones be bygones. So, what's up with you now besides holding down that number one spot on the charts?" I asked.

"Yeah, that's all good, but it ain't the same without my crew here with me. Latrell is gone, and me and D are on the outs," she replied.

"Yeah, that was messed up how Latrell died. I read about it in the paper. That girl always had a wild streak to her, though."

"Never mind me. What are you doing with yaself now?" she asked me.

"Well, you know I got royalty money still coming in, so I'm just chilling. I'm done with trying to be an artist. I'm content living large off of my old money. You know me. I was a hustler first, so money is never an issue," I replied.

We chatted a little while longer until we pulled up at her house. When we were ready to exit the limo, she told her security detail it was cool that they left. She felt safe with me. Big mistake! They complied with her wishes and left with the limo driver.

"Damn, T! You livin' it up for real. Can a brother

get a loan or what?" I asked jokingly, when we went in her house.

"Can I get you something to drink, Scar?" she asked.

"Yeah, let me get a Henny and Coke," I replied.

T looked finer than she did when I first met her. Getting money certainly had agreed with her. She brought me my drink and sat down beside me on the couch.

"So, Scar, what made you come to the show today after all this time?" she asked.

"I saw the previews on BET last week and noticed that you were gonna be on the show, so I decided to swing through. I used some of my old clout with the producers of the show to get in. Besides, you've been on my mind for quite some time," I replied.

"And why is that?" she asked.

"'Cause, T, you know you were the one for me. I just wasn't ready at the time. I was too busy doing me," I replied.

I could see I had struck a nerve by the look in her eyes. She wasn't totally over me. I was her first love, and I could always hit her soft spot. A nigga knew when he had a girl hooked for life, no matter who she got with after him.

"Yeah, well, that's the way life goes. I got a man now, and I'm happy with him. We've been together for—"

I pulled her toward me and kissed her mouth. She didn't resist as our tongues embraced in the most sensual fashion. She relaxed her body in my arms and my hands began to explore her frame.

I could tell her panties were wet from the moaning sounds she made when my hand made its way up her blouse to toy with her nipples. I ripped open her blouse to fully expose her breasts, and eagerly took them in my mouth.

As I made my way down to her midsection, she had already pulled her skirt off and kicked it onto the floor. In no time, my face was buried between her legs. I gave her oral pleasure from the friction of my tongue as it rubbed up against her clit. I had her at the point of climax when she suddenly pushed me away.

"Scar, I can't do this. This is wrong. I have a man. Shit ain't the same no more. You need to leave," she said.

"T, stop tripping. You know you like that shit. Don't act like you done got all siditty on a nigga. Let's do this for old times' sake," I said.

I moved toward her to finish what we had started, but she pushed me away. This bitch was playing games with the wrong nigga.

"I'm serious, Scar. This was a mistake. I need you to leave. I'll call you a cab," she said.

"Bitch, fuck you. I don't need no cab, ho. You got a lotta game with ya dumb ass. I was trying to be nice to you, but that shit is dead. Let's get down to business so I can be done with ya lame ass. I just wanted to fuck you one last time for the road," I said.

She had managed to pull herself together and threw on her clothes. I could see she was fuming about my last statement. She shook her head and gave me a look as if to say, *You ain't changed one bit. You still the same no-good dog.* That was true. I was still that same nigga, but worse.

"Scar, get the fuck outta here before I call the police!" she yelled.

"Before you think about doing that, I think we need to talk first. I got some things to say that might be of interest to you," I said.

"And what is that?" she asked.

"Look, bitch. I know you helped Rock and Rachel set me up to take that rape charge. That was fucked up. Don't even try to lie about it, because Rock snitched on you before I killed him and that trick," I said.

She was totally thrown. She stood frozen in the middle of the floor. Her mouth was open, but no words came out.

"Oh, but there's more. I fucked your scandalous girl, Latrell, before I had her killed too. She helped me set that punk-ass Samson up before I offed that chump. Before I killed him, though, I made sure I got a copy of that freaky tape you made with that dude Ricardo," I said.

I was in a zone and didn't give a fuck. Takeisha was dumbfounded. She knew I held a smoking gun in my hand with that tape that could ruin her career.

"Scar, I'm sorry. I know I was wrong to set you up. Please don't ruin my career. If you ever cared about me, don't do this!" she pleaded.

"T, please. Save that dramatic performance for the silver screen. It's too late for that. Your tape is gonna be the talk of the industry by this time next week. I sent a copy to the *Enquirer* and Wendy Williams. I put ya ass on blast. Payback is a bitch, ain't it?" I asked, snickering devilishly.

"You dirty motherfucker. I'ma kill ya ass!" she said.

Takeisha ran into her kitchen to retrieve a large butcher knife. She came racing toward me with the knife, but I eluded her attempt to stab me. I managed to get behind her and grabbed her arms in an effort to knock the knife outta her hands, but her grip was too strong. I threw her to the ground and the knife fell from her hand.

She made an attempt to get to the knife, but I got on top of her and pinned her to the floor with my body weight. I slapped her across the face several times as I laughed in a sinister tone.

"You tried to kill me, bitch? I would off ya ass, but I wanna see you live and suffer. Once that tape is aired, your ass is gonna be through. Oh, and wait 'til your bean pie-eating daddy sees his little girl being the queen slut that she really is. He's gonna flip and disown you," I said.

I began to beat her senseless, pounding on her face and arms as she yelled in pain.

She managed to wiggle her arms free and dig her nails into the side of my face. Filled with rage, I got up and kicked her in the ribs and groin area. She yelled at the top of her lungs with every blow I landed.

"You better not let me live because if I do, I'ma kill ya ass if it's the last thing I do," she said.

I landed a sharp blow to her temple and she was knocked unconscious. I checked her pulse to make sure she was still alive, then ran into her kitchen and grabbed a towel to wipe the blood from my face. The wound that she had engraved in my left cheek would be a permanent blemish I would wear for the rest of my life.

As she lay unconscious, I searched her house to retrieve anything of value I could take with me. I discovered a couple hundred grand worth of jewelry I could fence on the streets.

I rummaged through her purse to find her car keys. Once I found them, I was on my way. I took one last look at her lying helpless on the living room floor.

Dumb bitch, you shoulda never set me up. You brought this on yaself, I thought as I walked outta her front door. I jumped into her car and was onto my next destination. I would ditch her wheels after I got there.

The only ones that knew I was with Takeisha were her bodyguards. That didn't matter because I would be long gone by the time them or the police tried to catch up with me. I had it made.

I knew it would be too risky for me to try to get any royalty money from Marquee Records from this point on, so I said "fuck it." You win some and then you lose some. I still had enough money to live well for a long time. I got my revenge on all of my enemies, I had a shit load of money, and I was free. It was off to paradise. I was sure that Takeisha's life would become a living hell soon.

43

Danita (D-Boogie)

I had just watched Takeisha's show on *106th and Park* when I began to miss talking to my friend. When I saw her on TV, I realized what an important part of my life she was, and she was the only friend I had left in this world.

She had apologized to me several times and had called me on countless occasions, but I ignored her. All the confusion from Latrell's and Samson's deaths had me in an emotional tailspin at this point in my life. As a result, I lashed out in anger at her over finding out about her deal secondhand and not from her. I felt that if we were friends and we were a group, I should have been the first person to know.

In reality, it wasn't a big deal that she did a solo album. I was actually happy for her. T was born for the spotlight, and she deserved to be the center of attention. God gave her the natural talent and personality to wear the diva title like it should be worn. Latrell always wanted to be just like her, but didn't have the right equipment to do so. That was the reality that fueled her jealousy. Me, I was content to play the background as a member of the crew. All in all, Takeisha was entitled to be successful because she worked hard at her craft and had what it took to be the Beyonce of the rap game.

I decided that it was petty to hold a grudge against her. That was why I went to her house that night to make up with her and tell her how proud I was of her success. When I used my key to let myself into her house, I had no idea I would find her lying on the floor, near death. I checked her pulse and was relieved to find out that she was still alive.

"T, wake up! Wake up, girl!" I yelled. I shook her several times, but she didn't respond. To see my homegirl lying in a pool of blood had me bugging the hell out. I wondered how the hell this had happened and who had done this to her.

My efforts to revive her didn't work, so I called the police. The operator told me an ambulance would be on the way. I cradled her in my arms and prayed that she would be all right. Minutes later, the paramedics were at her front door.

T came to when they placed the smelling salts' under her nostrils. She began to mumble something, but I couldn't understand what she said. The paramedics placed her on the gurney and carted her off to the hospital. I stayed behind to talk to the police. I told them I had no clue who had done this to her. They took down my information and said they would be in touch with me in the near future for a more detailed statement.

After dealing with police, I made my way over to the hospital to check on her status. I was relieved to find out that she was gonna be all right. The doctor she suffered blows to the head, and that was why she was unconscious when I arrived. She had several broken ribs and a broken arm. Her bruised face would heal in time, and he assured me she would be as good as new with proper rest if she followed his orders to the letter.

She was sedated and resting peacefully, so I decided to come back the next day to see her. I called her father to let him know what happened. He said that he would be in New York immediately. I also called Travis, who said he would be on the road within an hour to come to see about his sweetheart.

Of course, the press got a hold of the story and it was all over the news. They got it all twisted up, reporting that she was raped and beaten by a crazed fan who followed her home from the show. I got the real deal when I talked to her the next day.

"D, I'm sorry I didn't tell you about me going solo. I've made so many mistakes in my life, and I don't wanna lose ya friendship. I need ya support right now more than ever. Is it still KS crew for life?" Takeisha asked me.

"Girl, you know it. All is forgiven. I love you like a sister. Now that Latrell is gone, we're all that's left of the group. I wish you two could have reconciled your differences before she died, but we can't dwell on that. We have to deal with fixing the things in life that we have the power to still change.

"I said some mean things to you as well. I apologize to you for that. Now, I wanna know what happened and who did this to you," I said.

She told me it was Scar who did this to her. She also told me he was responsible for Latrell's and Samson's deaths. He had turned the tape of her sexcapade with Ricardo and Latrell over to the media to ruin her career. When I asked why he would hurt her like this, she confessed her role in setting Scar up to go to jail.

It bugged me out for minute that she would do something like that to him, but then reality set in. Their relationship was a never-ending saga of drama and infidelity that culminated in both of them going over the top to get back at each other.

Scar was evil as evil could be and deserved whatever he got in retaliation for what he had done. I instantly relayed the information she gave me, except for the part about her setting Scar up, to the police, and they put out an APB on Scar for his arrest.

Rashid and Travis arrived later that day. She was delighted to see the two most important men in her life. She tried to smile, but the pain from the bruises on her face made it difficult.

I could see that she was worried about what the tape would do to her career and how her father would react. However, I knew that with faith and time, she would weather the storm that was about to come. She and I were family again, and I prayed that nothing else would come along and attempt to tear apart that bond.

44

Scar

Scar had manged to elude capture by the police. After the incident with Takeisha, he and Trevor made a quick escape outta the country before the authorities detected their crimes. They already had fake IDs and passports made before they had put their plan into effect. They had a gang of money to live off of the rest of their lives, and new identities that would allow them to maneuver around the world without drawing attention to themselves.

They decided to settle in Rio de Janeiro. The warm Brazilian climate and the vast selection of beautiful women made this an ideal home for these two. They purchased a villa by the beach and spent most of their time sipping on Rum Runners and Long Island Iced Teas served by the country's finest eye candy. They partied all night and slept during the day. Life couldn't have been any sweeter for them.

Unfortunately for Scar, the demons of his past caught up with him. He underestimated the reach of Miguel Salazar's international connections. Miguel had discovered in conversation with detectives Horowitz and Drake, that Scar was instrumental in his arrest. He paid the detectives plentifully for their information, and swore revenge.

Miguel was the leader of the U.S. arm of the largest South American drug cartel, the Menendez family. If anybody could find Scar and Trevor, they could. They had the money and the resources on hand to find a needle in a haystack if they wanted to do so.

When it was discovered that the pair lived in Rio, a hit squad was instantly dispatched. When they located Scar and Trevor, they brutally murdered them, chopping their bodies into little pieces and leaving their remains on the beach for the birds and insects to eat. It just went to show that no sheisty deed went unpunished in this world. If you did dirt, then expect to receive the same in return.

45

Takeisha (T-Love)

"**A**nd the BET Music Award for Best Rap Single goes to T-Love for the smash hit, 'C.R.E.A.M.' "

The crowd erupted in applause as I made my way to the stage. I accepted the award from Magic Johnson and Lisa Raye then made my way to the microphone to make my acceptance speech.

"First and foremost, I wanna thank God for giving me the talent and drive to fulfill my dreams. Next, I wanna thank my father, for his love and understanding of me when, at times, I didn't understand myself. I love you, Daddy.

"I wanna dedicate this award to the memory of my mother, Rosa Jenkins, because without her and my father, I wouldn't be here today. I wanna thank Samson Miles for believing in the KS Crew enough to give us a chance. I especially wanna thank him for the energy he put into this album, and I'm sorry he didn't live long enough to see it to fruition. We had our differences, but I have to give him credit for helping me achieve my dream.

"To my girl, my sister, Latrell, known to y'all as Luscious, even though you're gone, you live forever in my heart. To my ace, D-Boogie, you have been my rock. You always said I was the strong one in the group, but I disagree because you were the force that truly kept me going. To Travis, my soul mate, I love you forever.

"Finally, to all of my fans, I just wanna thank you for all of your support over the last year. Even though there were negative forces that sought to destroy my career, you saw through the madness and accepted my God-given talent. Your appreciation of my art just shows me that if God is for you, there is no one that can come against you. Thank you! Thank you! Thank you!"

That was the best night of my life. I won three other awards before it was all said and done. My album had sold close to ten million copies to date. The negative scandal that Scar tried to create actually backfired and helped further boost my success. The public was sympathetic to my situation and embraced me. They saw that I was a young girl who had made a bad choice, and I was a victim of someone else's vicious plot.

I was never charged with anything in connection

with Ricardo's death. In fact, after I talked to the police, I convinced them that Scar had murdered him to get a copy of the tape to use against me. They bought this story hook, line, and sinker. I never told the police that Samson tried to blackmail me with the tape. I told them Scar killed Samson when his attempt to extort money from him failed. I mentioned nothing about Rock and Rachel's murders because that would've incriminated me. Their deaths would go down as two more unsolved murders.

D and Silk got married after their child was born. She gave birth to a little girl, who she named Latrell, after our deceased friend. That way she was always a part of our lives. Right or wrong, good or bad, the KS Crew was for life! That was the vow we promised to carry to the grave.

Travis and I were still together. He finished law school and was now a practicing entertainment lawyer. He had a growing list of superstar clients thanks to me. We had plans to get married and start a family in the next two years, after his practice was more established.

As for my father, he was once again proud of me as his little girl. He forgave me for the tape situation after he saw how much I had matured since that episode.

My life had taken so many twists and turns over the last five years. I went from a dream-chasing, money-hungry teenager to a multi-millionaire rap star. I had several movie offers that my manager, Ace, and I were sorting through. My future was as bright as the stars in the sky, and I appreciated my success, taking nothing for granted any longer. It took my trials and tribulations for me to be thankful for the little things life offered, like love, friendship, and family. The money was beautiful to have, but the value of having peace of mind was priceless.

Acknowledgments

Much love goes out to:

Carl Weber and Urban Books for the top notch job you do in promoting my work; all of my readers that bought *A Thug's Life* and *Around the Way Girls 2*—I told you I would continue to bring the heat! my down south homeys, Jihad and K Elliott, which one of us is gonna step up and claim Donald Goines' spot? Susan Hampstead and *Don Diva* magazine; Richard Holland and Urban Knowledge Bookstore; the streets of Baltimore for instilling these stories in my brain; all the starving rap artists coming up in the game—don't let your hunger push you into making unwise decisions; and me, for working so hard to make my vision a reality!

T. Long